THE
INDECENT
DEATH
OF A
MADAM

Former scriptwriter for *Spitting Image* and Sony Award winner, Simon Parke is the author of the Abbot Peter murder mystery series and the historical novel *The Soldier, the Gaoler, the Spy and Her Lover*. Away from publishing, Simon is CEO of the Mind Clinic and enjoys the loneliness of the long-distance runner.

THE
INDECENT
DEATH
OF A
MADAM

SIMON PARKE

First published in Great Britain in 2017

Marylebone House
36 Causton Street
London SW1P 4ST
www.marylebonehousebooks.co.uk

British Library Cataloguing-in-Publication Data
A catalogue record for this book is available from the British Library

ISBN 978–1–910674–48–2
eBook ISBN 978–1–910674–49–9

Typeset by Fakenham Prepress Solutions, Fakenham, Norfolk NR21 8NN
Manufacture managed by Jellyfish
First printed in Great Britain by CPI
Subsequently digitally printed in Great Britain

eBook by Fakenham Prepress Solutions, Fakenham, Norfolk NR21 8NN

Produced on paper from sustainable forests

This book is dedicated to the memory of
Paul Carter.
'Baffled, broken but compelled to praise.'
Rest in joy.

Author's note

Stormhaven is a thinly disguised version of Seaford, where I have the honour of living. The geography and the history will tend to be true, whether it's the town station's long platform or golf balls at the top of Firle Road. But the Bybuckle Asylum, the Stormhaven Etiquette Society and the *Sussex Silt* are invention, as are all the characters.

And Seaford's crime figures also differ a little from mine.

Prologue

'I'm not liking this place,' said James, looking into the darkness, something he'd been doing for a long time now.

They sat on the wet mosaic floor, just inside a door that said, in rotting lettering, 'Gladstone Ward'.

'It's a roof against the rain,' said his companion, younger than James and a fidget. 'Definitely better. Definitely.'

And it hadn't been hard to gain access; no one cared enough to lock this building any more. They hadn't cared for a long time. The flotsam and jetsam of empty cans, needles and discarded crisp packets lay scattered, shifting and scraping in the wind.

'But it's not, is it?' said James.

'It's not what? What isn't it?'

'It's not a roof against anything. Feel the damp.' He ran his finger down the dripping walls. 'We'd be drier in the sea.'

'How would we be drier in the sea?' Ben was literal, nervous and not best served by his energy drink. He was accidental company rather than chosen for James. They'd met outside the McDonald's in Newhaven. 'Anyway, it's hammering it down outside. Hammering.'

'I think it's stopped.'

'I don't know about that.'

'I'm going anyway.'

'You can go – I'm staying!' And then more quietly. 'I'm definitely staying.'

Silence.

'And I can hear the cries,' said James. 'Can you hear them?'

'What cries?'

'Listen.'

'Listen to what?'

'Can you hear them? The mad. They're still here, you know.'

'What are you talking about?'

'Don't you hear them?'

1

'I don't know what you're talking about sometimes. I need a piss.'

He got up in a hurry and chose a wall too close to James: the splatter and the smell of urine too close for decency.

'It used to be an asylum, Ben. A mental asylum.' He said it in anger because he still had standards. He'd fallen some way from his former life but still had standards.

'This place?' said Ben, doing up his flies.

'A loony bin. Used to hold hundreds of them here by the sea. This was the largest ward . . . Gladstone Ward.'

'How do you know?' said Ben, sitting down again. 'How do you know all this?'

'How does anyone know anything, Ben? Because they go and find out. It's called an education.' And James had had one. How else had he once been a solicitor? 'I read about places. You should try it sometime.'

'Why would I want to read about places?'

James had been sleeping rough for four years after losing both job and family through alcohol. But he still had his dignity, or shreds of it . . . it came and went. And he liked to know where he was sleeping rough, the history of the place, and there was a lot of history along the south coast – rocks, Romans, Normans and Nazis. He couldn't understand those who slept in a doorway without wondering who had passed this way before them.

Ben was now looking twitchy. 'I'm getting out,' he said, gathering his things.

'Why?'

'There could be ghosts.'

'Almost certainly,' said James.

'I mean there could be, if it was a nuthouse.'

'I wasn't thinking of staying.'

James found no peace here. The walls were not kind, he could feel that; and he still knew the difference between kind and harsh. Perhaps he noticed these things more acutely since the wheels had come off his life in such spectacular fashion.

And so together the two of them left the building, shuffling down the dark corridor with bags and overcoats. Not quite friends, not friends at all, but companions for now, stepping out into the night as the moon rose over the cold January sea. The rain had stopped.

'We could go to Newhaven,' said James. 'I think I will.' He wouldn't mention the beach huts to Ben; that wasn't knowledge he wished to share. Everyone has somewhere that they alone know. It keeps you sane. 'There's a shelter in the Sainsbury's car park.'

'I'm getting out of here,' said Ben. 'Simple as. Don't care much where we go; anywhere but a loony bin.'

They turned west towards Newhaven, a two-mile walk, away from the nuthouse, reckoned unfit for habitation. From its glory days – and there had been glory days – the Bybuckle Asylum on Stormhaven's seafront had fallen rather low. Eaten by salt and ripped by the wind, it couldn't even house the homeless these days.

Though, sadly, it had further to fall . . .

The abbot's heart bolted

like a startled horse.

It was *her*. It was Rosemary, surely? After all these years . . .

He'd arrived a respectful ten minutes early at the judge's house, darkly called Black Cap. Was it named in melancholy, perhaps? Did they miss the death sentence, the drama of the death hat, the power to dispatch the repulsive from this earth? Was there a judge within these walls raging at their impotence? It was possible . . . and it was cold. The abbot lifted the large door knocker with freezing hands and hammered news of his arrival with two loud bangs.

The door opened. 'Greetings – you must be the abbot.'

'The clues are there,' said Peter cheerily, his habit clearly displayed in the porch light.

The judicial welcome was polite, efficient and fast, and with his coat left on a hook in the hallway Peter found himself guided to a seat in the large front room, with the open feel of a medieval grand hall. The house grew out of this space, with Peter noting a gap where once an open fire had burned. The judge saw the direction of his gaze.

'Under-floor heating made it as redundant as a coal miner.'

'How very Roman,' said Peter.

'I'm sorry?' It was spoken with some aggression.

'Hypocausts were much used by the Romans in their villas throughout the colder climates in Europe and then Britain as they expanded their empire. They did need their heat.'

'I think we all need our heat, Abbot. I presume that's why you went to the desert? To catch some sun.'

The abbot smiled. He could think of no response to such an inadequate observation. He'd lived in a desert monastery close on thirty years, for reasons he couldn't necessarily name; but it hadn't been for the tan. And he remembered the chill as well as the warmth – the cold, clear-skied nights, which on occasion required three blankets for settled sleep in his cell.

'The open fire heats the chimney,' said the judge in declaratory fashion. 'My under-floor system heats the room.'

Peter sensed that she wished her heating to be a modern idea, rather than something ancient; her own discovery rather than anything Roman.

'It's certainly a warm house to walk into,' said the abbot, though his words were not emotionally true. The warmth was in the heating, not the host. They had met but not met; he'd been guided to his seat like a theatre-goer who was late for the performance, and now he sat with a cup of lemon and ginger tea in his hand, which wasn't really tea, not in Peter's estimation . . . and perhaps his face revealed his thoughts.

'No builders – so no builders' tea,' said Blessings with a tight smile. And she must have surprised a few defendants when she appeared in court to take her seat. A black female judge in her attractive forties was not what you expected in these parts. It was hardly America's Deep South, but Stormhaven was a place where the white population came to retire and further to harden their already harsh opinions.

All sense of cold was forgotten, however, when the abbot saw her, or imagined he saw her. Rosemary? Could it be? Indeed, his hand shook and his tea spilled, burning hot against his thigh through the habit. She'd appeared in the hallway, talking with Martin Channing who'd also just entered the six-bedroom house in Firle Road. Well, they'd entered together, here in the posh end of Stormhaven. So were they together? And how did Peter feel about that?

'So how are all our dear charities in Sussex?' asked the charmingly smooth Channing as he removed his coat with careless ease. He was editor of the local newspaper, the *Sussex Silt* – a publication also known as 'The Jackal'. It fed on the negative and nasty with a particular bent for celebrity shame, fraudulent local officials, any hint of adultery – and of course, Southern Rail. Or 'Southern Fail', as the paper always called it.

It was Martin's creation, this negative news-sheet, backed by a city hedge fund that handed over all moral decisions to their accountant, for while the paper was much reviled it was also much read . . . which was all that interested Channing. He'd never separated news from entertainment – 'There is no difference!' he'd say – and cared little for what the worried middle classes muttered over their claret and hummus. Here was a man who'd lunched with prime ministers in his Fleet Street days and knew only disdain for the rich and powerful. With a fine head of salt-and-pepper hair, he arrived on the south coast with a deep sense of mischief in the game that was life. 'Nothing to be taken too seriously, Abbot, otherwise where would we be?'

And so it was a polite question in the hallway, Martin to Rosemary: 'How are all our dear charities in Sussex?'

He was only feigning interest. The charities of Sussex were of no concern at all to Martin. And before Rosemary could answer, the editor's attention had moved on. He'd glanced through the hall to the front room and seen his guest of honour, Abbot Peter, sitting with tea and a haunted face.

'Looks like you've seen a ghost, Peter!' he declared heartily, and Peter smiled back weakly because it well described how he felt. A ghost from the past, yes . . . though not some shimmering ghoul but a flesh-and-blood memory, melting the years away, the edifice of time crumbling, as if he was back in the Highgate Asylum.

'Camomile, Rosemary?' asked Blessings.

'Thank you,' said the ghost, taking off her coat.

So it *was* Rosemary in the hallway, he knew now – or almost knew. What were the chances of another woman who looked so like Rosemary sharing her name? She was the right age, the age Rosemary would be . . . and suddenly the evening envisioned by the abbot was unravelling and a new fear appearing, making his neck sweat in winter. Would she recognize him?

He had to hope not; that would be best. It was forty years, after all, and he wore different clothes now, very different clothes. She'd have no idea of his life since then, of his long stay in the deserts of Middle Egypt, abbot of the monastery of St James-the-Less. They'd had no contact after they parted – and perhaps, in truth, they'd had no contact before. It had been Peter left restless by events; what Rosemary had felt, he had no idea . . . and it was all so long ago.

The front door opened again and two more visitors stepped out of the dark January chill. Polite greetings ensued, awkward more than kind, while hot drinks were organized and a plate of expensive biscuits appeared. Peter assumed they were expensive, as he'd never seen the like of them before and certainly not in the desert. Some even boasted gold foil, which was rather intriguing. And when all were seated, Martin – apparently chair of this select little group – made the introductions.

'It's quite wonderful of Blessings to play host again,' he said and the judge nodded graciously. 'That's the penalty for earning so much, of course. No one else here has the space for such a gathering!' Some nervous laughter rippled around the room. Channing had the ability to appear to be sniping at everyone. 'And not to forget our guest,' he said mysteriously. 'Abbot Peter!'

Heads turned.

'A rare species, abbots,' said Blessings.

'Well, a pretend abbot really,' replied Martin. 'He hasn't seen the inside of a monastery for a while . . . but clings to his old status for consolation.'

It was further sniping from Martin but true enough. Peter had been in Stormhaven for over four years now, while keeping his clothes and title.

'Word of warning, though, Abbot,' he said. Peter looked up.

'Yes?'

'I'm afraid we are a rather secret society.'

'Secret about what?'

'So we don't expect any sharing of details with the outside world. You must imagine that this place – and all that transpires here – is Bletchley Park!'

'Bletchley Park?'

'The code-breaking centre during the war,' said Channing. It was a sharply delivered put-down, an explanation that should not need to be given, one that was slowing Martin down – and showing his guest up.

'I'm aware of what it was,' said the abbot. 'I'm just struggling for the connection . . . with this.'

He indicated the circle of six in which he sat, comfortably settled with tea and biscuits and with no obvious link to high-pressure code-breaking in cold huts designed to foil the Nazis.

'The secrecy, Abbot! It was secret squirrel at Bletchley. No one could speak of what they did there, even to their nearest and dearest . . . just supposing the two are ever the same.' Martin looked around with a naughty smile. 'And when Churchill congratulated the staff on their work at the end of the war, he told them, "You were the geese who laid the golden eggs – but never cackled."'

'I see,' said the abbot. 'So this is a call not to cackle?'

'They went to their deaths saying nothing, revealing nothing. Such honour! And we expect the same, do we not?'

He looked conspiratorially around the group, who seemed to be in agreement with their leader on this one. Perhaps they were flattered to be part of a secret society, though Peter felt only the strangeness of the call.

'There is an irony in a newspaper man demanding that no one tell their story,' he said.

Channing told everyone's story, and still more eagerly if they asked him to keep it quiet.

'There's a season for everything, Abbot. You're forgetting your Scriptures again.'

Peter smiled . . . and tried not to look at Rosemary, who sat to his right in this strange circle.

He was regretting coming. At Martin's invitation, he was a guest speaker tonight at the Stormhaven Etiquette Society. He enjoyed speaking, believing himself not without skill in this particular line of work. But how he was regretting coming . . .

There was a knock

on Tara's door.

'Come!' she said briskly, settling her glasses in her thick blonde hair, cut shorter now she was in her forties.

It was Katrina, one of the working girls – though at thirty-two she was hardly a girl; her son was a teenager. Tara had seen them together in Morrisons, plundering the freezer section. She had warned her about shopping locally.

'You never know who you might bump into,' she said.

'I don't mind who I bump into,' said Katrina dismissively.

'No – but your client might. Particularly if his wife's in tow. That's heart attack territory.'

'That is not my issue,' said Katrina.

'Why not shop in Eastbourne?'

'Eastbourne is a graveyard.'

'And Stormhaven isn't?'

But today they were alone, no teenage son in sight, with Katrina looking concerned in a Virginia Woolf sort of way. Her long mousy hair was pulled back above her serious lagoon eyes. She stood in the doorway with a cross around her neck, like a disturbed nun seeking the advice of her Mother Superior. But this wasn't an abbey, it was Stormhaven's only brothel, Model Service.

'I've had a visitor, Tara.'

Her voice was a little shaky. Tara had no time for shaky this morning.

'It's your job to have visitors, Katrina. Was he nice?'

'He was a man.' She did not say this as a compliment. She earned her living from men; she did not have to like them.

'Did he pay?'

'He paid.'

'So all's well.' Why was Katrina disturbing her? But she clearly had more to say. 'You didn't indicate any trouble, Katrina.'

They had a system at Model Service. There were cameras in the corridor and a buzzer by the bed, mainly for the girls' protection, of course. But there was also the revenue to consider. Money was the first matter dealt with in this business; clients paid in advance for services rendered, and only after cash was handed over did things proceed. The girls had a small safe in their room where the money was deposited. Only once had a client tried to force the code from Katrina. She'd used the pepper spray on him, after which Tara had escorted him out with a rolling pin for support.

And so Tara was thinking this was unusual ... unusual for Katrina to be concerned by a man. She wasn't the high-maintenance sort, one of those girls with endless needs and fragile time-keeping. She'd been a model employee since arriving from Poland three years ago. And she wasn't your average sex worker – no one could call her that. She followed the pontiff on Twitter, and was inclined to offer papal pronouncements, which was unfortunate. Papal pronouncements were rarely helpful here – or indeed anywhere, in Tara's estimation.

But Katrina had a work ethic to die for, so who cared about her religion? She got on with it – as long as they wore a condom and refrained from violence. And if they smelt, she gave them a bath and made them enjoy it. Aside from her Catholicism, her core belief was this: 'A man is always better for a bath.'

So it was odd that she was standing here with a problem. Cherise, the other girl – she was much more likely to be having a whine. Since her arrival from Romford, there'd been good and bad. She'd taken them all forward a century or two with her understanding of the internet – well, she'd changed the business, to be honest. No more pictures in phone boxes, which the police had never liked, apart from to have a good stare ...

But oh! Did she have a grumble in her, that one? Cherise was never far from a grumble about her percentage of the takings or a noisy water pipe or the springs in the mattress, damp in the bathroom, her boyfriend or whatever. While Katrina – standing here wrapped in a bathrobe – she got on with things ... and then went home to her son. And that's the difference between Krakow and Romford, thought Tara.

So whatever was disturbing Katrina this afternoon, it must be serious. Did she want to leave? Had the pope finally got to her conscience? They say there's no recovery for a Catholic conscience. Or did she have family to return to in Poland? Her boy was growing up; did she want Polish schooling for him? That would be a shame for Model Service. She was a good girl, Katrina.

'He left a sticker,' said Katrina.

'I'm sorry?'

'A sticker.'

Tara wondered if this was crude – some slang she hadn't heard. But that was more Cherise than Katrina, who was never crude.

'You know – a message.'

'What sort of message?'

'You come and see.'

'Can't you tell me?'

She didn't want to move. Katrina had the room at the top of the house and Tara had done her ten thousand steps for the day . . . her Fitbit had buzzed its applause a short while ago. She didn't need more exercise.

'You come and see,' insisted Katrina.

They went up the narrow staircase, two flights, to Katrina's room, which still smelt of sex.

'You didn't give him a bath?'

'He did not want a bath. He wanted to be hit . . . with happy endings.'

Tara eyed the various tools of the trade in the corner. Clients were given a choice of instrument when it came to punishment and the weapons were not always predictable. Katrina had once come down to ask her for 'the kitchen tool – the flat bendy blade'.

'A spatula?'

'Yes.'

They'd had to go next door for one of those, where their neighbour Eileen was a keen cake-maker. She had a spatula and handed it over with some excitement.

'What are you baking?' she asked.

'Katrina's doing something spankingly Polish,' said Tara.

'Ooh, I'd like to see that!'

11

No, you wouldn't, thought Tara, and they didn't return it after use. They bought Eileen a new spatula, claiming 'an accident'.

This afternoon, however, it had been the good old-fashioned cane.

'Well, I hope you hit him hard,' said Tara. 'Now, what's the problem?'

Katrina was usually quick to clean and air the room; she used to be in hotel work. But not this afternoon. She was troubled and pointing. There on the open door was a blue sticker which read: 'TO THE SLUT CREW OF CHURCH STREET, BE WARNED: YOU'RE NOT QUITE WHAT WE WANT. THE STORMHAVEN ETIQUETTE SOCIETY.'

Rosemary had recognized him.

She'd recognized Peter as soon as Channing looked across to him, sitting there in the judge's lounge, holding his tea. He'd appeared to avoid her gaze, but she may have imagined that. He'd always had an avoidant trait in him . . . though that was a long time ago. But do people change – really? They say time's a great healer, but Rosemary had never met anyone healed by time.

Peter had been an unusual arrival at the unit in Highgate; that was clear enough in her memory. There was never a happy story on patients' notes when they arrived, but 'violence in a church service' was more entertaining than some. She remembered it all rather clearly, because he'd told her the story. He'd started attending a large and successful church in Oxford where he was at university, and all seemed to be going well until the day he began throwing hymn books at the preacher, accusing him of talking 'crap'. Apparently he kept shouting just that: 'You're talking crap!' and 'This isn't true!' And when a steward came to remove him, he took offence at the physical contact, a firm grip on his arm, and swung round and hit the steward in the face . . . and when the preacher said, 'I see our friend has a problem,' he turned and shouted, 'No, you have the problem – you're talking crap! And I'm not your friend!'

The steward, whose nose was broken, had insisted on pressing charges, feeling that he would be 'a poor witness to our Lord' not to do so, and once the police were involved it all got rather complicated. But for reasons Rosemary knew nothing about, the young man ended up at the Highgate unit, where she was just starting out as a young mental health nurse.

And he was different, Peter; Rosemary had never met anyone quite like him. He was dangerous but not in a physical or emotional sense, like most of her patients. You could just see that he wasn't going to fit into the world, that he'd always be throwing hymn books – or any other missiles to hand – at those in authority, at

13

those speaking, well, 'crap'. And while she knew it wasn't a good idea, that you couldn't always be throwing hymn books, she quite admired him for it. Perhaps Rosemary would have liked to throw a few things at people herself. But she'd erred more towards duty in life, towards being responsible, helping people, sorting things out; she was good at this. And what was the point of getting angry? It didn't achieve anything, really it didn't.

Peter had bought her flowers sometimes. Patients were allowed out towards the end of their stay, to do a little shopping at the newsagent's on Highgate Hill, accompanied by a member of staff. And he would sometimes bring her back flowers. 'Just a small thank you!' he'd say and then disappear. And that was all fine. But when he'd started writing letters to her after he left the unit, she'd ignored them – or occasionally offered rather distant replies, because professionally it was the right thing to do. One couldn't form a relationship with clients, it wouldn't look good. It could be perceived in the wrong way.

Though she'd always remembered him and, yes, never met anyone else like him. They say you only meet one person, and for Rosemary, perhaps that had been Peter. And if her letters had been a little warmer, who knows? But life had been busy, with no time for complications of the heart. There had been more important matters to attend to; and then forty years went by.

So, it had been quite a surprise to see him – and in those clothes! – at the Stormhaven Etiquette Society the night before.

And the surprises were not finished . . .

Tara breathed deeply

as she pondered the sticker on Katrina's door. Not a woman shocked easily, Tara was shocked now. What was that sticker about? Well, she could see what it was about. 'TO THE SLUT CREW OF CHURCH STREET, BE WARNED: YOU'RE NOT QUITE WHAT WE WANT. THE STORMHAVEN ETIQUETTE SOCIETY.'

'What is this etiquette society?' asked Katrina. She pronounced the 'u' as a 'w'.

'Lord knows,' she replied, trying to sound religious.

'And what does it mean?'

'It doesn't mean anything.'

'Everything means something.'

Tara continued with her breathing. She'd once tried meditation, learned that breathing was her friend, a refuge from anxious thoughts . . . and she was having a few right now. She knew all about the Stormhaven Etiquette Society. They had a record of nastiness, targeting organizations with their stupid stickers and then vilifying them in the press. And that was the last thing Model Service needed, quite the last thing, because then the police would have to get involved. So Tara breathed in and out, her lungs trying to soften the blow, to ease the waves of fear. She knew of the Stormhaven Etiquette Society, but Katrina needn't.

'I don't know what it means, dear,' she said, looking round the room. Everything was in order otherwise. Tidy girl, Katrina.

'You look worried,' said Katrina.

'I'm not worried. I'll talk to the boss, but life goes on. Probably some sad little joke.'

'You think so? If he returns, I'll kill him.'

'Just make sure he pays you first . . . and doesn't enjoy it.' Tara peeled the sticker from the door but held back from destroying it. 'And you think he left it on the door when leaving?'

'Well, who else put it there?' Then Katrina had a thought. 'Look at the corridor film. He's on camera. You can see who he is.'

But Tara knew that there was no footage to look at. He'd been the first client of the day, her mind had been elsewhere, she hadn't turned it on. She often didn't, to be honest. It was more for show and to keep the boss happy. The boss liked to look after the girls, as if this was some hostel for abused women, when in truth it was nothing of the sort. It was a business, with everyone – clients and staff – here out of choice, and with much better customer/staff relations than the post office up the road.

'So there's no footage?'

'The important thing is, you saw him.'

'I saw him, yes.'

She'd seen him from all angles. The identity parade would have to be a little unusual.

'And you hit him.'

'But he enjoyed it!' said Katrina with frustration. 'That's no punishment . . . no punishment at all.'

It's no good if you enjoy the punishment. What's punishing about that? It turns hell into heaven and Katrina did believe in punishment – or what hope was there for society?

But with no name or address, the young man who liked to be hit with a cane and left offensive stickers on doors had slipped anonymously away into the sea breeze.

Who else could have left it?

Geoff and Martin

were an odd couple, sitting on the seafront bench in January. Geoff Berry was a successful Stormhaven estate agent. They were talking about the Stormhaven Etiquette Society and Geoff had some issues.

'I just don't feel terribly comfortable there,' he said.

'Oh?' Martin tried to sound concerned.

'In the meetings, I mean. Though it's a great honour to be asked, Martin; absolutely a great honour!'

'It's an honour to have you among us, Geoff.'

Martin could not imagine less of an honour and was irritated that he needed this man; that he had to play at flattery on this freezing shoreline.

'But, well – do they *get* me, Martin? I do wonder if they really get me?'

'Oh, I think the discerning get you, Geoff. And really, does anyone else matter?'

Was Geoff happy to be loved only by the discerning? He'd perhaps like a few of the undiscerning on board as well.

'I wonder whether I'm a bit zany for them,' he said. 'Whether I move through the gears too fast and they can't keep up.' What was Geoff talking about? Was he describing his inability to focus, wondered Martin; his mind did drift rather. 'I just don't always feel comfortable.'

'Comfort will come,' said Martin with a reassuring smile. 'A fine wine takes time, Geoff.' And then as a clincher: 'You're a great hit with Rosemary, of course.'

'Really?'

'Very much so.'

Geoff was relieved. He loved being a great hit with people and felt considerably heartened by the news. He also liked being compared to a fine wine ... well, he liked any compliment really. And it was possible that with a little more patience, as Martin suggested, comfort in the group would come; though he wasn't sure. They were a pretty odd bunch, were they not? And if they didn't 'get him' now, then when would they?

He'd started attending meetings of the Etiquette Society because Channing was a hard man to say no to. The notorious editor had strolled into his Geoff Berry estate agency and said, 'I need you to step outside for a cup of coffee, Geoff. Do you have a moment?'

It was a bit presumptuous, of course it was, as if he didn't have a business to run and a thousand things to attend to. But Geoff had found a moment, a window in his diary, because he was intrigued, not to say flattered, by the interest of a man such as Channing. He was also a little bored at work, to be honest. 'No two days are the same,' he'd say to new employees. But actually, they were. Most days were exactly the same, tediously so, and he needed other interests, always had done. Geoff liked to be spinning as many plates as possible, and if he let a few crash to the ground, well, so be it.

'And I now want you to become a full member of the Stormhaven Etiquette Society, Geoff,' said Martin, looking straight out to sea, like an admiral eyeing the horizon. He spoke with that sort of confidence. 'It's decision time. You've been to a few meetings, you know the work we do – the good work we do. And God knows we need local figures of substance, some big hitters, to give us ballast . . . some gravitas.'

'Well, I hardly think I have much to offer!'

'Stop right there, Geoff!' Channing waved his finger at the property man in comedic fashion. 'Successful local businessman for twenty years, respected member of the Rotary Club, star of the wonderful local theatre – this is no time for self-deprecation!'

Channing was aware he'd forgotten the name of Stormhaven's wonderful local theatre. He'd been taken there for a performance once, and it had been appalling. Geoff may have been playing the lead – he probably was – but thankfully, the whole affair was erased from Martin's memory, so he couldn't be sure.

'I suppose I have become something of a local celebrity,' said Geoff, his feathers puffing a little.

'I even saw your photo on the wall in the post office, listing your achievements! Move over David Beckham, I say!'

18

'Well, that's just a company advert, Martin. Not quite Beckham-esque.'

He was hardly David Beckham; Martin had gone a bit over the top there, this is what Geoff was thinking . . . though maybe there were similarities. Geoff was open to the possibility.

'Not smouldering in your underpants, I grant you,' said Martin, pulling back a little. Flattery worked best when at least briefly acquainted with reality. 'He really does that very well, the smouldering thing.'

'He does,' said Geoff, though with hesitation, because he didn't want to sound gay.

There was a momentary pause on the seaside bench, though no quiet, thanks to the large machines bulldozing the Stormhaven shingle back towards Newhaven. They came every winter, after another year of tidal shift. And as the town's only sea wall against flooding, the banking of the shingle mattered.

'Not pretty,' said Channing, eyeing the huge-wheeled monsters shunting the stones. 'But I suppose we can't always have beautiful saviours. This is Stormhaven, after all – not Hollywood.'

'And it's all about decency, that sort of thing?' said Geoff wishing to get back to the Etiquette Society and his place in it. As Martin said, he'd been attending meetings for a year; it probably was time he made up his mind about joining. But the issue was a long way from straightforward.

He'd known of the society before Martin had approached him to join, and the fact was, no one was exactly complimentary about it. He wouldn't be telling Channing, but one colleague had called it 'a dangerous gathering of control freaks', while his wife, Mandy – who had just walked out on him again – had said, 'The Stormhaven Etiquette Society legitimizes snobbery, disdain and disgust, Geoffrey – sounds perfect for you.'

Mandy could be a bitch, but she wasn't stupid.

'Decency,' said Martin, reassuringly. 'Well said, Geoff. Decency. I know that's what your life has been about and it's what the society aims to promote.' Martin paused for a moment. 'And perhaps sociability is another important word for us.'

'Sociability?'

'It's a commitment to sociability – to being sociable, to noticing one's neighbours and behaving in a considerate manner towards them. Is that hope so very wicked?'

'Not in my book, Martin.'

It all sounded very decent indeed.

'So of course there's some shaming to be done – and quite right too!' Geoff nodded. 'Spare the rod and spoil the child. Shaming is the only way some people change.'

Shame did make Geoff feel uncomfortable, but if it was someone else being shamed, he could cope with that. Indeed, it was almost a relief.

'No one wants to receive one of the society's stickers, that's for sure!' said Geoff. Some of his Rotary colleagues lived in dread of a sticker being left at their business, because the unwanted delivery always went public. Anyone who received a sticker also found themselves portrayed darkly in the *Sussex Silt*.

'Group cooperation and norms for hygiene stand at the heart of evolution,' said Martin, doing his best to sound like David Attenborough. 'Of course there's shame and quite right too! This is about the survival of the human race!'

The survival of the human race? Geoff hadn't realized the stakes were quite so high here in Stormhaven . . . but Channing did have a point.

'It's about boundaries, about civilization, Geoff . . . about keeping those brutish twin scourges of selfishness and bad taste at bay.' Martin was looking out to sea again, as one pondering the profundities of life. He was a better actor than Geoff; he just didn't need tights and make-up. 'The Church used to do these things, of course, give us some rules . . . but alas no longer. Who knows what the reverends do these days? Run homeless shelters as far as I can make out!' Martin was pushing at an open door here, and Geoff nodded in shared and bewildered amusement. 'So the Etiquette Society fights alone for a proper, correct code of conduct – for simple but life-saving good manners.'

Geoff had not enjoyed the recent meeting. Martin had invited some abbot fellow to give a talk, which he didn't much take to, or even understand. But generally, meetings combined some rather enjoyable local gossip with a strong thread of negativity, which had its own joy. It was a particular pleasure to run others down and feel righteous as one did so. Like on a seesaw, when they go down, you go up!

The society met in an expensive property in Firle Road, adjacent to the golf course, owned by the judge, Blessings N'Dayo – and by the by, worth around £990,000 if put on the market today. Geoff couldn't help but know these things; to him, a house was always a property and never a home. This is what Mandy said, when he complained about her expenditure on curtains for the lounge, or new tiles in the en-suite shower.

'There'll be no return on the investment, that's all I'm saying, should we decide to sell the property.'

'This isn't a "property", Geoff – it's our home.'

'Everything's a property, Mandy.'

Geoff didn't like going home, this was the trouble. Others in the office looked forward to going home at the end of the day; he didn't. His life ended when he went home, as if he ceased to exist on going through the front door – no appreciation from anyone. He was appreciated at work, but not at home. And so the Etiquette Society provided another night out, another delayed return into the bosom of his unsatisfactory family.

And he had Martin to thank for this, because he created it all. Why the others were there, he couldn't be sure, for nothing seemed to connect any of them. There was the major-general, Terence Blain, like some latter-day Lawrence of Arabia . . . an odd fish all round. He was painfully polite but mainly silent in meetings – and now working in the supermarket, for God's sake! A decorated war hero who gave it all up to work in Morrisons. You couldn't make it up! Geoff would have loved to hear some stories from Iraq, but that wasn't going to happen . . . because Terence didn't speak of it.

'What's been your most frightening moment?' he'd once asked him in a meeting.

'Asking Blessings if she had any sugar,' he'd replied with a wry smile. And the group loved that.

And then there was the judge. The name Blessings really didn't suit her; she was terrifying, absolutely terrifying. Martin had said, 'She's quite harmless, really,' but there was nothing harmless about her in Geoff's estimation. Fortunately, he'd avoided saying the first line that came into his head when she greeted him in the hallway: 'Well, you don't meet many black female judges in Stormhaven!'

It would have been true, but could have been taken the wrong way. And he didn't wish to fall out with her; a good relationship would be wise and useful, should she ever want to sell. The Geoff Berry agency would enjoy shifting that property on her behalf.

But if anyone could make him join the society, it was neither Terence nor Blessings – it was Rosemary. There was something about her: an older woman but an attractive one. Isn't sixty the new forty? Whether he had a future with Mandy, he wasn't sure. She seemed to be moving on, increasingly critical of him, and he really didn't need that. He didn't need anyone being critical of him. So Rosemary was an appealing distraction. It need be nothing serious, of course – though who knows? She seemed to like him, and Martin had suggested as much.

And if your wife can't be nice to you, is it really so wrong to look for someone who can? Hardly! He shouldn't have thrown the vase at her; he'd lost his temper, and now wished he hadn't. But then, any man would lose his temper with Mandy, and he really wasn't a violent man, not by nature. Rage had its own rules – it threw things and shouted – he couldn't help that. And he'd apologized; he always apologized, bought flowers or something. So why couldn't she just forget about it and move on? Well, she had moved on, quite literally. She was presently living with a friend in Peacehaven . . .

'So you'll join us, then?' said Martin.

'I'll join you,' said Geoff.

'Wonderful,' said Martin. 'The Etiquette Society gains a new warlord and Stormhaven breathes a sigh of relief!'

'Well, thank you.'

Martin smiled. He had his man.

'And now, while I've got you here, Geoff – and I know you're madly busy, as all successful men are. But there's one other small matter I may need your help with.'

22

'What's that?'

The two men continued their conversation looking out to sea, just a five-minute walk from the Bybuckle Asylum, a place of interest to them both and a murder scene in waiting . . .

'You can stay for a while,

and then we'll see,' said Blessings to Francisco on his arrival. 'Is this all you have?'

The young man had arrived with a holdall and rucksack and was standing awkwardly in the judge's hallway, where people hung their coats. It was about the size of the prison cell he'd left that morning.

'It is, yes – I like to travel light, always have.'

He had a springy Welsh lilt in his voice, as though fresh from *Under Milk Wood*. But his life had not been poetry in motion and he'd paid the price.

'I suppose, if we're being honest, you don't have much to travel with,' said Blessings in a corrective manner. One shouldn't make a virtue of necessity. This boy had nothing, this was quite clear. So how could he travel in any other way but 'light'?

And for the awkward guest, this was all rather sudden. Francisco, the son of two Welsh Catholics, had been planning on going to a hostel, a halfway house. It's what everyone did. And then, two days before his release date, the judge had offered him a room in her home and he'd said to himself, 'Honestly – why not?' No harm in being looked after by a rich woman, and a hot one at that, in an unavailable sort of way. His mates had made their jokes, of course: 'From arsonist to toy boy, Fran – surely now you believe in God?'

But it would take a little more than that for him to believe. He'd need to get past his Sunday school teacher, and he wasn't quite ready for that.

'I don't know what the gay scene is like in Stormhaven,' said the judge, bringing him back to the hallway.

'Oh.'

What were the rules of engagement here? He had no idea. He'd always found adults a mystery anyway. His father had lived in terror of his son being gay, when no girlfriend appeared. He'd use it as a weapon of attack.

'I don't want a gay son!' he'd say whenever Fran disappointed him, when he missed a goal or asked to sing in the choir, whatever it was. 'I don't want a gay son!' And now, some years later, he simply had a son who'd never speak with him again.

But Fran was in Stormhaven now and a long way from Taff's Well. He was in the house of a judge on the south coast of England – posh world – and she needed reassurance.

'The gay scene is not my first priority,' he said.

'So what is your first priority, Francisco?'

'Making myself useful around here, I suppose; and looking for a job. I just want to be normal.'

'You'll not be bringing young men back here, do you understand?'

'No, I won't be doing that,' he said.

It was strange, but when he'd faced her in court, she'd been kinder. She'd seemed like a friend in some manner. He had felt fairly treated and that's all he wanted, for things to be fair; because things hadn't always been fair in Taff's Well. Yet here in her home, away from the court, she was more like a warder than a friend, her tone full of rules and banging metal doors.

'I can do some gardening for you, Mrs N'Dayo. I've done gardening before. I used to do a fair bit of gardening. And I can cook.'

'Have you a good arm?'

'I'm sorry?'

'You'll find a lot of golf balls in the garden, over-hit from over the road.' With her head, she indicated the Stormhaven Golf Club. 'And when you throw the balls back, make sure you hit one of the club members. They're mostly old and unpleasant.'

'You don't like the golfers?'

'That's like asking me whether I like the Ku Klux Klan.'

Bit over the top, thought Fran.

'It's not big in Wales, really . . . golf, I mean.'

'Doesn't involve sheep,' said Blessings. Fran didn't like that; it just wasn't necessary. Not really the sort of joke a judge should make, in his opinion – but then what did his opinion count for round here? 'I'm away a lot when I'm working,' she continued. 'Follow me.'

They walked through the lounge. It was enormous – like, absolutely huge! There were no front rooms like this in Taff's Well. He'd never been inside a house as big, nowhere close; he was thinking this as they ascended the wide and slightly curving stairs. 'So it's useful to have a housekeeper here,' continued Blessings, 'to look after the place . . . especially if Dinah is home.'

'Dinah?'

'My daughter. She's at Roedean.'

'What's that?'

'It's a school, a big school outside Brighton, boarding obviously, and she likes to stay there as much as possible.'

'I always wanted to go to boarding school myself. Like Harry Potter!'

'But unfortunately she does need to come home occasionally to recharge her phone or whatever.'

'Right, well, that's no problem. How old is she?'

Blessings scowled. What sort of a question was that?

'You're not one of those gays who slip up sometimes?'

'No. I mean – I was just asking a question.'

'I need to trust you.'

'You can trust me, Mrs N'Dayo.'

'Any hint of anything – you know what I mean – and that will be that for you. Your probation officer will know instantly, is that clear?'

'Yes.'

This was more demeaning than prison had ever been. He'd walked in the door and assumptions had spilled from this woman like a river in flood on his father's farm, ruining the crops, drowning the pasture, killing good growth. He'd written a poem about that when he was inside; he'd called it 'The killing flood'. They'd had a poetry class, which everyone thought was a joke, but he enjoyed it, writing things . . . when no one had ever told him he could write.

And things would settle, he thought as he put his holdall and rucksack down on the bed in the small room at the top of the house. It had pink wallpaper, and with its angled roof you had to bend in places. It was like the servants' quarters, if Blessings had had servants. Perhaps he was the servant. He had to be positive, though, look on the bright side. He told himself this because he didn't want to get angry again; and she was giving him a home, when he couldn't go back to his own. There'd be no welcome for him in South Wales, not after recent events.

He didn't like Blessings. He knew that, as he wondered where he should put his clothes. He couldn't see any drawers. Was he supposed to live out of his holdall? He hadn't expected bunting and a Welsh choir – but everyone wants a homecoming, don't they? And she'd given him the smallest room in the house, that was obvious. Who knows how many other rooms there were? Plenty. But he'd been given the pokiest room by his new landlady . . . so that was clearly his worth to her.

He sat on the bed and looked out of the skylight. It was good to see the sky and really, he didn't have to like her. He had a room, that was the main thing and Fran could be stubborn and see things through. It seemed like the judge wanted to use him as some sort of houseboy, though they hadn't spoken of pay. Well, two could play at that little game; and perhaps he could use her.

As everyone said in prison, 'The only crime is getting caught.'

Terence would attempt the drop.

He'd ease back the throttle, slow the plane in the sky until the wings juddered their disapproval and the nose dipped, sending the craft spiralling down. Classic stuff from any pilot's manual, but still fun – the ability to recover the plane from the drop, early or late, depending on your nerves . . . Terence preferred late.

Flying was an addiction for Terence, a need, an obsession; but not a love.

'You love your flying,' they said to him at Shoreham airport where *Desert*, his little plane, lived. But this wasn't true, he didn't love his flying. He wouldn't call it love. He was simply drawn to the sky like a moth to the flame; and where was the love in that? Flight might offer wonder; there were some views to be had along the coast. Or it might fling him uncaringly to the earth in a tailspin of panic and chaos. This was adrenalin, energy, exhilaration – but not love.

Only the thrill of battle compared to this suspended existence in the sky. He'd gaze down on a distant world, tiny cars and patchwork fields, remote from its feelings, free from its pull and, by accident or design, close to death. He always felt closer to death in the sky; a more provisional being, one merely passing through this earthly space.

He'd flown for years. It was cheaper than seeing a therapist and a hundred times more effective. Therapists took you into your troubles, flying took you above them, which was a far happier place. Up here in his flying machine, different rules applied . . . rules of flight. When weight was balanced by lift and thrust balanced by drag, he and his plane found steady, straight, level flight . . . they found equilibrium. And when did he find that down below?

So Shoreham airport had become his shrine, the place he went when he had to, when he simply had to go there, when the noise inside got too much to handle and he could get into *Desert* and rise above it all. It wasn't the biggest airport in the UK, but it was the oldest, opened in 1911 – 'before planes were even invented!' as the tour guide joked. It earned its stripes in the Second World War, with Spitfires and Hurricanes scrambling into action from the grass runway, seeing off the Hun who flew missions along the coast, attempting to identify possible landing sites for an invasion of England. Cuckmere Haven, towards Eastbourne, was their desired entry point but they knew about Shoreham and often attacked. A Messerschmitt 109 was downed by ground fire on one occasion, sliding at wild speed across the grass, crashing near the terminal building. No one got out.

And though things were quieter now – no enemy fire in Shoreham – they weren't silent. The recent horror at the air show had brought a change in mood around the place . . . though not in Terence, for no one should be surprised by death. Why does death surprise? And so he avoided the hysterics, the anniversaries and the grief. Flight and danger had always stayed close, which was why he was here in the cockpit now, tipping the wing, looking down at Newhaven and the harbour walls, taking his plane out over the sea, flying low over the water before returning to base.

Mission, for now, accomplished.

'A madam has been murdered,'

said Tamsin on the abbot's wet doorstep. The rain wasn't giving up.

'A madam?'

'She ran a brothel.'

'Well, I'm sorry—'

'Can I come in, before I'm washed away?'

The abbot liked some notice when people came to visit his seaside home. It helped him prepare a smile. But Tamsin had given no warning.

'In Brighton, presumably,' he said, opening the door to this unexpected invasion.

'Brighton?'

'The brothel.'

Brighton and brothel seemed to go together in Peter's mind. London-by-the-Sea they called it, and home to all sorts of goings-on, according to the *Sussex Silt*. Marjorie, an old lady he visited, merely reinforced this image: 'London is Sodom and Brighton is Gomorrah – mark my words, Abbot!'

He didn't mark her words. Marjorie was full of unexamined nonsense and living proof that 'many years lived do not make one wise'. You could live the same stupid year eighty-five times over, and she had, determinedly so. But there was something there, some grain of truth in her repetitive tongue. Brighton was dangerous in a way Stormhaven could only dream of. In Peter's mind, the two towns were separated by a bus ride of fifty minutes . . . and a cultural eternity.

'I just assumed,' said the abbot.

'And thus became a fool,' said Tamsin cheerfully. It was the sort of thing he'd usually say to her, so it was nice to return the compliment.

'I have no defence.'

'You don't, no,' she said, removing her soaking coat. 'No defence at all.'

'Careful you don't die of self-righteousness.'

'Well, you've survived.'

The rain had been relentless since Christmas, driven today by a south-westerly, which threw itself at Peter's front door, as if in torment, twisting and thrashing about like a man possessed.

'The brothel's in Stormhaven.'

'Oh.' A brothel in Stormhaven? That did come as a surprise ... and now he was wondering where it was. Was it in the town centre? Or perhaps on the Eastbourne road – though why the Eastbourne road came to mind he wasn't sure. He'd never seen a brothel in the town, but then he hadn't been looking and you don't see what you don't look for. He couldn't have said where the clothes shop was, either.

'Surprised, Abbot?' Tamsin was doing something with her dark, Middle Eastern hair, adjusting it with her hands, calming it a little, though it didn't look greatly disturbed by the short walk from the car. This was perhaps something women did.

'Well, I suppose ...'

'Disappointed, almost certainly.' Tamsin was on the attack and delighted to be so. 'You perhaps thought your little town was above such things?' She often did this, referring to Stormhaven as 'your little town' as if it were a stick to beat him with. Playful banter; though not all play.

'I wasn't aware it was my little town.'

'Oh, come on – you secretly love the place, you know you do.'

'It must be very secret. I haven't even told myself.'

They found themselves at close quarters in the abbot's small front room, which was fine for a hermit, but not for a hermit with friends. There was one comfortable chair, left by the previous occupant. Everything else came from the beach, deposited there by time and tide.

'And what *will* it do to the value of your property?!' added Tamsin joyfully. 'I can see the estate agent's brochure now: "A seven-minute walk to the station – and handily placed for the knocking shop!"'

'That's not a big issue for me,' said Peter, sitting himself on an old herring box.

'What isn't?'

'The value of the property.'

The house had been left to him by a relative he'd neither met nor heard of, when his stint in the desert had come to an end. It was a godsend at the time, because he'd no other home on earth. But that, in a way, was the point: Stormhaven hadn't been a choice. He'd arrived here from the Sahara as a refugee, with nowhere else to go. On a good day there was gratitude in his soul; but not all days were good. Certainly this day had nose-dived a little with the unannounced arrival of Tamsin. 'Though strangely, it might be for you,' he added.

'How do you mean?'

'The value of this property. It's of no interest to me. But to those who come after me . . .'

Tamsin was his niece, after all – his one known relation in the world. So who else would inherit this two-bedroom home, with a study at the back, and just a salt-soaked seventy yards from Mr Whippy's summer pitch and the variable moods of the English Channel?

'Oh, yes.' She was embarrassed, an infrequent emotion in Tamsin. She hadn't thought of this when she teased him – the fact that she might inherit this home in which she sat – and she didn't wish to dwell on it now. This house was the abbot's house; she didn't want it to be anything else, because – and she'd never really noticed this before – she didn't want him to die. She really didn't want him to die.

'We've known about the brothel for a while,' she said, gathering herself, hardening herself, becoming a detective inspector once again, perching on the comfy chair.

'Is this the royal *we* – yourself and the Queen?'

'The police.'

'But, for whatever reason, you've let it be.' He said this as an observation, quite without the sauce of accusation, but Tamsin tasted that sauce in everything.

'We've *let it be*, yes – and I'm sorry if that offends you, but if there's no coercion involved and no drugs, we do have other priorities.'

'Until the madam is murdered, I suppose.'

Now Tamsin looked prim. 'It does change things, yes.'

They sat in silence for a moment, a question begging to be asked.

'And so why are you here?' asked Peter. 'Why are you soaking my carpet this morning to tell me about a murder in a brothel? It can't just be a search for a good cup of coffee.'

Tamsin laughed. 'If I wanted a good cup of coffee, I wouldn't come here, Abbot, believe me.'

'I'll speak to my staff about your dissatisfaction.'

'I blame your suppliers.' There was a Poundshop mentality in Peter and it showed in his coffee. 'You can't polish a turd.'

'How nice to see you.'

'But the idea of something hot is not unattractive,' she said, deciding to stir his hospitality muscles. 'Just supposing you had some decent coffee in the building.'

'I'm not sure I do . . . not *your* decent, anyway. But if we were to skip the coffee – which feels like prevarication – what would we be talking about? Or, to return to my previous question, why have you come?'

He knew why she'd come – but she'd have to say it. They'd worked together on a number of cases, supported by the Sussex police's 'trusted citizen' scheme, which permitted civilians to be brought in on police investigations where their experience and knowledge were deemed helpful to the enquiry. Their partnership had not always been easy, and neither had the Lewes HQ looked kindly on the fact that they were represented by 'a bloody monk'. It wasn't their idea of modern policing. But they couldn't argue with the results, and as the chief constable reminded them with some regularity, 'Policing is like Premier League football – a results-based business.'

The fact that on their first investigation the abbot had discovered that Tamsin was his niece had not changed matters a great deal. Both wished to keep family at a distance; it was the murderers they wished to get close to. So yes, he knew why she'd come and wasn't sad. The murder of a madam in Stormhaven sounded most intriguing. But she would have to ask him because neither liked to make it easy for the other. And then, as if to save her, her phone rang.

'Excuse me,' she said, reaching for the ringing in her bag.

Why do people allow themselves to be so ruled by a phone? wondered Peter. Why the compulsion to answer? They'd been talking, hadn't they? But answer she did, and as Peter watched, he saw a strange transformation occur. Tamsin took the call, stayed seated and said little . . . but her dark and well-trimmed eyebrows furrowed and some sort of fear – or perhaps confusion – crept across her face. Something was changing before his eyes. Tamsin was normally curt over the phone, dismissive and brief, as if the caller was an idiot. 'Idiot' was her most common response to a phone call. But now she was lingering, containing her bafflement, seeking confirmation, not in charge of whatever was happening. Whatever she was being told surprised her. Something had altered.

'Bad news?' asked Peter, as she returned the phone to her bag in a measured way, as if still thinking.

'That's right, yes,' she said quietly.

'What sort of bad news?' Peter was unused to her hesitancy.

'Well, someone's died, haven't they?'

The abbot smiled at the sudden sanctity of the occasion. Tamsin was not famous for her emotional attunement to feelings around death.

'It's never been an issue before, Tamsin.'

'How would you know?'

'When you're showing concern, I do *know* it's acting,' he said. 'Would you like some coffee?' He got up from the herring box to show willing. But she shook her head and looked at him; for a moment, she felt sympathy towards this man. After all, his world was about to be blown apart. No, really. No doubt he'd had difficult times in the desert; she sensed he was not a stranger to darkness. But he was walking into a lot more darkness now. When a sordid secret is exposed in a small town like Stormhaven, there's nowhere to hide, especially with the *Sussex Silt* on the prowl . . . and multiply that tenfold if you wear a monk's habit.

'Do you want to sit down, Peter?' How was she to handle this?

'I've only just got up.'

'You might want to sit down.'

'You're the one who seems uneasy, Tamsin. Almost compassionate . . . and it isn't your style. It's quite unnerving.'

Tamsin raised her eyebrows. 'And you don't know why that might be?' she asked.

'Why what might be?'

'Why this conversation might be difficult for me – given what I've just told you?'

'What have you just told me? You told me my coffee tastes of turd and that there's a brothel in Stormhaven . . . oh, and you worried a little about the effect on house prices.'

'I also told you about a madam.'

'You told me she'd been murdered, which is significant for her nearest and dearest; but not hugely revealing.'

Tamsin paused at the cliff edge . . . and decided to jump.

'We know, Peter.'

'You know what?' He was frustrated now.

She got up because she couldn't think what else to do, feeling trapped in this small space. She went over to the window.

'I need you to make this easier for me,' she said. The rain smashed against the glass, and through the spray she watched the wind-stirred sea, rising, crashing, foaming across the shingle.

'In your own time,' said Peter.

'No one's judging you, Uncle.'

Uncle? This was getting worse. She never called him *uncle*.

'I don't know what you're talking about.'

'Then let me spell it out.' She'd given him enough time to cooperate. He hadn't helped her, so kindness could be withdrawn. 'The madam of the Stormhaven brothel, Model Service . . .'

'Yes?'

'She had you down as her next of kin. As her partner.'

Peter stood silent, bemused. 'Next of kin? To the madam? Me?'

Tamsin nodded.

'Well, who was she?'

'I think we were hoping you could tell us . . . as next of kin.'

'I mean her name.'

'Rosemary Weller.'

Peter was stunned. 'Rosemary? What's Rosemary got to do with this?'

Rosemary had found Tara.

The relationship had started on her doorstep, with Tara very nearly slamming the door in this bold woman's face.

'How did you find me?' had been her first question, after Rosemary had knocked loudly and made her brief introductions. Tara's initial response had been defensive, and who could blame her? She did not appreciate the arrival of strangers on her doorstep, particularly one so clearly 'professional' as Rosemary. Was she a social worker, or worse, an Inland Revenue agent here to snoop, probe or condemn? Not everything in her life was above reproach.

'I spoke with the police,' said Rosemary cheerfully, which wasn't a good start.

'The police?'

'Well, how else would someone like me find a practising madam?'

This all seemed eminently sensible to Rosemary – and the end of the conversation for Tara.

'I'm sorry, but I . . .' Tara couldn't finish, she was aghast. She tried to stay out of police sight, as far away as possible. Why had this woman been speaking to the police? It didn't matter; it was time she went. 'I don't know what brings you here, Mrs Weller, but—'

'Er, Miss.'

'I don't much mind, Mrs or Miss, but I think you'd better—'

And she'd begun to close the door.

'It's nothing like that,' said Rosemary, pushing the door gently back open. 'I come as an admirer, Tara.'

'An admirer?'

'An admirer of the business you run here in Brighton.'

What did this woman know of her business? 'And what particularly do you admire?'

'You look after your girls, I'm told.'

'Who told you that?'

'The girls.'

'You *have* been busy.' There was something irrepressible about this woman.

'Could I come in just for a moment?' said Rosemary. 'I'd like a brief word, one I think you may like. I mean, I hope I'm coming with good news. But perhaps it's best shared in a slightly more private setting.'

Tara had opened the door, taking Rosemary through the hallway into the front room, where she sat her down on the white leather sofa.

'Very nice,' said Rosemary, looking around at a stylish room of wooden furniture and modern art. 'Really very stylish. You decorate your home like an arts graduate. And that's meant to be a compliment.'

Who is this woman? 'So why are you here?'

'I want to give you premises, Tara.'

'Promises?'

'No, premises. Well, promises as well, I suppose.'

'Premises.'

'Yes.'

'Premises for what?'

'For your current business. You don't have any, do you?'

'Well, no, I don't.'

She ran a network of sex workers in Brighton, hosting a communal website for them and offering various forms of both financial and emotional support. But it was geographically scattered and slightly chaotic.

'Right,' said Rosemary, reassured that her research had not been incorrect. 'So I want to give you a base, a home ... better protection for the girls than working alone in their flats where they're vulnerable. Men can be forceful; particularly groups of men. And it's better for their self-worth, don't you think, to work away from home? They then leave home to work and return there to live.'

Tara paused for a moment, to absorb the news so far; and all delivered at such a pace, as if everything was sorted. Rosemary, as she would learn, was brisk in her business.

'Where?' asked Tara.

'The premises?'

'Yes. Where are they?'

'In Stormhaven.'

'A brothel in Stormhaven?' She couldn't help laughing.

'Well, we already have a church and a post office,' said Rosemary.

They were now both laughing. It was Tara's first glimpse of Rosemary's humour, which surfaced only occasionally, but could be outrageous.

'Are you going to buy?'

'I already have.'

'Oh.'

This was all moving very fast.

'Yes, I have some premises in Stormhaven that are ready to move into. Well, they need a little decorating perhaps, a lick of paint, some furnishings, but that can be all arranged.'

'Right.'

'And you'd oversee that, knowing what's necessary.'

'Towels, mainly.'

'Towels?'

'You can't have too many towels.'

'Quite. But I'd need you to run it, to be there. Yes? Obviously you could continue with other work, as long as it wasn't to the detriment of the new business, whatever you choose to call it. Something tasteful; we could perhaps agree together about a name.'

'Stormhaven is hardly Sin City.'

'And we won't be making it so – not at all. This is a business, not a sin . . . a gift to the people of Stormhaven.' Tara was warming to her. Should she offer tea? 'And a gift to our employees. Like any employer, we simply give people work and protect them as they go about their business.'

'Who are you?'

'I'm Rosemary Weller, as I said.'

'No, I mean, why do you . . .'

'My work is mainly in the charity sector. Mainly charity – though I'm also churchwarden at St Michael's.'

'Churchwarden?'

'So I'm branching out a little.'

'I wouldn't be running a charity, you do know that?' said Tara.

'No. As I said, you'd be running a business, which must wipe its own nose financially, but one that respects its employees.'

'Would you like some tea?' This felt like the right time to offer.

'We need to talk about money first,' said Rosemary. Tara had been wondering about the finances. 'Once we've sorted the money, then perhaps a cup of tea would be nice.'

And that's how Tara had first met Rosemary.

They now had coffee

though neither looked pleased.

Tamsin had taken charge. She'd sat Peter down in his own front room, gone to the kitchen and returned with two steaming cups of an instant she'd never heard of.

'I hope this *is* coffee,' she said, waving the jar in the air. She wondered if they were gravy granules, with the aroma giving no clues either way.

'Lidl's finest,' he said. 'Well, Lidl's only.'

Her kitchen fears had been confirmed; the provenance of the coffee was deeply suspect. She'd pretend to drink it, she was trying to be kind, and this required deliberate thought in Tamsin. Kindness was not a flower that grew naturally in the fields of her being. But in the end, beyond kind thoughts, this was a murder investigation. And the man she wanted to work on the case with her had disqualified himself before they'd even started – by being next of kin to the victim! And she was angry about that.

The abbot knew the deceased well, this was quite clear. Yet in a rather absurd manner, he was attempting to bluff his way out of the mess, shiftily denying all knowledge. And yes, that also made Tamsin angry.

'So you obviously know Rosemary well.'

'I don't know her well.'

'You're down as her next of kin, Abbot. That's a few steps on from having once sat next to her on the bus.'

'It's quite inexplicable.'

'I doubt that somehow, Abbot. Everything has a reason, once obfuscation is peeled away.'

'Have you been going to English classes?'

'I'm quoting you.'

'Really? Well, I suppose I'm flattered.' And he *was* flattered. 'And clearly it's true. Nothing is inexplicable; everything has a reason.

But I'm sitting in a big soup of madness here. I don't know what to say.'

'You can start by saying how you knew her.'

'How I knew her?' He wasn't sure how he had known her. 'I knew her once. A long time ago, a different life.'

And then Tamsin remembered. Oh my goodness! Was this his first love? Was her uncle's past returning in a most uncomfortable way?

'This wasn't nurse Rosemary, who you fell in love with at that psychiatric unit in Highgate?'

Peter had regretted telling her. He'd let this slip on the last case they'd shared – the murders up at the school. He'd mentioned, in passing, his first, and failed, love affair . . . though to call it that, even to use that phrase, was to over-egg the pudding. It was neither love nor an affair. And he regretted telling Tamsin, immediately, because information is power.

But that was that; he could not call back the words. The deed was done, the information had wings, and Tamsin knew about Rosemary when he'd have preferred her ignorant.

'Yes, I did once have strong feelings for her.' That was not a phrase he'd used before, and he listened to himself saying it. These things had lived for ever inside him, but never outside, never spoken.

'How strong?'

'They weren't returned, that's all that matters, and the sap of obsession dried quickly enough in the desert sand.'

Let that be that . . . end of story.

'Or appeared to,' said his niece, inquisitorially.

'It was more than appearance, Tamsin. I stopped writing, she didn't write, we never met. The clues are there, even for the police. Whatever it had been, it wasn't any more.'

'Well, it clearly was for her. You're her next of kin.'

Peter shrugged. The coffee was too weak, as it always was when others made it. Could he reasonably go to the kitchen and strengthen it a little? Probably not . . . not now. Tamsin was obsessed with his relationship with Rosemary. And the more he explained how little it really was, the more it seemed to exist.

41

Deny something and it grows in size. She'd soon be saying he 'doth protest too much'.

'What can I say?' he said. 'I have absolutely no understanding of this development, Tamsin.'

'None at all?'

'My only thought – and it's a sad one – is that she must have gone on to live a rather lonely life. A full life, from what I hear, but perhaps lonelier than it looked. And our brief acquaintance – towards which she contributed very little, beyond being a most excellent nurse – perhaps became something more important to her in retrospect. These things can happen . . . a sense of something lost, yet which barely existed at the time.'

'You did suddenly become rather unobtainable, didn't you?'

'How do you mean?'

'After it was over. I mean, the monk's outfit and all that. And the desert. You suddenly became impossible for her, which might increase the longing, I suppose.'

Peter was struck by her insight – an unusual occurrence. Had she known such feelings herself? Had she once loved the unobtainable? She wouldn't be telling him if she had. As for Peter, he noticed his breathing deepening, as one stirred. He found himself strangely moved that anyone could put him as 'next of kin'. It awakened something inside him, there was no question of that. Rosemary's rejection had been the easier path, removing hope, which could be so difficult to live with.

But now he found himself troubled, wondering how different things might have been if he'd done something else? And in the light of this, another question: had his stay in the desert been nothing more than one long escape from his feelings? Imagine if he had stayed in England, for instance, if he'd persisted with the relationship – might things have been different between himself and Rosemary? He had to wonder . . .

'I wanted you on the case,' said Tamsin.

'I thought you might.'

'But that's not possible now, is it?' She was still angry about this. 'Why not?'

'You're too connected.'

Peter paused. He must think clearly. He wanted to work on the case. He'd wanted the case before he knew it was Rosemary. Now he wanted it even more.

'Am I a beneficiary of her death?' he asked.

'How do you mean?'

'In relation to her will? I'm sure you've seen her will.'

'I have and no, you're not. You're next of kin, but you receive nothing in her will. Absolutely nothing at all.'

'Don't sound so pleased.'

'So no more surprise houses coming your way. Everything has been left to charity – apart from the business.'

'The business?'

'Model Service.'

'Of course, yes.' He would have to get used not only to her death but also to Rosemary as the owner of a brothel called Model Service . . . when it appeared the most unlikely thing in the world. It wasn't that he now thought worse of her; he just thought differently. She was becoming a different person in death and therefore strangely alive, leaving so much to be re-evaluated. 'So that's good news, isn't it?'

'What is?'

'I'm one of those rare souls delighted to be excluded from the will.'

'Because?'

'It frees me to work on the case,' he replied. 'Where's the problem in me investigating the murder of someone I last spoke with forty years ago?'

'You haven't seen her since?'

He'd have to tell her; there were too many witnesses. 'Once.'

'You *have* seen her again?'

'Yes.'

'Recently?'

'Yes.'

'Why did you see her again? You said it was over.' Tamsin's frustration could not be hidden.

'It wasn't planned. We met at the Stormhaven Etiquette Society.'

'*Where?*'

43

'The Stormhaven Etiquette Society. It's a . . . well, does it matter? It's a society.'

'I'd got that far.'

'And I gave a talk to them the other night on the relationship between morality and grace.'

'A ticket to die for.'

'You weren't invited, dead or alive. You're not a member, it's invitation only, very secretive. But she's a member . . . or was.'

'Rosemary was there at the meeting?'

'Yes.'

'And you had no idea she would be?'

'No idea at all.'

Tamsin took in the scene, finding it hard not to be amused. The pain of others had this effect.

'That must have been a shock for you; a large ghost from the past walking through the door.'

'My feelings exactly . . . from the past. I don't imagine she recognized me and the evening came and went without incident.'

'You didn't kneel down before her and declare your love.'

'No.'

'Or meet for a clandestine liaison of wine and roses later in the week?'

'There was nothing between us, Tamsin. Too many years had passed under the bridge of time. I'm quite ready to assist on the case.'

Tamsin considered the situation. She wanted to believe him but felt unease. She had no interest in the lovesick or the self-pitying. If the abbot turned out to be one of those, or both, their investigative partnership would not end well.

'It may stir things, Peter.'

'What sort of things?'

'Well, perhaps you won't like what you discover about Rosemary. I mean, you probably never thought . . .'

'That she was a madam? No, I didn't. I can't say I came even close to imagining that.'

'And perhaps she had other liaisons that you'll find . . . upsetting.'

'What other liaisons?'

'We don't know the nature of her involvement, but she ran a brothel, for God's sake. It's different from a sewing club. You may discover things that provoke you, and rage is not a helpful tool in the detective's armoury.'

'No, but anger is – clean anger, unattached to the ego. And perhaps I'll be allowed that simply because a good person has been killed.'

Tamsin wasn't listening, caught up in her own line of enquiry.

'I mean, you say you're over her, Abbot, as if the desert was your real lover. But do these things ever die? Especially your first love . . . or perhaps more truthfully, your first obsession. Obsessions are stupid but powerful.'

Peter was not keen on this lecture and felt a tide of fury crashing against his shoreline. He didn't trust the lecturer for a start.

'How can you presume to know of my feelings, Tamsin, when you are so ignorant of your own?'

He looked at her to emphasize the force of the question. Tamsin was clearly in the turmoil he should have been in. She even took a sip of the coffee she'd been trying to avoid. The fact was, she didn't know what she wanted; or rather she did, but couldn't see how it could be.

'I do want you on the case, Peter, but I don't want you with any baggage, because you'll slow us down. And there's an airport-full of baggage here.'

'There's baggage on every case, Tamsin – *every* case. I've seen the police at very close quarters, remember, and been able to evaluate their performance. The scores aren't high.'

'You haven't perhaps met the elite of the force.'

Peter laughed. 'And then you're hardly a clear pool of consciousness yourself. It wasn't so long ago you ran away from a therapist who was just beginning to help you. And you ran away because you couldn't face what was coming to the surface. So where's that baggage now? At least I'm aware of mine.'

Peter was dragging up events from an old case, but they were ones she could not deny.

'So no lectures on baggage,' he continued. 'Or I might ask you precisely what it is that you fear?'

45

A haunted look on her face became – slowly – a guilty smile, a small act of awareness, and somewhere inside she was glad he was fighting back.

'All you're doing, Tamsin, is allowing me to find the murderer of someone I knew a long time ago.'

'Next of kin.'

'Her words.'

'Why would she lie?'

'She's not lying. It's just her interpretation.'

But she'd have to press him on this, really she would. Tamsin didn't want to get crucified by a wrong decision along the way, nailed on the cross of public perception.

'Interpretations are usually based on something.'

'I don't know why she called me next of kin . . . as I've said. You'll have to believe me on that one. But I do know I've had no serious contact with her since those faraway days. And I also know that I do not feature in her will – a fact that speaks loudly on my behalf, when I ask to be involved.'

'Perhaps you discovered she ran a brothel and felt betrayed.'

'And then killed her?'

'Perhaps.'

She might as well say it at the outset. 'Are you the murderer?'

But the words sounded stupid even as she spoke them, and Peter was inclined to agree.

'That Rosemary was a madam, I can cheerfully accept, believe me. It was her membership of the Stormhaven Etiquette Society I struggle with.'

And most of what he'd told Tamsin was true, though not quite all. He wanted to work on the case without awkwardness, so hadn't mentioned their meeting in Broad Street last Tuesday. It wasn't pertinent, he told himself.

'Then we need to go to the asylum,' said Tamsin, getting up. She'd made up her mind, public perception be damned. Peter had just joined her team.

'Which asylum?'

'Bybuckle.'

'Bybuckle? Why do we need to go there?'

'Didn't I tell you? It's where Rosemary was killed.'

'In the Bybuckle Asylum?'

'Keep up.'

He knew the place. It had been taken out of service in the late eighties and been a controversial folly ever since. It was a five-minute walk away, a near neighbour on the wind-battered Stormhaven seafront. After all these years of distance, Rosemary had been killed very close to his front door.

'And we need to go now?'

'You know SOCO, Peter. They'll have the murder scene packed away in no time – dabbed, brushed, pictured, sealed and sent. We need to be there before it is. We need to see the body.'

'Fine,' he said, but it wasn't. It was some way from being fine. His innards felt compressed by the thought of the scene that awaited him. Tamsin hadn't disclosed how Rosemary was killed and he hadn't asked. But now the decision was made and he was on the case, her ruthlessness returned. She wouldn't be protecting him.

'Still got the light, I see,' she said.

'Which light?'

'That one.'

Tamsin was putting on her coat and looking up the stairs to the candle that burned in the small landing window. It had been there for as long as she'd known him; she'd just never asked why.

'Yes, it still burns,' said Peter.

Not giving much away, then.

'Does it burn for a reason?'

'Must light have a reason?'

Tamsin wanted an answer, not a meditation.

'What you do in the privacy of your own home is entirely up to you, Abbot,' she said dismissively. 'We need to get to the asylum.'

Peter put on an old duffle coat. 'How did she die?' he asked.

He needed to know; and didn't want to know.

'You'll see soon enough. Ready?'

Police were everywhere

in this Impressionistic seafront scene. The Bybuckle Asylum was obscured in a wet mist, as Tamsin and the abbot approached on foot. There were high-vis jackets around high-vis cars, parked at angles, blocking off the seafront road. There were watercolour reds and blues, one becoming the other, and a salt-water shine on the road. Slippery steps took the visitor up to the front entrance of the asylum, a once strong and solid Victorian front door. Around them, evidence-protecting outfits moved with purpose, like Arctic explorers on a trip to the sea.

'Have you been inside before?' asked Tamsin.

'No,' said Peter, speaking through the wind. 'Though I've walked past it enough.'

'No walking by on the other side today, Abbot.'

'Have you been inside?'

'No,' said Tamsin. The place spooked her. 'Never had cause to, not being mad. But I have seen the crime-scene pictures. Not great. Are you ready?'

'I'm ready.'

'Seriously?'

'I'm ready.'

How could he ever be ready for this?

The police cordon was lifted with a wave of Tamsin's card and they climbed the ten steps up to the entrance. The salt wind ruins every frontage along the seafront, rusting Sky dishes, eating at the paint. Even the grandest dwellings suffer; though the Bybuckle Asylum had never tried to be grand. Sturdy red and grey brick in civic patterns, an earnest establishment, a place of both detention and reform, but decomposing now, rusty metal window frames, bereft of their panes, long smashed or blown away.

Inside the dark entrance hall they stood for a moment, struck by the damp desolation of the building.

'A place of ghosts and screams,' said Peter.

'Don't get weird on me, Abbot.'

Though she was glad he was here. There was something about this place, as if its history lived on, insanity permeating both walls and air. The mad had been removed, but their despair remained. Or was that all in her imagination? There was a rumour of developers turning this place into luxury flats, the vision for every half-decent space these days. But Tamsin wouldn't be buying one. How could this space ever be free of its history? And now this . . .

She spoke with the constable on the door. 'Where's the body?'

'Through there, ma'am.'

He pointed down the long corridor to a door on the right.

'Shall we?' said Tamsin.

They made their way into the darkness, reaching some swinging doors. 'Gladstone Ward' was the sign above the entrance, though nothing prepared them for the size of the room they walked into, a truly vast space.

'DI Shah?'

An officer approached them.

'Yes.'

'The body's over here.'

'Right.'

The officer looked at the monk, uncertain about procedure. 'Is he coming?'

'He is, yes. And he has a name. Peter. Abbot Peter.'

'Right.' What was a monk doing on a crime scene? 'And he has, er, clearance?'

'You get on with your job, sergeant, and I'll get on with mine.'

'Yes, ma'am.'

They were led towards a metal bed in the middle of the ward, partially hidden by the remains of a curtain, hanging from rusted rails in the ceiling. How many beds had been here once was hard to tell – fifty? A hundred? Now, only a few remained – a random scattering of bare metal frames. Only one of these was of interest today, however, and they approached it now.

'When was she found?'

'Eight o'clock this morning. A tip-off.'

'Phone?' He nodded. 'And how long dead?'

'About twelve hours, more details to come, but cause of death not hard to establish.'

'No,' said Tamsin, looking down.

Peter looked . . . and looked away, numb to everything, quite unable to feel. It had the appearance of an execution. A trial, a judgement and then . . . an execution.

Twelve hours earlier,

there had been no police in Bybuckle Asylum; they do tend to arrive late when it comes to murder. Rosemary had been here alone, wondering if her 'carer' would return. She was hoping they wouldn't, of course . . . really hoping they wouldn't.

She wondered, as she lay there, if this was some sort of revenge stunt, to frighten her, perhaps? If further harm was planned, then surely they'd have finished the job? So was she to be left here? Left here to scream until someone came to free her? But who'd ever come in here? People walked past this place with averted eyes. And who'd hear a scream from a building designed to muffle such things, to keep the public safe from the awkward noises of the mad and the tied-down? And she was tied down, her movement painfully limited.

Was this how Sarah had felt? She suddenly thought of Sarah, though she didn't want to. She had done her best for her sister, everyone knew that, done as much as she could, though it hadn't been enough . . . well, it was enough to get her drugged-up body away from the men – those repulsive men. But after that?

Rosemary didn't know much of the story. Her little sister had disappeared into the London scene after the arrest of her 'boyfriend'. She'd been determined to make her own way, breaking all contact with the family. And perhaps Rosemary could have done more to find her? But Sarah hadn't wanted to be found, this was the thing, and if she had, then she knew where Rosemary was. So surely it had been her responsibility to make it happen? You couldn't always rely on your big sister to do everything.

'I didn't need you to save me,' was all Sarah had said to Rosemary after the police had raided the flat. She *had* needed her, that was quite clear. But what can you say to someone like that?

And were things any better between them now? She hoped so. Sarah had reappeared after a while, found herself a perfectly decent job in London, something in accounts, seemed happy enough, and they'd met on occasion for a meal. They didn't talk about the past, they shared more recent events; though the past sat there with them, shouting loudly through their small talk ... and Sarah should probably have said thank you. She'd had time to reflect on what she'd been saved from. But she never did, or she hadn't yet. And she continued to choose rather unfortunate men.

But this was not the time to think of Sarah. Rosemary needed to think of herself, because no one was coming to save her. There was no big sister out there for Rosemary, no cavalry on the way. There never had been. She must focus on the bed on which she was tied, or perhaps on events that had brought her here. She'd review the evening, she'd reclaim control ... or at least some understanding. She liked solutions, she liked to sort things out; and everything could be sorted out with a bit of thought and elbow grease, even if you weren't always thanked for it. So what had happened?

Rosemary remembered the phone call she'd received the week before. It was an author researching a new history of the asylum; that had been their slant. They'd wanted to meet old employees and former patients to get a sense of the place. They offered both a reunion and a goodbye – some sort of closure – and a chance to hear of people's stories since. It had seemed a good idea at the time. The author spoke well; Rosemary felt she could hardly refuse. So she'd said yes and thought no more about it.

And this evening, she'd arrived at the asylum around six to find the doors open, the lights on, music playing inside. There was some trepidation – this place had memories for her – but hope was the stronger sense as she stepped inside, looking for a friendly or familiar face. But she'd got no further than the entrance hall before ... before what? Before being knocked to the floor. Yes, she remembered now.

Knocked to the floor, a pain in her head. She'd heard the front door closing behind her, sensed the lights being turned out, felt the cold mosaic stone on her face. And then she was being dragged, with difficulty ... she saw the corridor walls passing, the peeling paint, the damp matting, through open swing doors, hinges all rust and decay and into the main ward ... she knew it was the main ward, she knew this place, the bed curtains blowing a little in the wind through the broken windows.

And then nothing, until she was lying on the bed – though this wasn't a bed, or not a place of comfort. It was a bare metal frame. She'd tried to move and was slapped hard, like an explosion in the brain.

'Don't make me do more,' said the voice, its owner tying her harshly.

And then they'd left her and Rosemary lay listening to the sea heaving on the shingle and those words came to mind: 'Time and tide stayeth for no man.'

But perhaps they would stay with her tonight; because she needed their company in the gutted remains of the Bybuckle Asylum.

'Time and tide, please stay,' she whispered, like a child frightened by the night.

'Blessings' all mine!'

Martin Channing, the bad-boy editor, possessed a mischievous charm, determined to take nothing too seriously. 'She's not, of course; I don't think Blessings is anybody's.' He smiled. 'Although one or two brave souls have *attempted* ownership.' He pondered their attempts. 'They remind me of those pale-faced trophy hunters who stand in their stupid safari shorts next to dead lions. Only Blessings is very much alive . . . and she ate them all.'

Tamsin and Peter were visiting Martin at his place of work, having driven the seven miles to the historic town of Lewes. 'Everything happened here,' Martin had said, indicating Lewes in its entirety. 'They're all terrible history snobs, of course. If it isn't the battle of Lewes, it's their famous Protestant martyrs' bonfire narrative or Thomas Paine's favourite hostelry. They've probably got the original Garden of Eden somewhere off the High Street!'

They now sat in a side room off the airy office that housed the *Sussex Silt*. The newspaper had been revitalized by Martin's happily shameless editorship, and the building was an old warehouse now renovated and gentrified. Formerly, it had been a beacon of engineering, making agricultural machinery by the tidal River Ouse. But no one made things in Lewes any more, apart from fudge brownies for the tea shops and expensive candles for the gift shops. Only the river remained the same – the eternal flow, rising and falling at the tide's bidding.

And they were here to see Martin Channing with a particular matter on their mind. As the founding member, he was going to tell them all about the Stormhaven Etiquette Society . . . everything.

'It did surprise me,' said Peter as they settled.

'What surprised you?' asked Martin.

'Well – a man like you starting the Stormhaven Etiquette Society, when you hate Stormhaven . . . and etiquette.'

'Call me a missionary, Abbot!'

'I choke a little on that description.'

'Civilizing the natives!'

Tamsin joined them from the ladies', suitably impressed by their scented cleanliness and Molton Brown hand cream. If you judged a man by his shoes and an organization by its toilets, then here at the *Sussex Silt* she was in the presence of greatness. Channing had very nice shoes.

'And, of course, your little talk on morality and, er . . .'

'Grace.'

'Morality and grace, yes – it went down very well. Very well indeed. Not sure any of us philistines knew what you were talking about, mind! Too much time in the desert, Abbot! You've forgotten what the real world looks like.' Peter smiled for now. 'But you were a different voice, no question of that and novelty value with the monk's outfit, and just what we needed. You bestowed vicarious holiness on us all! We're a slightly odd bunch, obviously.'

'Slightly?'

'You can be honest, Abbot.'

'Well, I don't know what the opposite of community cohesion is, Channing, but you've certainly managed it with that group. Together you took dysfunction to a new level.'

'Marvellously modelled for us by the Church, of course.' Martin smiled with thinly veiled aggression. 'I mean, who has done dysfunction like God's robed ones, Abbot? The rest of us are just a pale imitation.'

'I'm not here to speak for the Church.'

'No, you'd need a defence lawyer with balls of steel and a complete disregard for the truth to do that. But we're digressing from the story.'

'What story?'

'Because after you'd left the gathering – you were a little hasty, I felt – Rosemary actually claimed she knew you.'

'Really?'

'Or thought she knew you.'

Tamsin flinched. What did Channing know?

'Well, hardly,' said Peter.

'I'm sure there's nothing in it; nothing in it at all.'

55

'So am I.'

'You weren't lovers in the desert, were you? How exotic, Abbot!'

Peter shook his head. 'Nothing like that.'

'So what was it like? I do sniff a story here.'

Peter wanted there to be no story. Tamsin's body tensed.

'Our paths crossed briefly a long time ago.'

'Some charitable endeavour no doubt!'

'You know me, Martin: always saving the world.' It felt like he might be out of the wood. 'Saving myself is rather harder, of course.'

'You were telling us about the membership,' said Tamsin, intervening. She didn't want Martin sniffing around the abbot's relationship with Rosemary. 'Blessings, for instance.'

'What of her?'

'She's your tame judge, isn't she?'

'Tame? Blessings?' Martin played surprised. 'Not tame in any manner at all! Cold and hard as an ice pick in Alaska . . . but who wouldn't be, frankly, having to deal with all those lawyers, who probably confuse her with their housemaids.'

'You don't like lawyers?'

'Lawyers are jackals of misery.'

'So a similar profession to yours, then.'

'Detective Inspector!' He enjoyed her verbal assault no end. 'Mind you, if you can survive the bitching at Roedean, you can survive anywhere.'

'Blessings went to Roedean?'

'I never did think single-sex schools were a good idea for girls. Without a few idiot boys around, girls can really be very nasty to each other. Though I think it was the incident with her father, Providence N'Dayo, that she . . . well, found rather difficult.'

'What incident?'

'A little interested, perhaps?'

'Maybe.'

'I shouldn't say, really . . .'

'It's never stopped you before, Martin. He was a diplomat, wasn't he?'

'A Ghanaian diplomat, yes. That's what brought them to this country; and Blessings never quite left. Her father left, but she didn't go with him. He returned to some minor posting in Ghana – only to be found dead by one of his sons.'

'Well, it comes to us all.'

'In the toilet,' added Martin.

They all paused. None of them wished to die in the toilet.

'It's hardly a crime,' said Peter.

'Not glorious, though, is it? I mean, there are better places to be found.'

'Where like?'

'Well, in a rocking chair, gazing at the setting sun, perhaps? Or reading my own editorial in the *Silt*? But as you say, no crime, so God knows why she's so sensitive about it all.'

That was probably enough about her father.

'So Blessings is a force, is she?' asked Tamsin.

'She's feared by other lawyers, this is what they tell me. And when the sharks fear you . . .'

'Quite. Well, we look forward to meeting her.'

'I don't think she likes the police very much. Just a hunch.'

'And you're supposing I care?' said Tamsin. Martin smiled. He could see a battle ahead.

'I'm old and wise enough to know the police never care.'

'A little harsh,' said Peter.

'But only a little.'

Tamsin stepped in again: 'So moving round the circle in the Stormhaven Etiquette Society, who's the mysterious Terence Blain?'

'Terence?'

'Former major-general, isn't he?'

Terence would miss the lifts

home in Rosemary's car. He had taken to enjoying her curt offer of help as the Etiquette Society disbanded for another night, with Blessings moving them firmly towards the door. She didn't encourage any hanging around at Black Cap; she liked the courtroom cleared.

'Lift, Terence?' Rosemary would say as things broke up. She asked cheerfully but without warmth; a casual enquiry that meant nothing. It was simply an offer of help from a professional helper.

'Don't mind if I do,' said Terence with equal distance, though Rosemary would have made a good military wife, with her no-nonsense approach. 'As long as it doesn't put you out.'

'I'm going your way. It would be rather odd not to offer.'

'People will start talking,' said Blessings on one occasion as she noted them leaving together.

'Talking about what?' asked Rosemary, putting on her coat.

'A lift in the car today, a shared hotel room tomorrow, in some out-of-town Premier Inn. I see it all the time. In court, I mean.'

'We're not in court, Blessings, we're in Stormhaven. And it's a lift, believe me.'

'I'm sure it is, Rosemary.'

'Though why you're quite so interested . . .'

'She's worried you might attack me,' said Terence and that had defused the moment. It drew a chuckle from Rosemary and Blessings had never returned to the theme, though the lifts in Rosemary's red Skoda had continued. She'd take him to the end of his road, King's Drive, and stop there.

'You can walk from here, can't you? You probably could do with some exercise after all that sitting.'

Parking at the end of the road ensured he never invited her in, never had to pose the question, which suited them both. And a walk from the car was no hardship for Terence. He'd close the door and be on his way, not good at farewells and the niceties of departure, feeling abrupt and awkward. He'd sat with dying comrades – gasping, choking, disappearing from existence – and he'd never said goodbye. He'd look them in the eye, hold their wild gaze . . . but never a goodbye, too final. Goodbyes were a bloody stupid nonsense for Terence; though sometimes, before his leaving, he and Rosemary would talk in the car, in a clipped manner and with an eye on the time. Perhaps Rosemary would ask him about his army days, which he spoke of as a faraway time, like one still in recovery, trying not to touch the scars.

'The army is the army,' he said. 'It captures people, protects people, breaks people and kills people. And that's just its soldiers.'

'Do you miss it?'

'I don't miss things as a rule,' he'd reply. Missing things was dangerous to Terence. It gave them too much value . . . as if anything had any value. 'One must not imagine anything matters,' he added.

It was a bit of a bombshell. The close confines of the car intensified the nihilism.

'Oh, I think some things matter, Terence,' said Rosemary firmly. 'Surely some things matter?' But he sat still and unresponsive, looking out of the window down a dark street of bungalows and their endlessly well-tended gardens. He was feeling as dark as the sky. Was this retirement – endless trips to the garden centre, a relentless trimming of the borders? And retirement could last thirty years . . .

'Well?' said Rosemary. Stormhaven was quiet at night, quieter than a corpse. 'What's life about if nothing matters, Terence?'

I don't know, he thought.

'I'll be getting home,' he'd say and get out of the car without a further word. Rosemary would watch him walk up the road towards his 1980s bungalow home – one of Stormhaven's finest, a military man in civvies.

But that was then and now Rosemary was gone, removed from sight, so no more lifts. The only challenge left for Terence was not to die of boredom.

Perhaps his flying would keep him alive now Rosemary was gone.

Sidney stopped filming.

He put the camera down with care and went to the kitchen to make a cup of tea. He moved slowly, not being as young as he once was. 'You're not as young as you were, Gramps,' as his granddaughter Sally told him. 'You should live in Eastbourne. That's the mecca for oldies, isn't it?'

She wasn't a sensitive woman, his granddaughter, and he had no affection for her, none at all. Why did he see her? Because she was his granddaughter. Would he see her if she wasn't his granddaughter? Not in a million years; not in two million. He disliked her. But she dropped in – perhaps she was bored – and liked to see him keep up with his filming. 'No, I think a hobby's good for you, Gramps,' she'd say, in her patronizing way. He hated being called Gramps. And she didn't know what he filmed; she wasn't that interested. This was a visit, not a relationship. He could have told her what he filmed, but she never asked. Sidney was interested, though; he'd always been interested in what he filmed.

He'd been taking photos since the war – or just after the war. He'd been sent to Nuremberg as a young reporter for the trials of the Nazi command. Amazing he'd recovered, really, because they were dark times, heavy with the awful truth. He remembered the bleak souls in black and white print, their Führer dead, the insane bubble burst. Some chose bluster and fight; but Sidney remembered their nervous, distracted looks around the courtroom, as if waiting for their saviour to arrive. Only their saviour was dead: suicide and then incineration. They were on their own in front of the world's cameras.

And from then on, Sidney went wherever his editors sent him, whether it was a Caribbean island and Princess Margaret's love life – 'involving no love at all,' as his colleague observed – or the starving in Ethiopia, also lacking love. He'd been there at the beginning of all that: those early scenes that shocked the world. You just recorded what you saw. Others could decide what they thought about it, what to do about it. He didn't feed the dying, he filmed the dying. And so now he filmed Church Street where he lived, and on rather better equipment than he once held in Nuremberg.

Though in the end, as editors told him, it was about the story, not the equipment. And the story today, from his bedroom window, was a brothel across the road. A brothel in Stormhaven; he was fairly sure of that. A special sense for scandal had been his stock-in-trade, after all. And this young man in his lens was a frequent visitor to number nine. He'd caught him on film several times, pressing the doorbell – looking around, always looking around, like a nervous war criminal, that's what brought it all back – and the door opening but no figure in the doorway. The young man just stepped into the darkness and closed the door behind him.

And there were other men, Sidney had noticed. Men arriving alone, visiting the house in Church Street, lunchtime or late, curtains always closed upstairs, lights on at odd hours. And no greeting at the door; there was never a greeting at the door. He just recorded the scene, he didn't judge. That was for others.

And now the rumour around town that the brothel madam had been killed.

He went out to get a copy of the *Sussex Silt*. It was a terrible rag, really, but he'd worked for worse, and it did tell a good story. And this one would be right up their grubby street.

'Terence is a soldier,'

said Martin, warming to his role as the Grand Explainer of Secrets to Tamsin and Peter . . . and the Stormhaven Etiquette Society had a few. 'And a first-rater,' he added. 'I mean, he's a genuine war hero; one of those who went above and beyond in the battle zones of Iraq and Afghanistan. Pulled off some crazy stunts in the desert, apparently – quite unimaginable. And his men loved him – "careless for his own life, careful for the lives of others," as one of them said rather memorably.'

Channing had an ear for the memorable quote, and was happy to invent one when necessary.

'Not something anyone will be saying about you, Mr Channing.'

'I think there'll be more people at my funeral than yours, Detective Inspector . . . just a hunch.'

'I suppose any celebration draws a crowd.'

Channing laughed loudly. 'Is this your way of flirting, Tamsin? You're reminding me of Beatrice in *Much Ado About Nothing*! Every put-down to Benedick, every insult – a hidden cry of love, as warily they circle each other!'

Tamsin's dismissive sneer was almost that of a teenager. 'I don't know what you're talking about,' she said.

'And Terence?' asked Peter, wishing to get back on track. His colleague's digs were needless and disruptive. Tamsin was not in love with Martin, but she was in love with attack and belittlement and this rarely furthered the investigation.

'Terence, yes. Well, he returned to this country a hero, more decorated than a Christmas tree – and then the bugger promptly turned his back on it all! He resigned his commission and disappeared off to stack shelves in a supermarket! Completely mad, but a good story, eh?'

'You wanted the story?'

'He had all sorts of offers, obviously. The army wanted him to reconsider, to take up a post at Sandhurst training heroes of the future. The government wanted him as a consultant and publishers tempted him with large advances and pressed him for his kiss-and-tell story of life in the war zones. I even offered to be his agent.'

'How thoughtful,' said Tamsin.

'I try to help where I can. What else are we on earth for?'

'You and Mother Teresa.'

'But he said no to us all, stubborn as a mule, and opted for days spent in Morrisons, surrounded by vegetables, not all of whom are management. I mean, why a supermarket?'

'It does have an appeal,' said Peter.

'Only to the dead, Abbot. And I think your colleague is with me on this one.' He looked smugly at Tamsin, who knew he was right. Working in a supermarket was unquestionably for the dead. 'But an interesting man, I thought; that ability to stick two fingers up to everyone.'

'Including yourself, I suppose.'

'As all good men must, Abbot! But I did pause for a moment and think he was a strong candidate for the society. A feather in our cap, so to speak.'

'So what's in it for him?' asked Peter.

'Well, I'm not sure he knows what he's doing there, to be frank. You'll have to ask him; and if you're lucky, he might even speak.'

'He isn't talkative?'

'Getting words out of Terence is like drawing water from a deep well with a rusty winch. It takes both time and effort.'

'But worth it?'

'No one's that interesting, in my experience,' said Channing, an agent scorned. There was spite in the editor.

'And Rosemary?' asked Peter. 'Was she equally uninteresting?'

Tamsin threw him a glance. She didn't want this to become personal. Peter had loved Rosemary, in some way or other. Was he about to be offended, about to blow his cover?

'Rosemary?' said Martin with a twinkle in his eye. Peter hoped it didn't mean what he thought it might mean.

'How did you know her?' he asked.

'You mean, how did we meet? How did I meet the splendid, and formerly virtuous, Rosemary?'

Rosemary had chosen the venue

for their lunch date – the lunch date unmentioned by Peter to Tamsin. After the Etiquette Society was done, and guest speaker Peter had left, Rosemary had coaxed the abbot's address from Martin, under some pretence. Though whether Martin had been fooled . . .

She'd chosen a deli on Broad Street. One or two had begun to appear alongside the charity shops. Peter had not been there before – he didn't eat out – but Rosemary knew it well and was waiting for him when he arrived. She had a laptop on the table and was working away in her steel-rimmed glasses, which she removed when he walked in. And the laptop was instantly closed and put away.

'You found it,' she said as he fended off one or two odd glances and sat down opposite her. It was not a large space, tables close together, and he couldn't remember feeling so out of his depth since . . . well, he couldn't remember, though Rosemary looked bright and unflustered. Brisk was the word that always came to mind with Rosemary, and perhaps she'd always been brisk; perhaps he'd never got beyond her brisk cheeriness . . . and perhaps when you're ill, that's all you need. As he looked at her now – as friend rather than patient – the cheeriness had a slightly determined and frightened quality.

'So, who'd have thought it?' he asked, with a confidence he'd been practising. 'I recognized you as soon as you walked in the door.'

'I recognized you once I sat down. At first, I saw only the habit.'

Peter felt the first wisp of disapproval. 'And most don't get beyond that, of course,' he said.

'So perhaps you shouldn't wear it!' she replied with teasing firmness.

'Perhaps I want to,' said Peter now wishing he hadn't come. What good could come of this?

'So what are you going to have?' asked Rosemary. She was already in charge.

'The soup and a cheese roll,' he said because it was the first thing on the menu. This wasn't the time to be thinking about what he wanted. It was the time for keeping everything as simple as possible. 'You can't go wrong with a cheese roll.' It wasn't his finest line . . . and then Matthew arrived to take the order. Rosemary seemed to know Matthew. She smiled at him heartily and, well, briskly; treated him like a member of the family, a family where people get on well with each other.

'So you live in Stormhaven?' said Peter encouragingly.

'Yes, Claremont Road.'

'Claremont Road? Not far from me.' It was only a five-minute walk.

'My father died and left me some money. I invested in property. Well, a couple of properties.'

'That was nice of him.'

'To die?'

'I was more thinking of the money.'

'It was nice of him to die as well.'

'So doubly generous.'

'What he couldn't give in life, he gave in death. A six-figure sum instead of a relationship – a sort of pay-off. And I was the only child still speaking with him. My sister—'

'You have a sister?'

'A younger sister, yes, Sarah. But she's made her own way.' Her throat had tightened. She was clearly angry.

'I see,' said Peter. He left a pause, and Rosemary stepped into it.

'And her way didn't include her family.'

'Right.'

'Or not my parents at least. The two of us have had some contact. Not the happiest of stories, but no matter.'

Peter nodded. She'd opened it up, and was now closing it down, withdrawing back into her shell like a frightened snail.

'And have you been here long?' he asked.

'About seven years, after London finally spat me out. And you?'

'About four – I was spat out by the desert. I don't know whose phlegm is more lingering on the soul.'

She wasn't sure about that remark.

'I don't miss London,' she said. 'I mean, I miss it and I don't miss it.'

'Glad we've cleared that one up.' She didn't quite laugh.

'The Charity Directorate post came up – well, they approached me – and it just seemed the right time to jump. And I think it was. I tell myself it was. You can't dwell on what might have been.'

'So you were head-hunted?'

'I suppose so. I'd done a piece of work here before, which gave me a local profile, I suppose.'

'I've never been head-hunted.'

'It's not so special. You're just a word on some twenty-something recruiter's to-do list. They have a fake interest in you, and a real interest in their commission.'

Abbot Peter looked out of the window on to the slow-moving street . . . and took in the moment. Here he was, forty years on, with someone he would have married with indecent haste, had he been given the slightest encouragement, yet he hardly knew her. He really didn't know her at all; though what or who had changed was difficult to say. Who knows anyone at twenty-one?

'Strange how these things happen, isn't it?' he said.

'How do you mean?'

'Well, I hadn't even heard of Stormhaven until I was told – standing in the Sahara on the end of a remarkably clear phone line – that a house had been left to me here.'

'Unusual.'

'I mean, I would have gone anywhere in the world probably, if someone had said "Come". But I came here, I came to Stormhaven, because – at just the right moment – someone died and left me their home. And now it's my world, really.'

'Stormhaven's your world?'

'In a way, yes.'

'Then you should really get out more!'

The abbot smiled. 'I've been out, remember. I've been out for

66

a long time. And now I've come back.' It struck him that she was possibly more nervous than he was. He was losing his nerves as they talked. 'And I suppose one thing my travels have taught me is that wherever I've gone, I'm only ever the size of my mind. Air miles are not the same as enlightenment.'

It was spoken in quiet rebellion against her briskness. He could see why she was where she was. Here was a woman who could sweep through her various good works with barely a glance either side. Chairing meetings would not be a hardship for her; it was *not* chairing meetings that would pose problems. She'd been a wonderful nurse to him in Highgate after his breakdown. The first woman in his life who cared for him: how could he not fall in love? But he wasn't that young man now . . . or only part of him was.

'So did you have a good time in the desert?' she asked. It wasn't an entirely friendly question.

'It's never been put quite like that,' said Peter, with mirth. 'I'm not sure you go to the desert for a good time.'

'So why did you go?'

Was that anger or just cheery no-nonsense questioning?

'There wasn't much to keep me in England. My step-parents weren't happy about me reverting to my birth name; well, they weren't happy full stop. I needed to get away from them.'

'And you managed that well enough.'

'Strange – but even as I think of them now, something in me dies.' He paused. 'And you didn't answer my letters, of course.' He needed to mention that, and as he did he looked her in the eye . . . and she looked away. 'Quite understandable, but not exactly an invitation to stay. And, as I say, I needed to go anyway. I went in search of sanity – and found it.'

'A long way to go for sanity.'

'If it had been available nearer . . .'

Rosemary had liked young Peter; there had been an innocence about him when the twenty-one-year-old walked through the door in Highgate. True innocence is a most subversive thing: quite unable to understand why things are as they are, why people are as they are and why they do what they do . . . and liable to point this out.

'It was the idea of a robed man in a pulpit, six feet above the rest of us, talking nonsense. Utter nonsense. And really, it was nonsense.'

This was one of the first things he'd said on the unit. She remembered the conversation even now.

'If you say so,' she'd replied.

'And the others just sat there!'

'The congregation.'

'Yes. They just sat there! And I couldn't understand why everyone else was letting it happen.'

'It's called being polite.'

'No, it's called being dishonest.'

'So you threw a hymn book at him.'

'He was patronizing me. I don't like being patronized. I told the police I didn't like being patronized. And I only hit the verger because he took hold of my arm. It's what my stepmother used to do when she wanted control.'

He'd been an interesting arrival. But clearly a relationship with Peter, however desirable, had not been possible . . . such a thing would not have been perceived well. There had to be boundaries in staff–patient relationships, even with former patients. It was a psychiatric unit, not a marriage bureau! It would have been frowned upon, this is what Rosemary had felt at the time, and she hadn't wished to be frowned upon; though maybe, on reflection, she'd been the one doing the frowning when no one else had been much bothered.

And maybe she should have answered his letters. She'd like to have done; he did have something, some presence, some quality of existence, which crept inside her bones. And the thought that she had turned that down, made an error along the way, a mistake – this was an uncomfortable thought. So she kept away from it, reminding herself of her professional boundaries, and how it never would have worked anyway.

'And there's a man I need you to look after,' she said, returning to the present.

'I'm sorry?' This was rather sudden, given that he didn't run a care home.

'I mean, watch out for. He needs a man to do that, I think. But not – you know – an idiot.'

'Right. Well, I'm glad not to be an idiot.'

'Everything's relative. And you have met him.'

'Met who?'

'The man I'm talking about . . . at the Stormhaven Etiquette Society.'

'A rather weird memory.'

'His name is Terence – the major-general.'

'Terence?'

'You know him?'

'We didn't really talk.'

'Talking is not his strong suit and that's his problem. Well, I don't know what his problem is, and it's none of my business, but his mother . . . well, where to start?' Rosemary leant forward across the table. 'She told him – and Terence revealed this while laughing – she told him he had a "heart of shit".'

She spoke the words as if they were nothing to do with her, like someone holding dirty washing as far from their body as they could.

'How touching.'

'And he doesn't seem to regard it as odd! He really doesn't. "Isn't that what every mother says?" He just agrees with her, so you need to talk him round.'

'Talk him round?'

'I mean, I told him it wasn't right what she said, but he didn't see that at all.'

'What's done to us when we're small, we don't regard as odd.'

Rosemary's shrug suggested she wasn't convinced.

'For our own survival,' said Peter, 'we have to believe it's normal and good . . . until we can no longer believe it. We believe the fairy tale until it's simply no longer possible. But she no doubt claimed she spoke those words in love.'

'Well, she did actually.'

'She would, yes.'

'I remember her words because he kept quoting them at me: "No one loves you like I do," she'd say. "No one loves you like I do, Terence."'

Peter winced. 'Which, of course, the child will believe,' he said, 'and crucify themselves for their heart of shit – instead of their parent. It's the price paid for survival. From there on, love will always be a monster, something grotesque and repulsive, to be mocked, scorned . . . avoided. Terence will struggle with love.'

The food arrived, Matthew delivering steaming mushroom soup and a cheese roll to Peter, with Rosemary looking at some pesto pasta with tomato.

'Thank you, Matthew,' she said, as if they'd been discussing their holiday snaps. 'It looks delicious.' And then to Peter: 'The food here is very good.'

Peter nodded.

And it had been good, and they'd talked of other things, with no further mention of Terence. Rosemary insisted on paying after some coffee; and they stepped out on to Broad Street in bright sunshine which was rather nice. And Rosemary looked happy, and said that they must do this again. Peter wondered if they'd kiss distantly, hug for a moment or simply shake hands.

They hugged, and then she turned and walked up the street towards the Poundshop on the corner. The abbot stayed where he was, catching the sun, watching her go . . . as he had for many years of his life.

He wouldn't see her alive again.

Tara Hopesmith sat at her desk.

And it was her desk now, with Rosemary gone. She owned the property in Church Street, fixtures and fittings. Queen of all she surveyed, as the solicitor, Trixie Brownlow, put it.

'You've done rather well, Miss Hopesmith,' she said from behind her legal glasses. Tara already knew that. Rosemary was an organized woman, prepared for all eventualities; you really couldn't have murdered someone more prepared for their death. 'Queen of all you survey!'

'This isn't a celebration,' Tara said firmly; though perhaps it was a small one.

'The police may have a few questions,' Trixie added. She was a lively woman in her mid-sixties.

'Oh?'

'Well, you have a motive for murder with bells on.'

It was strange how distant the police felt to solicitors. They shared the law as their business, but it wasn't the same business at all.

'I think I can handle the police,' said Tara. 'I've handled a few in my time.'

'Quite.'

Trixie wasn't sure if she approved. She was all for womanhood breaking the mould and doing their own thing. She was doing her own thing more than ever now, and enjoying the ride. Life really did get better with every year that passed. Whether this was quite the thing women ought to be doing, however – Rosemary and Tara's business – well, she wasn't sure. Though who's to judge? And she found herself saying this more and more these days. Who's to judge?

'She was a thoroughly decent woman,' said Tara.

'She was,' said Trixie. 'Absolutely decent . . . which makes it a most indecent murder.'

And Tara nodded, aware that she'd be missed for that reason. There had been a lot of good in Rosemary, Tara knew that, which had made her own resentment more difficult to justify . . . resentment at her 'junior partner' status.

But that's life and there was no resentment now. It had dissolved like ice in the sun, melting into nothing. As Trixie said, she was now queen of all she surveyed.

'How did I meet Rosemary?'

said Channing, enjoying his moment. 'Well, it won't surprise you to hear that she sent me a rude letter. Very rude.'

'Rude in what way?'

'Calm down, Abbot. Nothing involving photographs! She was simply appalled by my behaviour.'

'Any behaviour in particular?' asked Tamsin. 'There must be so much to choose from.'

'Just the usual dull and selective rage people see fit to dump on me. Water off a duck's back, really – but, well, it isn't always easy.' Channing managed an aggrieved look.

'Victimhood doesn't suit you,' said Tamsin sharply.

'No, but I do seem to bring out the self-righteous in people, and then they come at me like maniacs, powered by moral outrage, which is quite the nastiest of fuels.'

'But if we're being honest, Martin – which is occasionally possible – where would you be without it?' asked the abbot with a smile. Martin seemed to thrive on the rage of the self-righteous. In Peter's view, it was how Martin knew he was alive. What he'd become if it ever stopped . . . well, his decline might be very sudden. Martin needed the attention of public outrage like others needed calm.

'For some unknown reason, she didn't like my approach to all the loonies on the south coast,' he said. Raised eyebrows greeted him.

'I'm sorry?' said Peter, wondering if he'd heard aright.

'And we're not short of them, believe me. We have a stack of loony huts around here; or "care homes", as she'd prefer them to be called.'

He had heard aright. 'I can see why she might have been a little upset,' said Peter.

'But we stayed in touch. No point in falling out over something

73

like that, and I warmed to her campaigning spirit. We need more of that!'

'You mean you fancied her?' suggested Tamsin.

'Oh, really. Must everything come down to sex? Haven't we moved on from Freud?'

'I'm not sure men have,' said Tamsin.

'Well, we flirted mildly, I suppose; attractive woman, of course. And she wrote us some rather delectable pieces, full of virtuous fury, as chair of the Stormhaven Charity Forum.'

'And the Etiquette Society? Why did she muddy her feet in that?'

'Oh, she joined us on the "civility" ticket.'

'The *civility* ticket?' Tamsin couldn't say it without laughing a little.

'A desire to see the disadvantaged and needy treated with more civility,' said a straight-faced Martin.

'Your vision exactly.'

'Well, it was hardly the founding ideal of the society, no. In fact, the thought hadn't crossed my mind. But it worked for her. I didn't know she was a churchwarden at the time or I might have behaved better.'

'Really?'

'No. I'd have behaved worse, probably. I certainly had no idea she was running a knocking shop, which is really quite wonderful. Sly old thing! Ah, the opportunities missed!'

'Is this your version of grief?' asked Peter.

Channing paused, a brief sadness across his face. 'If we brought grief to our lives, Abbot, we would cry all day, don't you think?'

'Maybe.'

'So I prefer not to. I really prefer not to.' Peter nodded. 'And to be honest, your grief is rather more apparent than mine right now.'

'That may be true,' said Peter.

'And Geoff?' asked Tamsin, wishing to move on.

'What can I say about Geoff?'

'You can tell us what Geoff is doing in the Stormhaven Etiquette Society.'

'Geoff is an estate agent who would like to rule the world.'

74

Martin allowed a moment for impact. 'He actually hates the estate agent label. He doesn't think it grand enough for him – so I use it all the time. He thinks it demeans him, when he is so much more than that! He's an amateur thespian, of course, hogging all the best parts in the local theatre productions. But he probably wants to be mayor as well . . . he does like dressing up.'

'So again the question: why is he a member of the Etiquette Society?'

'I sold it to him on the elitist ticket. A secret society of the rich and powerful, keeping a paternal eye on the well-being of Stormhaven, exposing the bad eggs and the disreputable while applauding the righteous . . . like Geoff.'

'I sense it wasn't a hard sell?'

'Any opportunity to network and Geoff's in, believe me. But really, this is ridiculous, even for the police. You don't seriously think the murderer is a member of the Stormhaven Etiquette Society?'

'We need to talk,'

said Tara, now the sole owner of Model Service.

'If you're quick,' said Cherise. 'I have a client at three and I'm not missing 'im.'

'Such commitment to the cause.'

'Well generous last time, he was! Who said there aren't sugar daddies in Stormhaven! Up and coming town, this!'

Her emphasis on 'up and coming' left little to the imagination, but then that was Cherise for you, her sort of humour. Katrina didn't approve; she was Catholic, after all, and a close friend of the Virgin Mary. But whatever their jokes, Katrina liked her colleagues well enough. She felt safe here, which was not something she could say for much of her life. Here in Church Street she sensed they were in it together; they were sisters, watching out for each other. They did look after you here. Rosemary had made sure of that.

So Tara and Cherise were Katrina's colleagues, but not her friends. They didn't socialize away from this place. They met every Monday in the small reception area to talk through anything that had arisen in the week – another *double entendre* Cherise never let pass. Did the English never tire of this humour?

'It's what the seaside is all about, Kat!' Cherise would say. 'Double meanings. 'Aven't you seen the postcards?'

She had seen the postcards, even though she tried hard to avoid them. And she'd seen them because they drew Anastazy like magnets; he'd gaze upon each with fascination. She had found some under his bed recently, which wasn't what she wanted. The boy needed a father-figure to help him through the teenage years.

'I do not see the "double meanings" as so funny,' she said. 'What is funny about it? I think it is more disgusting than funny.'

'It's not like anyone takes them serious or anythin'.'

'Boys do. I have to tell Anastazy that nurses are not like that in real life.'

76

'He'll find that out soon enough.'

'What if he thinks nurses are like that – and says something? Or *does* something?'

'It's just harmless fun,' said Cherise. 'It's what men are like.'

'And I don't enjoy what men are like. Why do they have to look at women in that way?'

'How do you want them to look at you?' asked Tara, who really couldn't be doing with all this moral outrage from the second busiest prostitute on her books.

They were a good team. Tara looked after their website but Cherise was forever coming up with ideas as to how they could improve it. They'd recently added a Polish section, written by Katrina, which had made quite an impact. But with the death of Rosemary, what now of their future? That was the big question today.

Katrina had liked Rosemary. She'd been a mother to her on her arrival in this strange town. Clear, straightforward, practical, distant, but kind. Rosemary understood how to get things done, whether it was finding a school for Anastazy or setting up Stormhaven's first brothel. Perhaps Cherise struggled with her for the very reasons Katrina liked her, she thought. No doubt Cherise would have preferred someone more chaotic, more flamboyant – 'and less helpin' everyone all the time!' as she put it. 'I can't be doing with all this helpin' people!'

Or maybe Cherise was simply born to complain. She did complain a lot, while making a very good living through escort work, Skype performances and sex. Rarely would she take home less than £1,000 a week, and often it was more.

'I want to reassure you that everything will continue as it is,' said Tara.

'How do you know?' asked Cherise. She didn't take things on trust, never had. Why take anything on trust when the world so often let you down? This is why Cherise was a planner of future pathways. Keep your options open, girl, that was her motto. Never allow yourself to be trapped.

'Because I am now the sole owner of the business,' said Tara simply and clearly. Katrina and Cherise looked at each other and then back at Tara. 'Rosemary's death is a tragedy. But neither of you will be victims of that tragedy.'

'You're the owner now – of everythin'?'

'I am.'

'Rosemary was a good person,' said Katrina.

'She was a good person.' Tara could say that without feeling a fraud. 'But Rosemary is dead, and it's very sad, but I own the business now and I intend to make it work for us all.'

It was possible she wasn't expressing quite enough regret. But she was trying to be kind, to sound firm and certain, to reassure the girls about their future. Of course she was sad, but life had to go on. Rosemary would want that.

'My boyfriend won't be pleased,' said Cherise, idly checking her phone. She checked her phone without realizing she was checking her phone. Hers was possibly the most checked phone on the south coast.

'And wherein lies your boyfriend's interest?' said Tara, with disdain. Cherise's boyfriends never stayed long, the relationships always troubled. Tara felt weary at the thought of them, but this was how Cherise chose to live. Her first day of peace would be spent in a coffin.

'He wants me out of all this, doesn't he?'

'They've all wanted you out of it, Cherise.'

'I know,' said Cherise vaguely. 'But this one certainly does.'

'And can you blame him?' asked Katrina. It was not a profession that looked kindly on partners. When she got home, she did not want to see a man; she wanted to see her son.

'He knew what I did. It wasn't as if I kept it a secret or anythin'. Well, I told 'im on our second date. It didn't stop 'im then.'

'Until the thrill wore off,' said Tara wearily. 'And then he started getting all proprietorial.' This was hardly breaking news; it had happened before and would happen again. Sex workers spent half their lives on their backs and the other half trying to sort out their love lives. This was Tara's experience and it was laced with bitterness. The men she'd liked had not liked her trade, and so she found herself alone in her forties.

'He likes the money,' said Cherise.

'They do at first.'

'And does he really think I'd earn that in an office ordering paper clips or working in a care home? No way, José! And I've done office work, anyway, I was, like, *so bored*.'

'So perhaps he killed Rosemary,' said Katrina.

'What?'

'Perhaps your boyfriend thinks that if he kills her, there is no Model Service, you have to stop, you have to get a job in B&Q or something.'

And for a moment – though it was probably a joke, Katrina could be dry – Cherise did wonder if this might be true. Well, you don't know, do you? She'd only met him recently. And who else would want to kill Rosemary?

'All mothers hate their daughters,'

said Blessings. 'That's quite normal.'

She paused for a moment for effect. She was used to being heard, to being listened to, used to making pronouncements that people must take account of. And Blessings liked that: the fact that she was heard. 'Not all the time, obviously. One doesn't hate one's daughter all the time. But at certain moments all mothers wish their daughters dead.'

Tamsin nodded in acquiescence, as if nothing unreasonable had been uttered. 'And vice versa,' she added.

'Vice versa?'

'All daughters hate their mothers; most of the time, actually.'

Blessings was shocked. This was not meant to be a two-way street.

'And the commandments?' she asked with incredulity.

'Which commandments?' asked Tamsin.

'The *Ten* Commandments, Detective Inspector. I trust you remember them?'

'I'm not good with lists.'

'The commandments given to Moses, the great law-maker? I'm surprised a detective inspector needs an explanation.'

'I did see the film,' said Tamsin, aware this would irritate. 'Two hours of my life I'll never get back.'

'Find me two hours that you will,' said Peter.

'Honour your father and mother!' said Blessings, on a mission. 'That is number four in the list.'

The abbot wondered if Tamsin might need some help at this point; but from her reply, apparently not.

'You do know Moses wasn't brought up by his mother and father,' said Tamsin.

Blessings looked surprised. 'Is this relevant to the case?' she asked.

'They put him in a basket, as far as I remember.'

'They did,' said the abbot, feeling like a witness in this trial. 'They feared he might be murdered, so they hid him in a basket in the river.'

Tamsin framed it differently. 'They put him in a wicker basket in a large river and left him to the uncertain care of the water . . . and the local crocodiles.'

'Needs must,' said Blessings.

'Where fortunately – one in a million chance, really – he was found by the king's daughter and brought up as an Egyptian prince. Which probably saved his parents from a child neglect charge.'

'Your knowledge of Scripture is . . . well, exemplary,' said Peter.

'So he never knew them,' said Tamsin, triumphantly, like a barrister winding up a case.

'His mother *may* have been his wet nurse,' said Peter quietly.

'Doesn't count.'

'Right.'

'It isn't the same at all.'

'Is this going anywhere?' asked Blessings.

'Moses never knew his parents as parents,' said Tamsin. 'Which might have made honouring them a good deal easier. *That's* where it's going.'

Blessings smiled at the contest; professional respect, perhaps.

'And if we're using the Scriptures as testimony,' added the abbot, 'I'm not sure they commend hating your daughter either, Mrs N'Dayo. "Suffer the little children" and all that. Though I do understand that children drive parents to despair.'

'They do,' agreed Blessings.

'That's where I drove my parents anyway, and I was quite right to do so.'

How had they got here? Wasn't this a murder enquiry?

'And where's Dinah at school?' asked Tamsin, wanting to move on. She'd enjoyed the contest but had no interest in other people's commandments.

'Roedean.'

'Your old school.'

'If I had to put up with it, I definitely think she should. It's a hellhole, obviously, as I well know.'

'An expensive hellhole.'

Blessings smiled indulgently; she did not look like one concerned about cost. Martin had told them that circuit judges earn around £140,000 a year. And he knew the price of everything.

'I look forward to the day when one or two of my classmates appear before me in court,' said Blessings, 'and I use the word "mates" loosely. There are some scores to settle.'

Peter pondered the trials and tribulations of Judge Blessings N'Dayo: unhappy school days in a strange land; the decision not to follow her parents back to her homeland of Ghana; the historic racism and sexism of the legal world. 'Cold and hard as an ice pick in Alaska,' Martin had said. And a fighter, thought Peter.

'It's important she boards,' continued Blessings. 'There needs to be some distance between us. I'm sure she'd agree.' There was a pause. 'She's not an unhappy girl, of course – before you call for the social services. As I always tell her, only dull ordinary families have stay-at-home mothers – and we are neither dull nor ordinary.'

'No.'

'And I read through all her diaries. I mean, I think she means me to.'

'Really?'

'Leaving them in her drawer. Though she goes quite crazy when she finds out, in true drama queen style.'

'Does that surprise you?' asked Tamsin.

'Does what surprise me?'

'That she goes crazy when you read her private thoughts.' Tamsin was seething. 'I'm surprised that you're surprised.'

'They're full of teenage nonsense, of course,' said Blessings, ignoring the question. 'The diaries, I mean – all despair and heartache! Laughable, really. And so I call her "Nonsense" – a much better name for her – which just makes her angry again.'

'Not a good name,' said Peter.

'But she speaks nonsense most of the time, so appropriate. She'll get through it. Come to her senses.'

'She will,' said Peter gently.

'And then do something awful with her life, no doubt . . . but basically, a very happy girl. Very happy.'

Blessings had said more than she intended; but she wouldn't be judged by these people. She wouldn't be judged by anyone, never again. Not by her father or anyone.

'And how did you know Rosemary?' asked Tamsin. They weren't here to offer parenting classes.

'Well, I didn't know Rosemary, not really. Apart from her being a fellow member of the Stormhaven Etiquette Society. But it isn't like we all holiday together.'

'Who do you holiday with?' asked Tamsin, realizing her mistake instantly.

'I'm not sure that's any of your business, DI Shah. I understand the parameters of a murder investigation, both inside and outside a court, and that doesn't include random nosiness.'

Tamsin and the abbot felt the sudden presence of a judge and the dynamic changed for a moment.

'Did you like her?'

'Who?'

'Rosemary.'

Blessings made a face that ridiculed the question as a waste of time. 'Like her? Did anyone like Rosemary? She treated Terence like her puppy, which was somewhat amazing; but if that's what he wants. Tea, anyone?'

'Did you want Terence as your puppy?' asked the abbot.

Blessings stopped for a moment . . . and then dismissed the words. 'A laughable idea.'

'So you couldn't imagine anyone wishing to kill Rosemary?'

'I could imagine *everyone* wishing to kill Rosemary.'

'Because?'

Blessings got up from her seat and moved across to the old fireplace. 'Because she was so good, simple as that.'

'That's usually a reason for people to like you, isn't it?'

'You think so, Detective Inspector?' Tamsin didn't think so – she'd just been fishing. 'Being determinedly good is always an irritant in my experience, especially when, in death, the individual turns out to have been a madam and a keeper of whores.' Blessings rolled her eyes. 'Rosemary, it transpires, was the most appalling hypocrite.'

Rosemary's house

was a detached red brick property in Claremont Road, half a mile from the seafront. It had three bedrooms and a bathroom upstairs, with a large-windowed front room, study/dining room and kitchen downstairs. It was all wooden floors, organic tea, vegetarian cook books, ordered, clean . . . but not what you'd call comfortable – not cushioned and cosy.

'Not a place to relax,' had been Tamsin's first comment as they entered the house, now forensics had left. 'But then, did Rosemary ever relax?'

'I'm not sure relaxing loomed large on her horizon,' said Peter. 'She liked to make the most of each moment, felt guilty if she wasn't, always had things to do. I didn't realize quite how many things . . .'

'I like it,' said Tamsin. She sat down for a moment in the front room as the winter sun briefly touched Stormhaven like an angel of peace. 'I mean, I couldn't live here but I like it. No mess.'

'No mess, no.'

'Do you like it?'

'Er, yes,' he said, unsure, 'and no.' He did like it, in a manner. He liked the simple order, and some familiarity drew him; while something else pushed him away. It may have been the fact – yes, of course – that it reminded him of his childhood home in Eltham: ordered but not warm, and too much red and green paint making it dark . . . darker than it need be. Peter liked light.

'But could you live here, Abbot? You know, had you been an item?'

'We were never an item.'

'No – but you wanted to be.'

'A different person in a different life.'

'So could you live here?'

'I'd like more light.'

'Anything else?'

'I'd have a place to rest as opposed to sit. I've had a lot of sitting in my life. You sit in monasteries; you don't rest.'

'It was your choice.'

'And it is, perhaps, a little too ordered. I might have made the place untidy.'

'Ah, untidiness – a deal-breaker, Abbot, even for true love.'

'You speak from experience?'

Peter was forever asking questions about her love life, and she was forever closing the door on his inquiries. An uncle had no business to know these things; well, no one had any business to know these things. A private life was private. Though in truth, Tamsin had no concept of true love; it was a phrase she'd borrowed rather than one she'd known.

'Shall we take a look in her study?'

They stood for a moment in the doorway of Rosemary's work room. The wooden desk, holding a computer and two fountain pens, was placed by the window looking out on the street. There was an armchair with a light stand behind. It was a working armchair, one where she sat to read documents, away from the desk. There was a spare pair of glasses on a small table to the side. The only other furniture was a bookcase, holding reference books concerning charity law, a Virginia Woolf novel, several publications on walking holidays in the Lake District and a book called *Anam Cara* by John O'Donohue.

'Interesting reading,' says Tamsin. 'As in, not at all interesting.'

'If your bookcase is your soul, it does make it a rather personal affair.'

'What if it's just your bookcase?'

In the locked drawer in her study they found three files: 'Charity', 'Church' and 'Model Service'. They were all in good order, a gathering of legal and official documents. It was the last of these that most interested Tamsin, and here they discovered what the abbot already knew: that she'd bought the property in Church Street with money left by her father. The business appeared to pay her a rather minimal rent while Tara Hopesmith drew a basic salary of £25,000 as 'Premises Host'.

'Doesn't seem a lot,' said Tamsin.

'Sounds a fortune from where I'm sitting.'

'That's because you dwell in genteel poverty, Abbot. And Tara interests us, as the new owner of Model Service.'

'And Rosemary's friend.'

'So perhaps she'll give herself a huge pay rise to ease her grief, because she can, now that she owns it all. All in all, a pretty decent outcome for Tara Hopesmith once the dust of tragedy settles.'

'Bit obvious, isn't it?'

'Most crime is obvious, Abbot. It's just someone being impatient, someone snapping, someone thinking, for one mad moment, "Why not?" There's nothing clever or subtle about most murder.' Tamsin got up. 'Time to go, I think. There's nothing else for us here. I'll take the files.'

'OK.'

Peter had wanted to take the files, to sit with her writing, her work . . . her life; but it was better he didn't.

'It's better this way,' said Tamsin, discerning well.

'It is,' said Peter.

'And I'll be in the car. You may want to stay a moment. You know . . .'

'Thank you.'

Peter heard her open the front door, and then her feet on the gravel outside. Tamsin denied it, but she could occasionally be thoughtful. He sat alone in the front room with the winter sun and the ticking clock.

How strange, he thought. Time and tide stayeth for no man, as one scene becomes another. When he was being treated in Highgate by that wonderful young nurse, who would have imagined he'd be sitting in her front room forty years later with his body in a monk's habit . . . and her body in a morgue?

So who put her there?

And then he noticed the small photo on the desk, two young girls – Rosemary and Sarah, surely? He looked again. There they were, one taller than the other, doing the right thing, smiling as one should, the smaller girl less certain, more ambivalent, as though dragged into the picture. Rosemary and Sarah, all those years ago.

He'd like to find Sarah. She was out there somewhere.

'I am the hollow man,'

said Terence with a self-deprecating smile. 'Not much of me here, Inspector, never has been.'

Tamsin was wondering if he referred to himself or his home. It was a modern bungalow with functional un-matching furniture, as though bought as a job lot, a landlord in a hurry and without aesthetic care. Tamsin was struck by the absence of pictures, which left a lot of bare wall. There were one or two army photos, comrades in arms in faraway places, but no art to soften the wall lines or colour the space. They stood in a civilian barracks in Stormhaven, as though he was a lodger, someone passing through, with no sense of home. He could be packed up and gone in an hour; this is how it felt.

'You were a soldier, though.'

'I was a soldier.' He saluted jokingly as he said it.

'A much decorated major-general.'

'Like a Christmas tree, yes. I know the jokes, hung with baubles – and thrown out as soon as Christmas is done.' It sounded angry to Tamsin, though spoken in a carefree manner.

'Are you angry?'

'But then they never promised to care, did they? So what was I to expect?'

'I agree,' said Tamsin without sympathy. Why did people imagine their employers should care for them? Pay them, yes. But care for them? 'And surely the truth is that you actually threw yourself out, Major-General, with everyone begging you to stay.'

'I did evict myself, in a manner, I suppose. The Christmas tree that threw itself out the door – like a suicide bomber at a station!' Tamsin watched him. 'Don't mind me, Detective Inspector . . . old army habits.'

'You mean the self-pity?'

'The tasteless jokes. But you have to learn to laugh, because every day, they could be walking towards you. The bombers; anyone can be a bomber. The woman selling you vegetables or offering you some cake or asking for help. She might be wired up for paradise – hers, not yours.'

'So you left the army?'

Tamsin wanted to get back on track. Terence was dangerous; a disturbed and disturbing man, who stood some way outside conventional life.

'Threw myself out the door, yes . . . sometimes, you just have to go.'

'And a change of direction.'

'I'm not sure we ever change direction, do we?'

'I think you have.'

'No, we just change our employment, which is not the same thing at all.'

Nonsense, thought Tamsin. Your employment is your direction. What other direction is there?

'Still, from war hero to the supermarket? It's not a traditional career path.'

'The hollow man is hollow wherever he is, Inspector. There is no career path that can save him.'

Tamsin had no idea what made this man tick. Where was she to begin with him?

'And you enjoy your work in the supermarket?'

She tried to keep the question neutral, to keep the disappointment out of her voice. She understood ambition, but found the dismissal of ambition unsettling, cowardly even, risk-averse. Though those were not words ever used about the man on the sofa in front of her now.

'I do,' he said. 'A different sort of battlefield.'

Waitrose, where Tamsin usually shopped, was never a battlefield – except on Saturday mornings and Sunday afternoons; there could be some sharp elbows then. Morrisons was probably different. The poor and infirm shopped all the time, with so much of it on their hands.

'Though I don't remember seeing you on any shopping missions,' said Blain. 'Are you a traitor to the cause?'

'I don't shop there, no. I live in Hove, actually.'

'Very nice.'

Tamsin had never shopped in Morrisons, and could not foresee the moment when she would. She wouldn't shop at Morrisons even if she lived across the road with only a Zimmer frame for transport. She'd get a taxi to Waitrose.

'Daring raids into the warehouse for more yoghurt is the sum of my adventures now,' said Terence.

'They must be different days, Major-General.'

'As I've said, not for the hollow man.'

'But the loss of status? Surely . . .'

Tamsin clung fiercely to status. She could not imagine it so carelessly tossed away, as something of no consequence.

'Status is only in the mind, Inspector.'

Tamsin was feeling around for another angle. The major-general, perhaps unsurprisingly, was a well-defended man who seemed to see her coming before she even set out. She'd need to find a crack in the wall.

'So why membership of the rather exclusive Stormhaven Etiquette Society? It doesn't seem like you, man of the people and all that.'

Taunt him a bit, she'd try it.

'Why not?' The ex-soldier looked gently surprised. 'We must all fill our days on this earth with something and I rather like decency. Something to be applauded, I think. It's a terrible world without it.'

'Without decency?'

'What's the use of a bus pass, Inspector – which is not so far away for me now – if appalling behaviour prevails on the bus? You know the sort of thing: loud music, vile-smelling food, shouting, mocking youths at the end of a school day and what they now call "man-spread" taking up half your seat? A bus pass in such circumstances merely becomes a free ticket to hell.'

Tamsin had no immediate answer; she never used the bus.

'There was a whole page on it in the *Sussex Silt* recently,' continued Terence. '"Why public transport is hell!" was the headline. And while I don't care much for the paper – Martin is a mischief-maker, of course – there were strong feelings expressed in the piece, a lot of anger. Whatever happened to discipline? I wonder sometimes.'

Tamsin had heard that Blain had been popular with his soldiers, but she could not imagine him being soft on them. So a good man to follow, but not a good man to cross. His eyes bore into her now.

'Perhaps you find etiquette a rather fanciful notion, Inspector, because you don't travel on public transport. You miss a lot in a car, especially one as expensive as yours.'

Keep calm, Tamsin. 'So you like decency.'

'I do.'

'Did you also like Rosemary?'

'Full of good works, Rosemary. Almost exhaustingly so, and one must support good works.'

'But did you like her?'

The major-general smiled wearily.

'Must we descend into likes and dislikes?'

'They are normal human experiences,' said Tamsin, for whom 'dislike' was more normal and felt with force right now. An awkward silence followed, because Blain would not be jumped; though he did speak after a while.

'We were captured and held for five days in enemy territory,' he said. He spoke casually, as if this was of no consequence, as if he was telling her he'd decided to order an extra pint of milk.

'Where?' asked Tamsin, too eager.

'A dry place. I've been to a few of those. We were held by bounty hunters after some navigational issues in the unit.' He couldn't hide his disdain. God help the soldier who'd made a mess with the compass. 'I blame myself, of course. It was my team.'

'There's no accounting for idiots, though,' said Tamsin, who worked with them on a regular basis.

'They were just businessmen, our captors,' said Terence. 'Not soldiers, businessmen. People for whom war was business, but trying to arrange a handover to those less enamoured of us. These people could make money from us. Their potential buyers – well, they were different, and our prospects would not have been good had they succeeded.'

'No.'

He spoke slowly, words carefully placed. 'We were looked after by a young fellow called Zak, who brought us our food, talked with us on occasion, nice smile. Quite a charmer, in fact – happy eyes and probably a good son. He even joked with us, practised his English and we all told him how well he was doing. He liked that. But on the fifth day, I borrowed his gun and shot him in the forehead.' Tamsin froze for a moment. 'He looked at me as he fell, as if surprised that I had ignored his kind and caring manner. But I couldn't tell you whether I liked him or not. I just knew he was in the way.'

Silence.

'So did you shoot Rosemary?'

'You do ask a lot of questions.'

'You must know about interrogation, Major-General. It has a purpose.'

'More purpose than outcome, in my experience.'

'You're not answering the question.'

'And why answer such a damn-fool question? Would I be removed from the suspects list if I said no?'

Tamsin felt weary. This man drained her – no, crushed her. Tales of his virtuous acts littered his self-deprecating path. But all Tamsin heard was contempt for everything and everyone; and a meaninglessness that suffocated her.

This man could put a bullet in anyone, including himself. But had he put one in Rosemary?

'So why join the Etiquette Society?'

asked Tamsin, aware of the estate agent's eyes mentally undressing her.

'Oh, Martin can be very persuasive, as I'm sure you're aware,' he replied from behind his desk. His agency was round the corner from the station, along with the other estate agents in Stormhaven. They all nestled together, as if they weren't quite important enough to stand by themselves.

'This is you networking, is it?' said Tamsin.

'I'm sorry?'

'I'm told you are a compulsive networker.' She threw that in because she didn't like him. He was a lecher. 'Is that your main interest in etiquette?'

Geoff stayed calm. 'Is that a nasty way of saying I get on with people and I enjoy their company?' he said. Geoff had a large desk and was boss of his company; he felt a certain power here. And what did women know anyway? 'If it is, then guilty as charged. But if that's the best you can do, then really . . .'

'It's your wisdom I need – not your offence.'

'Then why be offensive?'

Good line, thought Peter, who wondered the same. He sat in the background, happy to leave the chair where it was. Maybe house buyers eagerly pushed their chairs forward, to discuss their dream home with Mr Berry. But the abbot didn't feel the need. He had a home already, was quite beyond dreams of that sort . . . and he was happy in the corner. From there you see everything, including Tamsin behaving poorly.

'Do you know of the Bybuckle Asylum?' asked Tamsin.

Geoff laughed. 'Of course I know the Bybuckle Asylum! It's my job. I know every property in Stormhaven, Newhaven,

Peacehaven – and Alfriston as well, if you're loaded. Used and unused, sold and unsold, to buy, to let. You must remember I've been an estate agent in this town for over twenty-five years.'

'Yes, I was wondering about that.'

'Wondering about what?'

'Well, with your experience, you'll be aware that it's a valuable site – the Bybuckle Asylum, I mean. You could build a fair few flats on that land.'

'Not the classiest part of Stormhaven, obviously.'

'You mean there *is* a classy part?'

'There are some very desirable areas of Stormhaven, Detective Inspector. The Etiquette Society meets in one of them. But houses by the sea, disintegrating in the salt air, though popular on the holiday market, are not so highly priced.'

'Oh?' said Peter.

'Fine views, obviously – if you like the sea. But terrible maintenance costs. So the seafront has great scenic qualities but is not one of the more sought-after areas in town. More for the Clacton clientele.'

'The Clacton clientele?' said Tamsin with undisguised merriment, all too aware that the abbot's property had just been well and truly junked. And the abbot was thinking the same. Not one of the more sought-after areas? For the Clacton clientele?!

'Brighton and Eastbourne have wonderful seafronts, of course,' continued Geoff, unaware of the abbot's address. 'Much grander affairs than Stormhaven, full of both style and life. Stormhaven, in contrast, offers a determinedly derelict shoreline: a couple of tea huts, some appalling sixties flats that are falling down – and that's your lot for seaside glory.'

'You think so?' asked Peter, who found glory in a beach pebble. But Geoff wasn't listening. He sensed – wrongly – that he'd been given a stage.

'Might all have been very different, of course; very, very different. The town was close to acquiring funding in the nineteenth century – significant funding that would have quite transformed the place. We would have got a pier of our own, a promenade with gardens . . . like Eastbourne.'

'So what happened?'

'Who knows what happened? But the money disappeared, the promises dissolved and they missed out. Brighton probably got it . . . they tend to. Brighton gets everything. Though they've now got the Green Party as well, so you can't win them all!'

'Quite.'

Tamsin hated the Greens messing around with Hove's parking. Momentarily, Geoff was a kindred spirit.

'So no seafront grandeur for Stormhaven,' said Geoff. 'Not that the locals mind. It keeps visitors away, and believe me, no one here wants visitors. The tourist office is run from a cupboard in the police station.'

'A cupboard with a desk,' said Peter, slightly on the defensive for his new home.

'But still a cupboard, Abbot. Everything in this town is designed to keep people away.'

And that's exactly how Tamsin felt in Stormhaven: an unwelcome visitor. The abbot had somehow become part of the local furniture, wandering around in his odd clothes and smiling at people. But Tamsin was an unwanted visitor . . . a stranger.

'And Rosemary?'

'Rosemary?' Geoff looked blank, like a child in class who has drifted off, suddenly caught by a teacher's question.

'She's why we're talking with you. We're not looking to buy.'

'I didn't know her; I mean, not well. I didn't know her well.'

This was an answer they'd heard before. No one seemed to know Rosemary well.

'You knew her from the Etiquette Society.'

'Oh yes, I knew her there obviously, but not otherwise. I mean, she was a churchgoer, I think, which is fine, it's a free world, but it's not a habit of mine, shall we say? The theatre is my temple.'

'And who do you worship there?' asked Peter.

'Very amusing, Abbot.' Geoff felt stung. 'But contrary to popular belief, not all actors worship at the shrine called "Ego".'

'I'm sure not.'

'Though I can't deny people do speak very well of my performances. So what is a man to do? Now, if that's all—'

95

'And obviously you'll know number nine, Church Street,' said Tamsin, stepping in. Geoff Berry seemed to seek approval as much for himself as for his properties.

'A desirable three-bedroom terraced house in the heart of Old Stormhaven; four-minute walk from the station, three minutes from the sea.'

'And also a brothel.'

'Well, so I hear . . . I mean, so I have read. There has been a little coverage in the *Silt*, and while I have no time for the paper usually—'

'You don't need to apologize.'

'I mean, I had no idea, of course. No idea at all.'

'I thought you knew every property in Stormhaven.'

'To know the property is not to know the activity therein.' Geoff looked smug, as though he'd delivered a good line rather well. 'That's the difference between an estate agent and a journalist, Inspector. What people do behind their firmly closed doors does not appear in our brochures.'

'It might make them more interesting if it did,' Tamsin said. 'So you really didn't know?'

The estate agent sighed like a slightly deflated balloon. 'There were rumours.'

'Rumours?'

'There was concern about house prices in the road dropping, if it turned out to be true . . . and became known. So obviously I wasn't going to publicize it; that would not have served my clients well. No one wants to discover that their precious little property, their life's investment, is two doors down from a knocking shop.'

'So you did know.'

'There are degrees of knowing.'

'And degrees of lying,' added Peter.

'And Rosemary's involvement there – what was your degree of knowing about that?' said Tamsin.

'I had absolutely no idea.' He sounded adamant.

'No idea as in *some* idea?'

'No idea at all. Really not. No. She lived in Stormhaven, so she was seen around, quite naturally. I do remember – yes, it's just come to my mind – a conversation about the place.'

'Amazing how the memory works.'

'Yes, I did actually ask her once if she'd heard any of the rumours.'

'You actually spoke with Rosemary about the rumours?'

'I did, yes. I recall it now.'

'And what did she say?'

'She said she had heard them and discounted them as the fanciful inventions of those with too much time on their hands . . . which included half of Stormhaven, by her accounting!'

Peter smiled. He could hear Rosemary saying that, so maybe it was true.

'When, in fact, all along she was just a common or garden tart,' added Geoff. He snorted a little. 'Quite a performance, really, if you think about it. There she was playing bloody Mother Teresa, when all along, well . . . though clearly someone saw through her.'

'Why do you say that?' Tamsin acted surprised.

'Well, why else was she killed?'

'Perhaps it has nothing to do with the brothel.'

Geoff's amused grunt indicated he didn't agree. 'If you play with fire . . .'

'Perhaps it's about the asylum. Who knows?'

'The asylum?'

'Well, it is rather staring us in the face, isn't it? I mean, that's where she was murdered.'

'It's what they call "a lonely spot", I believe. Not a place where you're likely to be disturbed.'

'True. Though also a valuable site, as we all agree.'

'I didn't agree.'

'You merely said it wasn't as valuable as some other sites. That could still leave it very valuable.'

'No crude pun intended, Inspector, but given Rosemary's apparently keen interest in sex – aren't you rather taking your eye off the ball?'

He was proving quite irritating.

Sidney Stokes was a short man, probably mid-eighties, and he sat before them now with a small case on the table. They were in the interview room in Stormhaven police station, which was open for four hours a day. Outside these hours, someone would have to come from Lewes to deal with a crime; and no one from Lewes wanted to come to Stormhaven. The police shared these premises with the Stormhaven Tourist Centre, with whom, in the cause of cost-cutting, they also shared a kettle, a fridge and an interview room – though the Tourist Centre called it their kitchen/diner.

An Elton John tribute act was the next big thing at the Barn Theatre, according to the posters.

'Looks mildly interesting,' Peter said, casually. 'He's a singer, isn't he?' He was thinking that he should involve himself more fully in the town's cultural life. Tamsin's mind was elsewhere. She'd booked the interview room, but now Shirley from the Tourist Centre wasn't happy.

'Where am I going to have my lunch?' she asked.

'We won't be long,' said Tamsin.

'How long?'

'Not long at all.'

'My sandwich and drink are in the fridge, and there's only one kettle here. So there's no tea for anyone until you're out.'

'Half an hour, max.'

'I'm not waiting half an hour.'

But what else could Tamsin do? Sidney Stokes had walked in here and demanded to speak with her. She could hardly say no to the man; hardly hold up a murder enquiry because it clashed with the Tourist Centre's lunch rota. So while Shirley ate her well-filled sandwiches on the front desk, which wasn't ideal – a strong smell of bloater paste everywhere – Tamsin and the abbot spoke with Sidney across the table in the 'interview room'.

'I don't want you to think I'm being nosy,' he said.

'We're not thinking anything,' said Tamsin. 'Just tell us what you want to tell us.' And hurry up about it . . .

'I've lived in Church Street for thirty-seven years.'

'Really?' said Peter encouragingly. Unlike his colleague, he liked history. 'You must have seen some changes.'

'No, I haven't seen any changes really.'

And that summed up Stormhaven, thought Tamsin. The land time forgot.

'Apart from the new beach huts; not sure what I think of them.'

'They do divide opinion,' said Peter, though he couldn't think of anyone who didn't like them. A seafront should have beach huts. If you haven't got a pier or sand, you really do need beach huts, especially in that whipping wind across the shingle.

'But there comes a moment,' said Sidney.

'How do you mean?' asked Tamsin.

'I mean, I don't want to waste your time or anything.'

'No, really, you're not,' said Tamsin, counting the seconds of her life as they slipped away. 'Not at all.'

'We're very glad you found the time to speak with us,' added Peter soothingly. 'Would you like some tea?'

He'd noticed the kettle in the corner, the shared kettle.

'I mean, neighbours come and neighbours go,' said Sidney, ignoring the offer. 'Nothing's for ever, I know that. I mean, I miss Mrs Carstairs obviously.'

'Mrs Carstairs?'

'I miss her.'

'No longer with us?'

'No longer with us, no. Passed away, sadly.'

'People do pass through our lives,' said Peter, 'and we miss some of them.' He wondered how Mrs Carstairs had passed through Sidney's, but had no time to ask. And he found himself missing Rosemary now, as he sat in this strange little room in Stormhaven police station; though in truth he hadn't missed her for years. It was just the finality of it all. She had been offered to him so briefly, so surprisingly – and then snatched away. Suddenly, here she was in Stormhaven! And then she wasn't . . . and had maybe become more interesting for that reason. Yes, that was possible. Would he be knocking on her door this evening if she was still alive? That was the question. It was possible he might . . . just supper or something.

'So how can we help you?' said Tamsin.

'I don't think you can.'

'So why are you here?' The tone betrayed her boredom, which could flare quickly into aggression.

'Maybe I can help you. I live in Church Street, you see.'

'You mentioned.' He now had half of her attention.

'And I have some film for you.'

'What sort of film?'

'Footage of the brothel at number nine. I thought you might be interested.'

He now had her full attention. 'What sort of footage?'

'It's been closed for twenty years,'

said Peter.

The abbot and Tamsin stood once again in the cold emptiness of Gladstone Ward. This time she looked around the place properly, with appalled incredulity. Old metal beds, which had somehow survived the slow looting of time, were scattered about round the vast and vacant space, as if awaiting the arrival of another tortured mind. Flimsy curtain partitions, disturbed by the wind, protected the privacy of ghosts long gone.

She looked across at Peter. 'Bleak.'

He nodded. The abbot stood in awe, as though in a cathedral, all other life brought to a halt. But his thoughts weren't heavenly.

'I'm not a fan of the mad,' said Tamsin.

'You surprise me.'

'I mean, they're deeply irritating. But who on earth thought this was a good idea?'

The abbot smiled sadly. 'It's had better days . . . well, glory days, briefly.'

'Glory days? This place?'

'Oh yes.'

'And when were those exactly?'

'It was built in 1849 and had seven hundred beds.'

'And that was the good idea?'

Peter had done the research that Tamsin could never do; he had to, he couldn't help himself. He had to understand how something came to be, the story of its origins, the place from whence it came. 'From no thing, some thing,' as writers from the East put it. Whereas Tamsin was happy to deal with what was in front of her, without so much looking back. Life was too short.

'Such intimate care,' she said, with due sarcasm. Seven hundred beds? Well, they could have fitted most of them in here. She held back from calling it a room because it wasn't a room; only in the way an aircraft hangar was a room.

'It's hard to believe, but it was forward-looking at the time,' said Peter, a student of lunacy for reasons he wasn't quite sure of. 'There was a sea-change of thinking about mental health around that time.'

'Tell me,' said Tamsin. She wanted to know. 'Perhaps just the highlights,' she added, because she didn't want to know that much.

'Well, in 1847, the Lunacy Commissioners—'

'The *Lunacy* Commissioners?'

'Yes, they existed then, and they made a very big announcement. They said that the shackles and chains traditionally used on the insane should be replaced by "mild and gentle treatment".'

'So what was it like before that?'

'Before that, they'd been fair game for any treatment – really any treatment at all. Physical violence, cruel restraint, emotional neglect, sexual abuse.'

Tamsin did not wish to dwell on that sort of stuff. It made her short of breath. 'So that was quite a change.'

'Oh yes, a brave new world in the universe of well-being. It was called "The Asylum Age".'

'That doesn't sound good.'

'No, but that's only with hindsight. At the time, it was very good . . . a phrase characterized by moral treatment of the patients and a new respect for them. The famous Hanwell Asylum was the model for others to follow – the centre of this enlightenment. Or "good practice", as we'd call it today.'

'I work for the police so it's not a phrase I recognize.'

Peter smiled. He understood cynicism, though tried not to let it be the final word.

'Instead of living in shackles, as in the previous model, the patients were set free . . . or as free as was felt possible. Visitors to Hanwell could witness patients enjoying gardening, attending chapel and even dancing at the Christmas party.'

'I've tried that. It's always unwise.'

Her boss had once hit on her at a Christmas party; it still soured her memory.

102

'But such things were unheard of in the world of the mad. This was all very different. As I say, the Asylum Age was a new dawn.'

Tamsin sighed and pulled her coat collar round her neck, against the damp chill. There was a window frame banging in the wind, through a door on the left. They approached the door now, a reasonable walk away, and looked through. There was no attempt to glamorize the space. Bare walls, bare concrete floor and space for a further twenty beds or so; no privacy curtains on display.

'This was Victoria Ward,' said Peter. 'It was where the most acute patients were put – or dumped – in the later years, at least. They were left here to rot among themselves, away from public view and staff care. It became known as "The End Room".'

'Hard to imagine this was ever a new dawn,' said Tamsin.

'Well, the truth is, the dawn didn't last long.'

'So what happened?'

'It's practicalities that kill a vision. There was overcrowding, of course, when the workhouses closed down and the pauper lunatics sought sanctuary in the new asylums. And then came the economic cut-backs – these people were no one's priority, when there was an empire to build around the world.'

'From one insanity to another.'

'And quite soon, the wheels had come off the whole mental health project. Overworked medical staff, untrained, unsupervised nursing staff – it all sounds pretty contemporary, really. And by the end of the century, the idea that anyone could be cured by kindness – the bold hope of Hanwell – well, that vision had died completely.' They walked slowly back into Gladstone Ward and towards the entrance. 'By the 1870s, most asylums had reintroduced straitjackets and other forms of physical restraint. And drip by drip, asylums and their decaying buildings became little more than prisons for the "degenerates" and "defectives" that lunatics had once again become in the public eye.'

'The death of a dream.' The phrase seemed strangely poignant for Tamsin. 'Though let's be honest, kindness never cured anyone,' she said, hardening again. And the abbot let it pass for now.

'Bybuckle Asylum was also part of the Victorian rush to the seaside.'

'They should have gone to Hove.'

'It's why there were so many private schools in Stormhaven. At one time there were fifty in the town.'

'Fifty?'

'Yes. It explains the very long station platform. It was for the Stormhaven schoolchildren at the end of term.'

'I did wonder at its length. Four people got out of the three-carriage train when I used it. I mean, it isn't London Victoria.'

'And of course, care homes for the troubled arrived here as well. It was felt that the mentally unwell would benefit from the sea air – though whether they did is unclear. And Bybuckle was finally closed in 1997, two years after the Colney Hatch Asylum. After a six-month investigation.'

'Six months? I could have done it in a week, with Friday off.'

Peter smiled. 'It was all very controversial. There were about a hundred and fifty patients resident at the end, and there was a great deal of panic about what was to become of them. Their families were concerned at the absence of care if Bybuckle went.'

'I can see their point. They'd suddenly be knocking on *their* doors. And who wants the insane sharing breakfast with them? I really couldn't be doing with that, even if it was my mother. Particularly if it was my mother.'

'There were the usual petitions and demonstrations, demands that it stay open, but the investigation was pretty damning. It famously declared Bybuckle a "human storage dump lacking in either care or stimulation". There was also the accusation that everything at the asylum – including shift patterns and meal times – was arranged for the benefit of the staff rather than of the patients.'

'Surprise, surprise.'

'And with Care in the Community the new "truth on top", Bybuckle closed, with much acrimony.'

They contemplated the long-neglected space. No acrimony now – just the wind, the rotting lino . . . and murder.

'Didn't someone mention a TV documentary?'

It was one of her colleagues at Lewes. She'd ignored him at the time but it seemed more pertinent now.

'Yes, a film crew was allowed access to the place as the end game unfolded. They interviewed patients, filmed the investigation – well, as much of it as they were allowed – and the cameras continued to roll after the closure order was issued, a very traumatic fight to the death. They called the programme *Bleak House*.'

'So Bybuckle Asylum is famous.'

'Famous for fifteen minutes. No one gets much more than that.'

'And after the closure?'

'After the closure the building was left to rot, as one scheme after another fell through, and nothing more was heard of the place until, well – this.'

'But why?'

'Why what?'

'Why kill someone here?'

'Well, maybe as Geoff said, it is a lonely place. It ticks all the boxes for a planned killing.'

They looked at the bed, the particular bed, the one used for murder, still cordoned off with police tape. The forensic sweep had come and gone in a rush of science and protective gear. There was little here un-dabbed, un-brushed or un-sifted.

'But she wasn't brought here dead,' said Peter.

'I'm sorry?'

'I'm saying we know she died here. She fell in the hallway, but she didn't die there.'

'So?'

'So we know she came of her own accord.'

'Obviously.'

'It made some sort of sense to Rosemary to come here. Why would that make sense?'

'Coming here makes no sense at all.'

'So either she knew her attacker . . . or she knew the place.'

'Or both. And I'm getting cold. Shall we move?'

But the abbot wasn't allowing cold right now. 'We have a brothel, an etiquette society and an asylum,' he said with force, grabbing an old broom handle and lowering himself on to his haunches.

'An unusual combination, I grant you. What are you doing with the broom?'

'If we were to make each of those a circle . . .'

'What?'

'If we make a Venn diagram of them – you know, the ones with the interlocking circles.'

And in the wet surface dirt, he began to draw. 'Three interlocking circles: the brothel, the etiquette society and the asylum.'

'Right.'

'And Rosemary is in the space where each of them overlaps. There!' He pointed with the broom. 'She ran the brothel.' He was slowly getting used to saying that. 'She was a member of the etiquette society . . .'

'And she died in the asylum.'

'So where's everybody else in the diagram?'

And then a noise behind them: a slight shuffle, nothing more, but enough to make both turn their heads towards the doorway. A silhouetted figure was watching.

'Can we help you?' asked Tamsin.

'Er . . .'

Tamsin recognized her. 'Tara Hopesmith, isn't it?'

'It is, yes.'

'Well, fancy seeing you here.'

'Rosemary was my friend.'

'Right. And I suppose the other headline is: you were the main beneficiary of her death.'

'I just had to see,'

said Tara, a little flustered.

So she can still blush, thought Tamsin. 'See what?'

Tara was standing in the doorway of Gladstone Ward, like a new nurse reporting for duty.

'Well, I've never been here before. I just had to see . . .'

'Where Rosemary died?' asked Peter.

'Yes.'

'So you don't come here often?' said Tamsin.

'No. I mean – never. Why would I? I just saw the door open.'

'It wasn't open. We closed the front door behind us.'

'Well, it looked open. Perhaps it was the wind.'

'Why don't we sit on the bench in the entrance hall?' said Tamsin, eager to be elsewhere, eager for light.

'Well . . .'

'It wouldn't do any harm to have a chat with the new owner of Model Service.' Tara looked troubled. 'We were going to drop round later today anyway – you've saved us the bother.'

'I always like to help the police.' She decided against adding 'out of their trousers'. She could handle this . . . though she found the DI intimidating. Women were harder than men.

They left Gladstone Ward and walked along the dark corridor to the entrance hall where evidence of Rosemary's initial fall had been found, both hair and blood. Tamsin and Tara sat, and Peter stood by the entrance, looking out to sea. The idea that she fell here, just where he was standing – without a friend to help, alone – well, he found it almost as upsetting as the murder. This place was like the Stations of the Cross, each a stage in Rosemary's passion.

'It's all turned out rather well, hasn't it?' said Tamsin, cheerfully.

'What has?'

'For you, I mean – Rosemary's death.'

'If you mean the will—?'

'So what got you into prostitution?' It wasn't a kind question; not warm with the presumption that women should do whatever they wish to. The aroma in the air was one of disgust.

'I was a Roedean girl.'

'Another one? You didn't know Blessings N'Dayo, did you?' Tamsin thought they must be a similar age, early forties.

'Blessings?' Tara laughed in amused shock. 'Well, I did as it happens.'

'A happy acquaintance?'

'It was over twenty years ago.'

'Don't tell me you don't remember. Everyone remembers their school days.'

'It was happy enough. We were teenagers, you don't ask whether you're happy; you just get on with things. It was pretty awful actually.'

'Did you like her?'

'I don't know. You didn't want to cross her, I remember that. Why do you ask?'

'No reason.'

'She was from somewhere in Africa. She was rather exotic at the time.'

'Well, I suppose you might meet her one of these days.'

'Oh?'

'She's a judge.'

'Lives in Firle Road,' added Peter.

'Very posh,' said Tara. 'One of my ... well, I know someone who lives there.'

'But you're quite posh yourself,' said Tamsin. 'Roedean isn't for paupers.'

'My father was a property developer, so money was never an issue. The logs of human warmth were perhaps in shorter supply – but that's life, isn't it? You get on with things.'

'And you've certainly got on with things.'

'I started sex work at uni in Brighton, yes. I presume you want my history?'

Tamsin nodded.

'I was working in a bar and hating it so I gave my notice in, and it was then that the landlord suggested sex work, "just to tide you over".'

'"To tide you over"?'

'It's what he said. And it made sense at the time.'

'He was your pimp?'

'For a short while, I suppose. Not for long. He was increasingly gross.'

'Now there's a surprise.'

'I mean, I never imagined it as a career, obviously.'

'Obviously.'

'But I had no interest in joining Daddy in the property trade; nothing could be as immoral or as soulless as that. So I worked for a housing association briefly, but the office politics bored me . . . and by then I was earning around a thousand a week as a sex worker, which twenty years ago was a very decent sum.'

'It's a fairly decent sum now,' said Peter, in awe. He simply couldn't imagine such riches.

'And all thanks to a university education,' said Tamsin.

'My studies did suffer – but I've always believed in apprenticeships.'

Peter smiled. Tara's story probably wouldn't feature on government posters – not really the apprenticeships they're trying to promote.

'And then I started helping others.'

'Oh, spare me – a tart with a heart?'

'No, a human being with organizational skills.'

'So you were organizing prostitutes?'

Tamsin refused to use the phrase 'sex worker' – as if the job was similar to a care worker or a health worker!

'A lot of the young women needed organizing for their own well-being.'

'And were the police ever interested?' she asked, as if the illegality was startling.

'I found the police very interested, Detective Inspector, but not in the legalities, if you know what I mean. Well, you know men.' Tamsin had walked into that one and now Tara was animated, stirred from defence into attack. 'I mean, does the abbot fully appreciate the ridiculous laws around sex work?'

'Well, I . . .'

'We could make a quiz of it. I did this at a dinner party recently. Do you like a good quiz, Abbot?'

'Not particularly.'

'So question one: is it legal to sell sex?'

Tamsin would allow this to play out. It might be educational for her uncle.

'I'd say illegal.'

'Wrong, Abbot. Sorry about that.'

'It's legal?'

'Quite legal, yes. It's legal to sell sex in your room, but illegal to do it on the street or in public.'

'I'll remember that – should funds run low.'

This was not a quiz he'd expected, and certainly not in the hallway of the Bybuckle Asylum. He'd done well in the monastery quizzes on high days and holy days. But they tended to be more theological in tone. He didn't remember a 'sex laws' option.

'So, question two: is it legal to work in a brothel?'

'Er, I'd say . . . not legal.'

'No, it's quite legal to *work in* a brothel, Abbot – but illegal to *run* one.'

'That does sound a bit odd.'

'Can I quote you on that? "Abbot says it sounds a bit odd." Question three: is it legal to advertise sexual services?'

'Well, I presume it must be, if it's a legal activity.'

'Wrong again. It's legal to *pay* for sex. But kerb-crawling is illegal, as is advertising sexual services online, in phone boxes or in newspapers . . . anywhere public, in fact.'

'I'm not doing very well here.'

'Final question, Abbot: how many sex workers in a house make it illegal?'

Peter's mind was now a mist of unknowing, as if wandering through a land of cheerful insanity.

'Ten?' He had no idea.

'No, two. One sex worker in a house is legal, but two is illegal.'

'That's when it becomes a brothel,' said Tamsin, offering legal clarity. 'Which the police may, or may not, choose to be interested in.'

'And that's also when it becomes much safer for the women,' said Tara, with an ace of her own. 'Strength in numbers. This was always Rosemary's view. She was very interested in their safety . . . in our safety.'

'I can see her point,' said Peter, warming to Rosemary's vision.

'A single sex worker is much more vulnerable.'

'Perhaps she should get a proper job,' said Tamsin.

'Like screwing people for money in heartless property deals?' Her father's dark exploits had been entirely legal, of course.

'There are other jobs.'

'All I'm saying is that we need to define "proper" – but don't worry, I won't be asking the Etiquette Society for advice.' They sat in silence for a moment. Tara suddenly looked weary, tired of the battle. 'I simply note the abbot scored nought in the quiz, which confirms what a madness it all is.'

Peter remained at the door, looking out to sea, but offered words of support.

'It is a nonsense, as you say, Tara – but then morality tends to be so when the law gets involved. Sheep and goats aren't easily separated, in my experience. Life is a speckled thing.'

'But what we do know is this,' said Tamsin, determined to have the last word, the knock-out blow here in the asylum. She didn't find the abbot's intervention helpful. 'Amid all the uncertainties, the madam is always illegal. Women can legally sell sex, men can legally buy sex – but the madam, the organizer of it all, is *always* illegal.'

She looked at Tara. 'My girls all pay their taxes, work in a safe and health-conscious environment, are all legal citizens of this country and are in no way coerced labour. Where really is the problem?'

'Well, how about this: why does the main beneficiary of the murdered woman's will now return to the scene of the crime?'

'Who said I'm returning?'

'So your lodger is an arsonist?'

said Tamsin. They were back in the large dwelling of Judge Blessings N'Dayo.

'He *was* an arsonist,' said Blessings, correcting her. 'There's a difference.'

'Really?'

'You were once a baby, Inspector, but you are no longer a baby.'

'She still has her tantrums,' said Peter. Perhaps a jest would ease the tension between these two upholders of the law. It didn't.

'Is the rehabilitation of arsonists quite so inevitable?' asked Tamsin.

Not in her book it wasn't . . . and her question was aggressive. She'd refused the offer of tea precisely because she wished to attack. You can't attack holding a cup of tea; you can discuss but you can't attack.

And Peter realized that he must allow things to be, just as they were. Both these women operated through aggression, through conflict. So maybe Tamsin and Blessings were destined only to clash, drawn together like warring armies, with hopes of partnership a dream that could never be. Or maybe conflict was the partnership; they would work together, but through hostility. They were both women who liked to lead. So who, wondered the abbot, would get to wear the crown?

'I wouldn't want us to give up on the principle of rehabilitation, Detective Inspector. Give up on that principle and things really do look bleak.'

'You can't give up on something you've never believed in; and I've never believed in it.'

'Is that so?'

'Prison is about punishment. Why do we insist on making it more complicated?'

Minimalist elegance ruled their surroundings in Blessings'

home – a triumph of style over life, with all clutter banished. There were vistas of shiny surfaces and clear space everywhere, interrupted occasionally by Ghanaian *objets d'art*. Martin had been rather rude about these, calling her 'a plastic African'.

'Her African furniture makes up for the absence of black names in her contacts list. All very white,' he said.

But they sat here now because of Francisco, the mystery man in the kitchen, as Martin called him. 'He floats in and out of view at Black Cap – now you see him, now you don't!'

So what did Blessings really know about him?

'Francisco does interest us,' said Tamsin.

'He interests many people, I'm sure,' said Blessings, with disdain. 'I can see their little minds whirring. But their interest doesn't interest me, if you see what I mean.'

'We just need to establish how he came to be here.'

'He's here because I sentenced him to three years in prison.'

That explained the criminal record.

'*You* sentenced him?'

'Yes.'

'You were the judge at his trial?'

Blessings' expression said, 'Keep up.'

'I was, yes. And we seem to be running a little ahead of your research, Detective Inspector. Don't ever become a barrister – you'd seriously struggle.' A low blow which found soft flesh.

'What was his crime?' asked Tamsin, raging inside.

'I think you know – or at least I hope you do.' She patronized Tamsin with her smile. 'He lit a fire in a church hall.'

'As you do.'

'And I'll always remember his reason.'

'Which was?'

'He said he didn't like his Sunday school teacher – which was rather sweet, but hardly a worthy reason. Otherwise, which church hall across the land would be safe? Certainly none in Ghana.'

'So you sentenced him.'

'Of course, he had to go down. Arson is not popular with the law-makers. It damages property, which is demonstrably more important than people.' She enjoyed her showy sarcasm. 'But I

113

was struck by his remorse at the time. He did seem genuinely sad.'

'Perhaps he was just sad he'd been caught. That's the only time I see remorse kicking in.'

'And then I was impressed by his use of the rehabilitation programme offered in prison,' said Blessings.

'You stayed in contact with him while he was behind bars?'

'Yes, I did actually.'

'Is that normal?'

'What is normal, Detective Inspector?'

'Judges are always staying in contact with those they send down, are they?'

'I'm afraid I'm not nosy enough to know. And I'm not sure there are any Home Office figures to help us.'

'How did you stay in contact?'

'Letters . . . and such like.'

'And such like?'

'I did visit him on one occasion.'

'Out of uniform?'

'No wig, if that's what you mean.' For the first time, Blessings was a little uncomfortable.

'Do you provide this visiting service for all those you send down?'

'Ah, the "num" question!' Blessings laughed at her own observation.

'You'll have to explain your hilarity.' Tamsin was thrown.

'It's a question that expects the answer "no",' said Peter quietly. 'In Latin, *nonne* at the beginning of the question expects the answer "yes". *Num* anticipates the answer "no". As in, "Surely you don't visit every criminal you send down?"'

'Very good, Abbot,' said Blessings. 'Very good! You were clearly listening in class. And of course the "num" and "nonne" questions are the bread and butter of any cross-examination. They're designed to expose a weakness in the other person's case – and they do it very well. In this instance, it's highlighting the fact that clearly I don't do this for everybody – so why do it for Francisco?'

'So why did you do it for Francisco?' Tamsin continued to fume.

'Everyone deserves a second chance.'

Now it was Tamsin's turn to mock with her face, suggesting an entirely inadequate response.

'So he's a lodger here?'

'Precisely.'

'He isn't more than that?'

'He does other things, if that's what you mean.'

'What sort of things?'

'He looks after the house when I'm away. Circuit judges travel a lot; I spend far too much of my life with room service in appalling hotels.'

The abbot quite liked the idea of an appalling hotel. He'd never actually slept in a hotel, so it couldn't help but sound intriguing. And room service sounded particularly exotic.

'Anything else?' asked Tamsin.

'He's a very good gardener, a pretty handy chef. And to forestall further questions from any grubby minds in the room' – she looked around cheekily – 'he's gay. He likes men. Is your interest calmed a little?'

Tamsin tried to hide her mirth at this suggestion. The abbot would later tell her she was only partially successful.

'Not really, no, Blessings. In fact, if anything, it's stirred a little.'

'Oh?'

'And we have old Sidney Stokes to thank – former newspaper man, but in retirement a keen-eyed amateur film-maker.'

'No doubt you will explain.'

'Well, according to his video footage, the gay Francisco, the one who likes men, has been a most committed visitor to a brothel in Church Street. Quite a regular there, apparently.'

'A brothel?'

'But perhaps he's doing their gardening. Or knocking up a soufflé for everyone?'

Blessings sat still as if stunned; and then melted and nodded in appreciation. 'You played your hand well,' she said. 'Expertly played, Detective Inspector.'

Tamsin could scarcely have been happier . . . such applause from a judge. Warmth towards this woman flooded through her body.

'And now, Blessings, I need to ask a favour of you. About tonight.'

'Brothel etiquette?'

said Tara. 'It's very important, of course it is. Rosemary was very strong on etiquette, as you know, Abbot.'

Peter sat alone with Tara in No. 9, Church Street. He'd been sent.

Tamsin's afternoon was to be spent arranging a meeting of the Stormhaven Etiquette Society that evening. Peter's was to be spent here, digging.

'I think we all need to sit down and have a chat together,' she'd told him earlier. 'Let's see what the oddest society in Europe has to say about the death of Rosemary. But while I'm organizing that, I want you to find out everything you can about Model Service. All right?'

'Yes.'

'I mean, you're OK with a brothel? You won't do anything stupid?'

'Like what?'

'You were a long time in the desert.'

'I'll try and limit my vice to ignorance. I didn't score well in the quiz.'

'Which makes you ideal. Play the idiot; you do it very well.' Peter was not sure if that was a compliment. But he did play it well, and knowingly when necessary. 'Ask every question you can. They'll talk more freely to you . . . what with your habit. You'll be cute, other-worldly. They'll want to help you, want to explain. They've probably never explained a brothel to a monk. And I think Tara's got a soft spot for you.'

'I hardly think so.'

'She kept looking across at you in the asylum, hoping you were going to save her. Are you going to save her?'

'You were being quite hostile.'

'Oh, you're not in love with her as well, Abbot? Is any attractive middle-aged woman in Stormhaven safe?'

Peter rang the bell of Model Service with trepidation. Four years earlier, as an abbot in the desert, he would not have expected to be visiting a brothel. But then the future does surprise, and here he was in Church Street entering a whorehouse. Model Service was tastefully engraved, discreet black on bronze, like a solicitor or financial adviser. And Tara was the perfect host, opening the door, welcoming him in and sitting him down in the reception area, as if everything was quite normal; which for her it was, to a degree. She pulled a curtain across, enclosing the space where they sat, like a nurse giving a hospital patient privacy.

'The girls will answer the door to their clients,' she said, explaining. 'But they won't want to see us . . . particularly a monk. You're not the first churchman, obviously,' she added, 'but you are the first monk. I'd have remembered a monk. Though I was once asked to dress as an abbess. Should that be your fancy.'

'You do realize I'm here on business.' He was suddenly concerned that he hadn't made himself clear.

'Everyone's here on business!'

'No – I mean, it's the investigation.'

'I do understand,' said Tara, smiling. 'Though disappointed, of course.'

Peter was finding this difficult and Tara's easy-going charm wasn't helping.

'So you might not see everyone who uses the place?' asked the abbot. 'I mean, if the curtain is drawn.'

The question felt clumsy; he felt clumsy.

'No, I don't see everyone and wouldn't expect to. The girls work independently and I trust them.' Peter nodded and wondered where trust came into it. Perhaps it was about the income, which presumably would be shared in some manner, Model Service taking its cut.

'It must have been a bit of a shock to find us in the asylum today,' he said, reminding himself that this was a normal investigation, where normal rules applied. Create a relationship and see what emerges.

'No – the shock was the place, believe me; I'd heard it was bleak, but, well . . .'

'Not a good place to die.'

'Someone didn't like her,' said Tara.

'No.' There was a slight pause. 'Did you like her?'

'Of course. She was a good person.' The abbot nodded. She was a good person. 'What – you think this place may have something to do with the murder?'

'It's possible.'

'She kept it very quiet and deliberately so, but she believed in the business, no question about that. It was her idea.'

'Her idea? The brothel?'

Tara recounted her first meeting with Rosemary.

'She had her reasons. I don't know what they were, but she had them. She was very clear about what she wanted, particularly concerning the care of the workers.'

'That was uppermost in her thinking?'

'It was, yes. Which is fine, I had no problems with that, but it has to work as a business as well. I told her it wasn't a charity.'

'No, I think that would be stretching it.'

'Not that she expected anyone else to understand her involvement. "It's the best thing I do," she once said, and I believed her. But she kept her ownership of this place secret. She only told her closest friends.'

'Quite.' He was hurt by that idea. 'And who were her closest friends?'

'I don't know.' Did anyone know? wondered Peter. 'But who here would want to murder Rosemary?' asked Tara.

'You might, I suppose,' said the abbot. 'You do now own the business.'

'I was warned by Rosemary's solicitor I would be the number one suspect.'

'So I'm sure you have a water-tight story, carefully prepared.'

Tara paused for a moment before speaking. 'We did have a small incident here the other day.'

'What sort of an incident?'

'Katrina found a sticker on her door, after one of the clients left.'

'Placed there by him?'

'Well, I didn't put it there, and I don't think Katrina did.'

118

'What sort of sticker?'

'It's the sign they use.'

'Who?'

'The Stormhaven Etiquette Society. A bit strange, really. Given that we now discover Rosemary was a member.'

Peter was thinking of his Venn diagram and the overlapping circles.

'And what did the sticker say? Do you still have it?'

Tara reached for the desk drawer.

'No, wait,' said Peter. He handed Tara a clear plastic bag. 'Fingerprints,' he said.

'Well, I've handled it already.'

'You just won't be handling it again and obscuring other prints. We wouldn't want you falsely accused.'

'I think I was falsely accused this morning by your colleague.'

'The detective inspector accuses everybody; it's part of the dance. She accuses me in most of our investigations – including this one. I was her first suspect.'

Tara held the sticker and read the message out loud: 'TO THE SLUT CREW OF CHURCH STREET, BE WARNED: YOU'RE NOT QUITE WHAT WE WANT. THE STORMHAVEN ETIQUETTE SOCIETY.'

'They don't pull any punches, do they?' Peter was now feeling a little ashamed that he had been their guest speaker.

'Other people have received them,' she continued. 'A flower seller received one for not putting the apostrophe in the right place on her sign. I mean, I ask you! Another shop got one after a wheelchair user was moved out of a shop, against their will, because they were blocking an aisle.'

'I sense Rosemary's hand there.'

'But, of course, nothing's attributable because no one knows who they are,' said Tara. 'So they can do as they please.'

'They make great play of their secret membership. On my visit there, I was told they were like Bletchley Park, pledged to silence.'

'Like a group of silly little boys.'

'And girls. So who's behind this one?' asked the abbot, looking at the sticker.

'How would I know? Completely sick, if you ask me.'

'Well, your old friend Blessings is a member . . . should it make any difference.' Would this stir anything?

'A judge in her free time as well? Well, I'm hardly surprised.'

'But you aren't in contact with her.'

The coincidence of Roedean and Rosemary seemed to link them, but Tara was having none of it.

'No,' she said firmly. 'Is there anything else?'

There *was* something else. But how could he say this? It was hard to drop casually into conversation.

'I need to understand,' said Peter.

'Understand what?'

'I know how a monastery works, Tara; and I don't need to know all the details, I'm not here as a voyeur.' Tara was now smiling. 'But, I mean, how does a place like this work?'

'A brothel, you mean?'

'Yes.'

'You want all the ins and outs, Abbot?' Tara was quite shameless.

'I just need to understand Model Service, how this place works.'

'You want a guided tour, Abbot?' She was enjoying his embarrassment.

'Well, not a guided tour. I just need to understand . . .'

'Follow me,' said Tara. 'And let me help you understand.' She got up from behind the desk, pulled back the curtain, and led him up the small but steep stairs, two floors, to the top of the house.

'I'm told that stairs are very good for you,' said Peter on arrival at the top. 'Perhaps you could advertise as a health club as well.'

They were now standing outside a door.

'So, this is Katrina's room, where the sticker was left – here on the door.' Peter noted that a sticky stain remained. 'She's not in until later. So shall we go inside?'

'It isn't optional, Martin,'

explained Tamsin on the phone. 'There will be a meeting of the Stormhaven Etiquette Society tonight.'

'But it isn't convenient,' said the editor, who had other plans for the evening. He really didn't feel like the Etiquette Society. Somehow the fun had left this particular adventure.

'Nor is the cold-blooded killing of Rosemary,' said Tamsin. 'It's ruining everyone's evening.'

He could hear she was in a determined mood.

'I just don't understand why the Etiquette Society is getting dragged into it, Detective Inspector.' Tamsin enjoyed his discomfort. 'I mean, it's our task to civilize people rather than murder them. So it's hardly likely—'

'Perhaps you murder them if they refuse to be civilized. Or, if they turn out to be the madam of a local brothel.'

'Well, I was as amazed as you are.'

'And I'm not at all amazed. So how amazed are you?'

'*Touché*, Detective Inspector!'

She did have a feisty spirit which he rather admired. And she wasn't finished.

'Are you seriously telling me, Mr Channing, that the *Sussex Silt* – which knows the name of every insect under every stone along the Sussex coast – knew nothing about Model Service?'

'I have a piano lesson this evening,' added Martin. 'It really isn't a good night.'

'A piano lesson?'

'And she's not a teacher who appreciates excuses, really not – rules me with a rod of iron. She'll think I haven't been practising, when truthfully young Mozart has had a great deal of my attention this week. Though I have to say, he's very awkward company – particularly the left hand, which he took very seriously. Did you know that, Detective Inspector?'

'You're presuming way too much interest.'

'Oh yes, it was all about the left hand with Wolfgang Amadeus.'

'Well, be glad for your left hand that you're free of Mozart tonight, Martin.'

She wanted to be clear.

'Oh, thankfully I am never free from genius – his or my own.'

'But you'll be there on time or you'll find every aspect of your life made very difficult.'

'Is that a threat?'

'It's just a fact, Martin, so it probably won't appear in your paper . . .'

There would need to be another murder.

The killer of Rosemary Weller had realized this at about nine o'clock that morning, while drying their cereal bowl at the kitchen sink . . . always good to clear away the meal. Who wants dirty cups and plates sitting on the sideboard all day? No decent human being wishes for that – though the thought of a further fatality brought with it a sudden tightening in the chest, tension in the body.

It was a reluctant realization, and brought a heaviness of spirit as blue sky momentarily appeared from behind the clouds. It was like the emergence of some magical turquoise ocean, another world, another life. But it didn't change anything . . . what must be, must be. The law of unintended consequences had a lot to answer for, and all very difficult because they liked Rosemary, as much as one could; just as they also liked dear— The doorbell rang.

A young postman handed over a large envelope, which, once opened, offered details of a number of properties in Suffolk – pictures, floor plans, prices.

A change of air might be good; perhaps inland, away from the sea. Everything could be moved, once this was over. They had thought it *was* all over, of course, all done and dusted . . . but no, it wasn't. And Suffolk was nice – saner than Norfolk, so perhaps there was blue sky beyond all this, a fresh start in Suffolk. Does God speak with murderers in this way, somehow knowing that not everyone can live, and that someone has to kill them? That someone has to play Judas?

There would have to be one more killing; and then, even as they watched, the cloud slowly covered the blue, as if it had never been there.

And never would be again.

'It might start with a bubble bath,'

said Tara. They were standing in Katrina's small bathroom, the tour of Model Service now under way. 'An assisted bubble bath.'

'Assisted? Is that for the more elderly clients?'

'Hunt the soap, that sort of thing.'

'Is it not in the soap holder?'

'It's in the bath, Abbot . . . sliding around in the bath.'

'Oh, I see.'

'And it does make life much more pleasant for the sex worker if the client doesn't smell. I'm sure you can imagine.'

'Oh quite, I'm against smelling. Some of the monks – you really didn't wish to sit next to them for the evening office.'

'But if you want the client to have a bath, it has to be fun, part of the pleasure.'

'I normally read a book.'

'That's because you're alone, Abbot, so your options are limited. Imagine if you had company. You might put the book away.'

'Or hold on to it more firmly.'

'A bath relaxes the client as well, so it's good in every way. After which you can help them dry, give them a good rub down.'

'I've probably heard enough now.'

'We've hardly started!' said Tara briskly. What was the abbot afraid of here? He did seem strangely vulnerable. 'And then you wrap them up in a bathrobe and give them tea and ginger nuts,' continued Tara, 'while you get everything ready.'

'Tea and ginger nuts?'

'It's strange, yes, but that is peculiarly enjoyable for a lot of them. Ginger nut biscuits are very important for a brothel, Abbot. I sometimes think it's more about the biscuits than the sex . . . particularly for those of mature years.' Instinctively, Tara was checking the towel cupboard, which displayed a good selection, neatly stacked.

'I suppose it's nice to be looked after,' said Peter, who never had been.

'A lot of them do want to be mothered, quite literally sometimes. One man came in recently – he was an older gentleman – wearing a nappy under his trousers. He wanted to have his nappy changed by Katrina. That's all he wanted. And now he comes once a week.'

'To have his nappy changed?'

'Yep. And to be washed and pampered a little as well.' Peter breathed a bemused sigh.

'And Katrina obliges?'

'Of course. We always try to say yes when we can. Another client, a good-looking young man – he stripped off to reveal his mother's knickers and stockings.'

'Why would he be wearing those?'

'I tell you, nothing surprises me about men any more, Abbot. Really – though no doubt I'll be surprised again tomorrow. The main thing is to have enough towels. A brothel can't have too many towels; activities take place on towels. And baby wipes are vital obviously . . . for spillages.' Peter had seen baby wipes in the super-market but had mistakenly assumed they were for babies. 'Excellent for all sorts of cleaning,' she said, firmly closing the cupboard.

'I'll bear that in mind.'

'And the rest you know!' said Tara cheerfully.

'Yes, I don't need to know any more,' he replied with some relief, moving towards the door.

'You perhaps start with a back massage after the bath, then a front massage moving into sex and happy endings.'

'And we all like those . . . in a story, I mean,' he added quickly.

'So you see, an hour's booking might involve only a few seconds or minutes of sex. Is that all so bad? Is that worth killing someone for?'

Abbot Peter smiled sadly as Tara left the room, her point made.

'Murder is never committed by the happy,' he said, joining her on the small landing. 'What's that door?'

He hadn't noticed the other door at the top of the stairs.

'It's the Glory Hole. Let's go downstairs, shall we?'

'What's the Glory Hole?'

'You don't want to know . . . or rather, don't need to know.'

'And now I'm fatally intrigued.'

'The clue's in the name. It's a very particular service . . . involving a hole in the wall. You were saying murder is never committed by the happy.'

'I was, yes.'

'Tell me more about that.' She spoke over her shoulder as they returned downstairs.

'Well, the unhappy can justify anything to themselves,' said Peter, letting go of the Glory Hole for now. 'The deeper the unhappiness, the greater the power for self-justification, however twisted the logic. But murder is always about unhappiness.'

'And so who *are* the happy, Abbot?' asked Tara, because she didn't meet many of them.

'Those content in their own skin. When we find someone like that, we can rule them out of the enquiry. So can we rule you out?'

'Definitely,' said Tara. 'Not because I'm content. I just didn't do it.'

'Well, thank you for the tour.'

'My pleasure, Abbot. There are unwritten rules in a brothel.' Tara was back at her desk in the reception area. 'No drugs, no under-age girls, no coercion and everyone pays their tax.'

'And those are rules you hold to?'

'Of course, which is why we're left alone. We're breaking the law, but I never feel that. I don't feel like a law-breaker – well, it's a joke. I'm just helping my girls to keep safe and find an income.'

'Very commendable.'

'Sex workers don't have a voice, you see.' Tara hadn't finished. 'The government thinks it's all very moral to make brothels illegal. It plays to their constituency. People like my father and his golf club friends. But I'm the good guy here – not them! They *endanger* women by making brothels illegal.'

Peter wanted to be out before a client appeared. His presence here, in his monk's habit, could be misunderstood. Though really why did he care?

'You did make your views on the law quite clear this morning,' he said.

'And you scored nought out of four, Abbot, because you're sane and the law is an ass.'

'I think your next step is to stand for parliament, Tara.'

And with that, Peter said his goodbyes and closed the door of No. 9 behind him. It was a place of danger for him, he knew this in his heart. And all he could think of now was the Glory Hole – though as he walked down towards the sea he pondered the fact that in the hands of Tara, his first guided tour of a brothel, far from being an apology, had ended up as a moral crusade. She seemed to believe in it, just as Rosemary had. It wasn't just the oldest business in the world; it was also the noblest, apparently.

But then that was true of all dark crime. Whether it was the wife-beater, the bullion robber or the abuser of children – they all felt a victim, all had a cause, all saw themselves as crusaders in a hostile world . . .

Tamsin found Terence by the apples.

'This is not a job you want,' he said as she arrived by his side in the many-aisled Morrisons.

'It's the one you chose, Major-General,' she said.

He put his finger to his lips to invite some hush. 'My past is not known here. I prefer it that way.'

'You don't want to discuss your Victoria Cross in your tea breaks?'

'And I meant the apples, by the way. The *apples* are not a job you want, because they all need rotating.' He indicated a deep drawer of Royal Galas.

'I'm sorry?'

Tamsin had never worked in a supermarket – never sunk so low, thank God – so incomprehension was natural enough.

'The ones at the back have to come out before the new delivery goes in.'

'That's a bit fiddly and time-consuming. I'm not sure I'd bother.'

'You'd simply put the new ones on top?'

'Well, who's to know? And if no one knows, what's the point?'

'Get behind me, Satan.'

'And I don't imagine the other staff are quite so thorough.'

Terence smiled. 'The evening shift does lack discipline,' he said, like a commander speaking of some raw recruits. 'But then they're students.' It wasn't a compliment. 'Lost souls imagining themselves found, their minds glued to their phones.'

'A cheerful observation.'

'I don't think you came here for cheer, Detective Inspector.' That was true. There was nothing to cheer her in this retail Hades. It was shabby, piled high – and full of special offers, which for Tamsin cheapened the place in so many ways. 'They're not here, most of them.'

'How do you mean?'

'Here in their uniforms, here on the shop floor – but not here, if you see what I mean. And as drugged as the apples.'

'The apples are drugged?'

'How else have they survived?'

'You mean the sign lies?' said Tamsin with mock surprise. She indicated a bright poster above their heads declaring: 'There's nothing like fresh fruit!'

'And this is nothing like fresh fruit,' said Terence, picking up a Pink Lady from the chiller cabinet. 'Some of these apples were picked over a year ago. I spoke to one of the suppliers when they visited the store. He was ex-army as well, as it turned out. He told me that most of these little beauties have been sitting for months in chiller cabinets around the world, waiting their turn.'

Tamsin decided on a change of gear. 'And away from the fresh fruit scandal, there's a meeting of the Stormhaven Etiquette Society tonight. So I hope you weren't planning anything – you will need to be there.'

'Why?'

'Because I'll be there as well. It's part of the police enquiry.'

'You mean a gathering of the suspects?'

'No, a gathering of the Etiquette Society – unless you know something I don't.'

Terence returned the Pink Lady to its place on the shelf.

'I'll be there,' he said, as though they hadn't talked at all. And turning his back on her, he began the rotation, putting the older apples from the back into a basket for temporary holding.

Tamsin took that as a dismissal. She was glad to get out of there.

'Sex work is a positive choice,'

said Cherise with confidence.

'Some might see it as desperate,' said Peter. 'I mean, I don't . . . but some might.'

'It's not at all desperate.'

'No.'

'Only the stupid and the ignorant think it's desperate.'

'Quite.'

'It's a positive choice. Totally. And I mean some just want a cuddle. There's a lot of lonely guys out there.'

Peter sat on a chair in her room, a floor below Katrina's. Cherise was sitting on the bed, in the absence of a second chair. Why would you want two chairs in here? It wasn't a library, as Cherise pointed out.

'Not a library, no,' agreed the abbot.

'Financial stability is worth way more than bein' with some bloke . . . or woman, if you're that way. I mean, most men are pretty flaky; sorry to say that, but it's true. And right now, I enjoy the money more. I mean, you're probably goin' to judge me, being religious . . .'

'I'm not judging you.'

She wasn't naturally attractive, or not to Peter. She looked like an over-painted wall, all original features lost. She had jet black hair, heavily made-up skin and various tattoos, which Peter, though tempted, did not gaze on too closely. There was a snake on her left arm, he saw that.

'You like the snake? All my men like the snake,' she said. 'Had 'im done in Southend.'

Somewhere inside him Peter did like the snake. 'It takes me to the Garden of Eden,' he said.

'Is that one of those eco parks?'

'Well, in a way . . . it doesn't really matter. We're here to talk about you, and about this place.'

'It's a service industry, like any other – it's not seedy or nothin'.'

'No.' Cherise must be allowed her self-justification. It really wasn't necessary; he didn't come to judge, but she wouldn't believe that. She'd been justifying herself for years, this was Peter's take, and here she was, cash-rich but still chased by a sense of exclusion, of having been placed outside the circle of love with the consequent need to please. Peter saw a child full of shame who, to make things better, felt compelled to please.

'Only ten per cent of prostitution is on the street now. Did you know that?'

'I didn't know that.'

'Those days are gone – penny drabs on street corners. The internet has changed everythin'. These days, men just click on, get in touch, say what they want. Simple. I'll do a full strip for a customer on the web cam, that's quite popular at lunch when they've got a break. And a fair bit of escort work.'

'Escort work?'

'You know, meet up somewhere for the evening. Sometimes they just want to take you out for a meal; that's it, that's all they want. And that's a pretty easy three hundred quid! And then sometimes they want more.'

'Did you like Rosemary?'

'Some girls see ten in a day. I don't do that, no way; that's cheap.'

'Ten? It does sound a lot. More than a therapist would take on.'

'I won't do more than five. Five's the limit. I've done twelve in a day, but that was mad.'

'Five seems a better number.'

Where had that line come from?

'Maybe six – I mean, you can't turn them away. But I want to be my best, you see. I used to work in an office. It's not like I 'aven't tried – but I 'ated it. Four thousand quid a month and I'm my own boss.'

'That's a lot.'

'It's sometimes more. The young guys treat you like you're a whore ... not always, but you know. Older guys are more respectful, treat you like a lady, some of them, anyway. Their wives have died, that sort of thing, but they still want sex. And why not? One of my clients is eighty-four, struggles up the stairs, but there's still life in 'im. Have you ever considered it, Abbot?'

Cherise smiled cheekily.

'Me? Well, it's a relatively new option given my past. I've been away a while.'

'You been in prison?'

'No, I was in a monastery in Egypt.'

'You should try it.'

'You're obviously happy with how this place is run?'

'Yeah.'

'Rosemary and Tara do a good job, I imagine . . . *did* a good job. And you can't think of anyone who'd want to kill Rosemary?'

'No, I can't. Only a nut job. I mean, there was a bloke last week who didn't want to be seen by her.'

'Oh?'

'Made me do a recce before he left; but that's not exactly unusual. I mean, it's not a place where people want to meet their friends.'

'And you think he might have been a friend of Rosemary's?'

'I dunno. And don't much care. Perhaps he was her vicar! She was a churchwarden, you know.' Cherise shook her head in amused amazement.

'Yes, so I've discovered. Unusual.' What else was he to say? 'Perhaps if I brought some photos in, you could tell me if you recognize any of them?'

'If you want – but client confidentiality and all that.'

'You're neither a priest nor a doctor, Cherise.' She looked sulky. 'And to be honest, I think we're a little beyond that anyway. Murder tends to blow life's little secrets out of the water. And you might be someone's little secret.'

'Whatever. I mean, it's only for a particular sort of person, I know that.'

'What is?'

'Being a working girl. It's not for everybody.'

'No, maybe not.'

'I mean, I have an accountant – I pay tax and everything, and it's not for ever. But I need the money right now . . .'

Katrina sat on the edge of the bed.

The abbot was again given the chair in a room not concerned with seating arrangements. He was back at the top of the house, next door to the Glory Hole, and Katrina had come in especially to see him. He noticed the cross round her neck and wondered if she wore it at work.

'You used to work in a club, you say?'

'In Prague, yes. Prague is famous for that sort of thing; and for its architecture, obviously. There are very fine buildings there.'

'But you left. You tired of the architecture?'

'I didn't like the men; not the men who came to the clubs. Too drunk half the time. They can't do anything . . . but it doesn't stop them trying.'

'Quite.'

'Sober men are quicker, and they get less angry with their performance.'

Various images passed through Peter's mind, which his stepmother would no doubt have deemed 'unhelpful'.

'You don't meet men at their finest,' he said.

'You mean they *have* a finest?'

'Well, health's a continuum and humans move up and down it, in my experience. Even women.'

'I meet men as they truly are, and some are all right, some are kind, respectful. But they come to take, all of them come to take. So I am not applauding too much.'

'You don't sound happy in your work.'

'It's like any office, Abbot.' Katrina was strangely flat in her delivery. 'There are some people you like, and some you don't like so much.'

'Though in most offices, you don't have to have sex with them.'

'That's something you just get used to,' she said with a shrug. 'I smile and get on with it. If you can't do sex with people, best not to be a sex worker!'

'No.'

'I mean, if you're going to complain all the time, don't do it!' The abbot felt told off and guilty as charged. 'You must just never *show* you don't like them, that's all. They must leave feeling good, as though they have made you happy. This is the thing. They need to feel they have made you happy.'

'The ego always needs comforting.'

'It is so with most of them, even though they pay.' Peter nodded. He felt like that with the staff in the supermarket; he always hoped they'd enjoyed serving him. 'But my son is getting older, Abbot.'

'Your son?'

'Is that so strange?'

'Not at all.' Why had he been surprised?

'He is now fourteen. So I'll have to stop or I might meet some of his friends . . .'

'Yes. Or even worse . . .'

'That too is also possible.'

There was a brief silence.

'No, that wouldn't be good,' said the abbot. 'That'd keep a therapist in employment for years.'

'He thinks I work in a bar. Best it stays like that.'

'Perhaps so.'

'No, it's time to stop,' said Katrina. 'This is what my priest would say.' She fingered the cross around her neck absentmindedly. 'My priest would say it's time to stop.'

'You've spoken about it with your priest?'

It was not conventional spiritual direction, but then things were different these days.

'No, I have not spoken with him of these things. He is a good man; but I do not want to give him fantasies.'

'It's probably too late to save him from those,' said Peter.

'It must be difficult for him already with no wife. Well, you will know . . .'

'Indeed.'

The room suddenly felt small and the abbot decided to grasp the nettle.

'And you knew Rosemary Weller?'

'Of course I knew her. She is – was – my boss. I am seeing more of Tara, she is the hands-on business person, but Rosemary would often be at our meetings, asking after our welfare. She was much concerned for our well-being . . . and our futures.'

'Did anyone here not like her?'

'I don't think so. Cherise complains about her but Cherise complains about everyone – she doesn't kill them, though.'

'And Rosemary and Tara?'

'They always seemed good partners to me.'

'Partners?'

'Business partners, yes.'

'Yes. And do they, er, work here? You know, er . . .'

'Do you mean sex, Abbot?'

'Well, yes. I'm just trying to sort out the roles . . .'

'Tara keeps some clients. Some she has been with for many years, they are almost married. She gets the nicest Christmas cards . . . posh ones. I don't think she takes on new clients, though. I am not sure, she might. We do not ask about Tara.'

'And Rosemary?'

It was the question he had to ask.

'No, Rosemary does not – did not have clients. I don't think she did that.'

'I see.'

'Though she has admirers. She told us about one.'

'Really?'

'We ask her if she is with a man, we were joking with her, and she said she was not, but that once she was . . . maybe a while ago. She did say she liked him. But really, she did not speak about herself and we did not ask.'

'And she didn't name this person.'

'No. He was in the past, I think.'

'Ah. Well, we all have a past.' His mind was racing.

'I think she was more the owner,' said Katrina.

'She was, yes.' Though not now. According to the will, Tara

135

had inherited Rosemary's fifty-one per cent stake in the business, making her the sole owner of Model Service, with rent-free use of the property for five years, when it would be sold, with half the proceeds going towards relocation of the business and the other half divided among various charities.

'I'm not sure anyone knew Rosemary,' said Katrina. 'Maybe the one who killed her knew her best of all. Who can say?'

'Or maybe they knew just one thing about her,' said the abbot, suddenly focusing on a truth. 'And that was enough. It's usually just one thing that does it.'

And suddenly, he felt alive with discovery. Together, Cherise and Katrina had opened a door. 'Are you attending Rosemary's funeral this afternoon?'

Rosemary's funeral

took place in the ancient church of St Peter's, at the top of Blatchington Hill. It was well thought of locally as it stayed open throughout the week, when so many other churches were locked and closed, wanting company only on Sundays. Even the abbot had dropped in once or twice to sit with the Saxon silence.

Rosemary's family had wished for the earliest burial possible and there'd been no reason to refuse. Nothing more would be learnt from her body, unless it returned to life and spoke its hidden truth. How helpful that would be, thought Peter, walking up the hill towards the church; how helpful to hear the post-death testimony of the victim, the pleading of the dead.

'This was done to me, *this* was done – by *them!*'

It may be happening in some séance nearby even now. Did a Stormhaven clairvoyant hold all the clues? After all, a clairvoyant had solved a murder in nineteenth-century Paris, according to Conan Doyle. Peter had told Tamsin the story once, just to irritate her. As he walked, he remembered their conversation.

'There were two brothers, Eugene and Paul Dupont,' Peter had said, setting the scene. They'd each had a glass of wine in their hands – a bottle brought by Tamsin, and the label looked expensive. 'Eugene was a banker, Paul a man of letters.'

'I've never known what that meant,' Tamsin had said.

'Well, a writer, I suppose . . . an unsuccessful one. But then Eugene disappeared.'

'As all bankers should.'

'And the police couldn't find him, so they gave up the search.'

'Good. So can we talk about something else? I've paid for the wine and I feel a dull moral in the air.'

'But Paul Dupont, his brother, did not give up so easily.' And nor would Peter. 'He visited Madame Huerta, a well-known clairvoyant.' Tamsin raised her eyebrows. 'And in a mesmerized state, she

137

got in touch with the dinner scene where the two brothers had last met. Following?'

'Yes, unfortunately. But happy to change places with someone who isn't.'

'She then followed Eugene's movements, in her mesmeric state, after he left the restaurant, until he vanished into a house which, when described, Paul recognized. She then told how Eugene, once inside the house, held a conversation with two men. From her description, Paul recognized them, too.'

'Where's this going?'

'Feeling threatened?'

'More bored than threatened.'

'Madame Huerta then described how Eugene signed some papers and received a bundle of banknotes. She then saw him leave the house, followed by the two men he'd met there, who attacked him, killed him and threw his body in the River Seine.'

'Did anyone believe her? She'd get short shrift in Lewes nick.'

'And she got short shrift from the police in Paris as well – until Eugene's body was picked out of the river and identified at the morgue.'

'Ta-da!'

'Mind you, the police still thought it was suicide. But Paul, his brother, carried on the investigation, going to the house she'd described in her mesmeric state. And there he discovered that the occupants, two men, did business with Eugene's firm . . . and also found the receipt for the money handed over in the clairvoyant's vision.'

'A fairy tale.'

'It wasn't a fairy tale for the two men in the house, who were then arrested.'

'Really?' Tamsin seemed genuinely surprised.

'Yes, really. They were father and son, named Dubechet, and further evidence quickly appeared. The pocket book that Eugene had in his possession the night of his death was found in the Dubechets' bureau. With other evidence against them, they were found guilty of murder and sent to penal servitude for life.'

'And the nutcase? How did her evidence work in court?'

'Well, it didn't. Madame Huerta was not summoned as a witness on the grounds that she was not conscious at the time of her vision.'

'Hah!'

'But conscious or not, her revelations undoubtedly brought about the discovery of the crime. Hard to disagree, isn't it?' Tamsin shrugged, hiding her discomfort. 'Who needs the CID, eh?'

'Quite,' said Tamsin, getting up to find some crisps in the kitchen. She'd heard enough. 'Much better to hand over detection to attention-seeking crackpots, the deluded or the insane.'

'That's no way to talk about your colleagues.'

They'd laughed. But here in the church, there was no clairvoyant to hand . . . though someone attending this funeral knew what had happened, and without the need for a mesmeric state.

They knew, because they'd been there.

*

The church was now full.

St Peter's was not a large space, having been designed for private prayer rather than gatherings. It could hold ninety souls at a squeeze – perhaps more at Midnight Mass, in the Christmas Eve crush. Stormhaven did expand at Christmas; children coming home to the sea, squeezed into the hard wooden pews to see in Christmas Day. But somehow this building felt happiest, most itself, when hosting one or two frail souls seeking solitude from the rush of life, seeking answers to prayers, lighting candles in the ancient stillness. It had the quality of a cave.

Peter looked around as the congregation waited. The Etiquette Society were out in force; and, while they would not be mentioned by the priest, the staff of Model Service were also present, closing for half a day out of respect for their entrepreneurial founder.

'Forty-two per cent of business start-ups fail because there's no market need,' whispered Martin Channing to Geoff. 'That's never going to be true of a brothel, is it?'

Geoff nodded appreciatively, always glad to be in on a joke, though it would have been better had he been the one to make it. He began to think of a smart reply with which to impress Martin.

'I'm all for supporting local business!' he said too loudly, and immediately regretted it. His words sounded clumsy and Martin's was only a half-smile.

Meanwhile, Blessings sat at the back, having made it – and with some flair – only just before Rosemary. She liked to be the last to arrive, whether in court or out. It made people pay attention to her.

'She'll be late for her own funeral, that one!' joked Geoff, straining again for comedic effect, though Martin's smile remained weak and slightly condescending. He'd prefer not to be sitting next to this rather needy clown. He'd prefer to be sitting next to the late arrival, Blessings, who did look stunning in black with the yellow earrings. And Martin pondered her love life for much of the service.

The coffin arrived to *Nimrod*. It was a professional recording, much to the annoyance of the parish organist, Oliver, who felt he could have handled it. After hearing him try that morning, however, the vicar had disagreed, with quiet force.

'I think we'll go with the recording, Oliver,' he'd said, as they stood together in the chancel.

'I don't see why.'

'I'm just not sure our organ is up to it.'

'Of course it's up to it.'

'I mean, you achieve wonders with the instrument, Oliver, but ...'

'You're killing live music,' said the organist.

No, that's what you do every Sunday, thought the priest. Oliver had taken himself and his huff off down the red-carpeted aisle, and for the rest of the day the vicar had received the silent treatment of a musician thwarted.

The coffin carriers made their careful way to the front – it was a narrow aisle – and the coffin was then set on the wooden plinth in the knave. There was an audible gasp, however, when the coffin was opened. The undertakers took the lid off; and there she was!

'What's he doin'?' asked Cherise, shocked.

'It is not so strange,' said Katrina. She had seen this before, in her homeland.

'It's bloody weird. There's a dead body in there!'

'That is the point. Sometimes the coffin is open so people can see the body and kiss the dead person goodbye.'

'Kiss a dead person? Like I'm doin' that,' said Cherise. 'That's gross.'

Tara glared at her. Like some Mother Superior, thought Cherise, when she isn't superior to anybody . . . and then the service got under way. Tara was glad she didn't recognize the vicar; that was always embarrassing.

Closest to the priest and the coffin, in the front row, was Terence, militarily square-shouldered. He was familiar with death, but not with churches. He had avoided army chaplains throughout his soldiering career, with no interest in their God of love, who offered sweet visions in the trenches to those with half a face or spilling innards. Their God of love was a beguiling fantasy for the weak; or for those coughing blood and shortly to die.

'Does God love me, Major?'

He'd never been able to say yes, even when the eyes screamed for it, pleaded for reassurance. But he'd sit in the front row now and give Rosemary a proper send-off, which she deserved.

Peter looked discreetly across at Tara. Women could look so demure at funerals, and Tara took demure to its extreme. Maybe death does this to males; mortality makes sex all the more urgent before the final dimming of the light. But he also looked at Terence, and with different thoughts. What to do with the material Rosemary had given him over their lunch together? Terence would not be glad he had it, nor could he admit to having it. It was really a set of therapist's notes, focusing on the poor man's relationship with his mother.

It had all been very difficult, apparently.

'You must look after him,' she'd said. But how was he to do that? Terence was not a man who invited help. And then, without a second thought, Peter was walking up the aisle towards the coffin.

After brief thoughts on resurrection, and edited highlights of Rosemary's life and work, the priest had invited any who wished to, to come forward and offer their personal goodbyes to Rosemary. The abbot had allowed one or two family members time and space to stand with the corpse in distant grief. It seemed that they found it hard to look at her, turning away in barely hidden revulsion.

And then for Peter, as he waited his turn, the shock of seeing Rosemary alive at her own funeral. She was walking up towards the coffin, her own coffin, the strangest of feelings – it was Rosemary! Only it wasn't Rosemary . . . of course it wasn't, just someone who looked extraordinarily like her. So was this her sister, Sarah? It must be her sister, the one Rosemary had mentioned, the one who'd 'gone her own way', a little younger perhaps, quick-eyed, embarrassed to be in front of everyone. There was a shyness about her, aware of watching eyes, not staying long by the coffin before hurrying back to her seat. So what was her story?

Peter knew he must speak with her; he was almost physically drawn to her. He'd catch her afterwards, he'd make sure he did. But with the family now seated, the abbot followed their path up to the chancel and the waiting corpse of Rosemary. Unlike her family, however, he did not wish merely to stand, or to remain distant; he wished to stoop and to kiss her . . . kiss her goodbye.

The face was a shock, though better than the one seen in the asylum gloom on that terrible night. They'd done their best, the undertakers, but only so much beautification was possible, given Rosemary's wounds. He paused, oblivious to all things but the woman before him. He had gone to the desert, and spent the years meant for her in the rocks and the sand. She'd been right not to come; she'd had another life to lead.

'You were right not to come,' he said quietly. 'Every second you lived was quite right and quite perfect.' And he then bent down and kissed her on the cold cheek offered.

It was not until he'd returned to his seat and the priest had announced the closing hymn that he realized his last kiss of Rosemary Weller had also been his first.

'Gallows humour,'

said Martin to Tamsin, noting the house name, gothic script carved in wood: Black Cap. The funeral that afternoon had been quickly forgotten. This was now a world without Rosemary, as the priest had said; and life must go on, as Martin had said. And here they were outside the judge's posh home. 'And I can quite see her wearing one! She'd enjoy sending someone to the noose and drop.'

Tamsin and Martin had arrived at the house in Firle Road together – or rather, at the same time, and this was not ideal. She'd wished to make her own entrance, unattached to a suspect.

'Have you seen her honour at work?' asked Martin as they crunched their way across the gravel drive towards the front door.

'No.' It somehow felt like a defeat.

'Oh, you should, really you should. She looks entirely fetching – even without the cap. Violet robe with delicate lilac trim, a short horsehair wig and a simply gorgeous red sash over the left shoulder.' Martin could sound very effete. 'She could try me any day!'

'And perhaps she will, Martin. I'd certainly be there for that one. Do you anticipate your conviction any time soon?'

'I think you'd have to catch me first and you're some way from doing that.' They were now standing at the door in the blaze of the security light. 'Blessings did look splendid at the funeral, didn't she? Made everyone else look quite the frump!'

And if anything, the judge was even more resplendent tonight, welcoming them in a Ghanaian robe of startling reds and yellows.

'You're on fire, Blessings!' said Martin. He seemed to have got over his missed piano lesson.

Waiting inside were the other members of the Stormhaven Etiquette Society. Estate agent and amateur dramatist Geoff Berry; war hero Major-General Terence Blain and their colourful host for the evening, Judge Blessings N'Dayo. Abbot Peter was also present, having walked the mile or so from his seaside home.

'Fashionably late, Martin,' said Blessings.

'Pot and kettle, my dear.'

'But rather stealing the inspector's thunder, perhaps?'

'Better than stealing Rosemary's!' said Geoff, followed by an embarrassed silence. Had he gone too far?

Blessings ignored him. 'I believe the inspector may have been counting on a dramatic entrance. We judges know all about those.'

And yes, a dramatic entrance had crossed Tamsin's mind. She liked people to stew a little before she arrived, for tension to build. Into this limbo of fear and unknowing, she arrived as both prosecutor and saviour.

'Never my intention, I assure you, Blessings,' said Martin. 'I doubt I could ever outshine the detective inspector!'

While Blessings, Martin and Tamsin jockeyed for position, Peter looked around at the faces in the circle, and was struck by the incongruity of the gathering. He looked at each in turn: a war hero ... an attention-seeking estate agent ... a cold-as-Alaska judge ... and an outrageous journalist. How had they ever come together? Rosemary had sat in this circle, of course. And what had she been in this strange alliance? Was she its conscience, perhaps? And if she was the conscience, then what was everyone else? Terence, he was its noble bravery, Blessings its savage legal clarity, and Martin its shameless community mouthpiece. But Geoff? What the hell was Geoff doing here? There was an inadequacy about him that made his presence strange. This group was clearly Martin's creation, gathered for his own purposes. But why Geoff?

'I'm grateful to you all for giving up your evening to be here,' said Tamsin. She wasn't grateful; it was required of them. They couldn't have said no. 'And, of course, our thanks to Blessings for being our kind host.'

Blessings' gracious smile was soon wiped from her face when she saw Fran loitering in the kitchen doorway.

'What are you doing here, Fran?'

'Just wondering if anyone needed anything,' said Fran, Welsh and proud. 'Tea? Coffee? Something stronger?'

'The only thing we need is for you to go away, Francisco,' said

Blessings. 'This is not your space, as you well know, and this is a private meeting.'

Fran said nothing, looking at them all, like a lingering camera shot, taking in their surprise and fascination, before slowly retiring upstairs.

'I was only asking,' he said, disappearing from view.

'Houseboy causing you problems?' said Martin. 'You just can't get the slaves these days.'

She ignored him and Tamsin continued.

'So what do you do here? That's my question. I mean, as a group. You send out unpleasant stickers, of course. We've had complaints about those, which we may or may not follow up. But apart from those, why is it that you meet exactly?'

'Haven't we gone over all this, Detective Inspector?' It was Martin. 'You somehow manage to make the promotion of good manners and civil behaviour sound like a crime!'

'In 1530, Erasmus of Rotterdam published a book on good manners,' said Peter.

'Definitely one for my Christmas list.'

'It was called *On Good Manners for Boys* and it contained advice about yawning, bickering and fidgeting.'

Geoff was yawning as Peter spoke, which caused a little mirth.

'Clearly one for Geoff's Christmas list as well,' said Martin.

'But the core tenet of his book was this,' said Peter. 'Erasmus defined good manners as the ability to "readily ignore the faults of others; but avoid falling short yourself".'

There was a short pause.

'Well, I'm sure we're all with the second half of that proposition, Abbot,' said Blessings, as though summing up. 'But readily ignoring the faults of others? I'm not sure where that would leave the world.'

'Well, it would leave you without a job,' said Martin.

'And you without a paper.'

The exchange was quick and ruthless.

'Rosemary would never ignore a shop with poor disability access!' said Geoff, feeling virtuous by association. 'So I don't think *she'd* be too happy about ignoring the faults of others – whatever this Erasmus fellow's views on the matter!'

'So who delivered the sticker to number nine, Church Street?' asked Peter.

'What sticker?' asked Martin.

'There was a sticker delivered to number nine, Church Street.'

'You mean the brothel?'

He did mean the brothel, but he preferred using the address.

'It was stuck on an inside door by someone – someone here, presumably. It seems unlikely to have come from Rosemary.'

'Perhaps she'd had a Damascus road experience and seen the light. A repentant sinner!' said Martin. 'You like those, don't you, Abbot?'

'It must have been discussed here,' said Peter, looking around. Respond, don't react, he told himself. 'When did you discuss delivering a sticker to number nine, Church Street?'

Silence. And then Peter took out the sticker in question, in its evidence bag, and held it up.

'Anyone's?'

'It does look like one of ours.'

'It does, doesn't it?'

'But we have never discussed it, as far as I'm aware,' said Geoff. 'Or not at any meeting I was present at.' He was a little shaken.

'Quite true,' said Martin, reassuringly. 'That sticker did not come from us. I mean, it looks like one of ours, but it didn't come from here.'

'Blessings?'

'They're right. We never discussed the place.'

Peter put the sticker away. What to believe?

'So either one of you, or all of you, are lying,' said Tamsin. 'Or, there's a rogue member out there, with access to your tools – but taking decisions for themselves.'

And now Fran was coming down the stairs again, and walking round the group towards the front door.

'I'm going out,' he said. 'I hope that's allowed. Or will I too be getting one of your stupid stickers?'

'He does have a temper, that boy,' said Blessings. 'He seems to spend his whole time angry.'

'We need to talk,'

said Fran, explaining his presence. He'd turned up at Model Service unannounced, which had freaked out Cherise. She'd told him to stop coming and now here he was again.

'What are you doin' here?' she asked angrily. 'I told you I didn't want to see you 'ere.' But she let him in; he'd have to come in off the street. 'I could have been working!'

It wasn't the best thing to say, Cherise was aware of that, but she was angry. She didn't like the unexpected – unless it was a lottery win – and anyway, if he didn't like what she did, he knew what he could do. They'd been through all this. And it wasn't as if they were an item or anything! They'd only been together a few weeks after he'd done some gardening work for her.

Cherise couldn't be doing with gardens, even her small one – and he was the cheapest quote. 'Gardener Man', he called himself in the popular *Stormhaven Scene*, delivered to every house in the area. So their relationship had started with laughter, her taking the mick.

'I saw a "Plumber Man" – did you steal the idea from him?'

'No, that's me as well,' said Fran, with some seriousness.

'You're "Gardener Man" *and* "Plumber Man"?'

'I was brought up on a farm, remember. And on page thirty-seven, I'm "Decoration Man" as well.'

And they'd laughed again. Though they hadn't laughed since, because Fran was making it increasingly clear that he didn't like what she did for a living and that he could look after her. Cherise didn't care, she really didn't . . . and told him it was none of his business.

'Look who's earnin' the money here!' she said.

'I'm doing my best. It's not easy with a record.'

'And good luck to you. I like a man who works and all that, but if you think I'm throwin' all this away . . .'

147

'There are other jobs.'

'But which one of them is going to pay like this one? I won't get a grand a week as a hairdresser, I'm tellin' you.'

'No one needs that amount of money.'

'Really? And how the 'ell would you know?'

But today Fran needed to talk because he was worried.

'I think Blessings might know.'

They were now sitting in Cherise's bedroom on the first floor. Fran looked around at the mirrors and the toys, and felt ill.

'Might know what? What is there to know?'

'That I've been seeing you. Or coming here, anyway, to this place. I don't know which is worse.'

'I don't see the problem. I mean there's nothing between us.'

He paused. 'She thinks I'm gay.'

'She thinks you're gay?' She started laughing. 'Why the 'ell does she think you're gay?'

'It's not funny.'

'It's quite funny. Are you gay?'

'No!'

'So why does she think you are?'

'Because that's what I told her, all right?'

'You told her you were gay?'

'When she visited me in prison and it seemed like there might be some accommodation. And I mean, it could be true, so it's not really a lie.'

'Well, it is a lie, because it ain't true.'

'Everyone wants a home, Cherise. We'd been talking about how difficult it was for gay men in prison, she'd been sympathetic . . . so why not make myself gay? It seemed a good path to go down, at the time.'

'Oh yeah, a really good path. Lie to a bloody judge, why don't you, about how gay you are?'

'I don't think she'd have me in her house if she thought I was straight. Then I wouldn't have met you.'

Cherise was still trying to get her head round it all. 'But why say you were gay?'

'I've just explained.' And he *had* just explained, but Cherise

148

wasn't really listening because she didn't ever listen and she was also expecting a call from a regular, someone she hadn't heard from for a while. She needed to be ready. 'So I was wondering if I could come and live at yours.'

'Live at mine?'

'Well, why not?'

'You can't live at mine, Fran. I mean, I haven't got room at the moment.'

'Well, you have got room.'

'No, but I mean it's not like we're together.'

'We are together.'

'Only in your head, Fran.'

'But I thought—'

And then the Skype call came through, the screen buzzing, and she said she'd have to take it, unbuttoning her shirt as she moved towards the computer.

'Hello, honey – I was wonderin' where you'd been!' Her voice was as soft as a peach. 'Just hold on a sec, big man . . .' she turned the camera away, and indicated that Francisco must leave, NOW! She was waving him out, and he left quietly enough; though as he closed the door, Cherise was speaking to 'big man' again. 'Now I hope you haven't been a naughty boy while you've been away, honey, because you know me, I'm always a good girl! . . . What do you mean, not always?! . . .'

Fran loved Cherise. He'd never loved anyone like he loved Cherise . . . so why couldn't she give this up for him? He was doing his best to earn money. 'Plumber Man' was busy – well, he would be, given time – and things would pick up, and when they did, he could provide for her. No one needed that amount of money, not what she earned. And how could they ever be together if she carried on doing what she was doing?

He'd done what he could, but that clearly wasn't enough. She was a bad girl and he'd need to teach Cherise a lesson.

'It must be a regret, Abbot.'

Blessings spoke with the confidence of one who knows for certain and who cuts through the flannel of polite discourse.

'What must be a regret?' he asked.

She'd told him to stay for a moment, when everyone had left after the evening meeting convened by Tamsin. He was looking forward to climbing the stairs of his house by the sea. The end of the day was calling him, as always it did; his bedroom, at the end of the day. But Blessings might have something useful to tell him and so he loitered in the kitchen as the others departed. They were back in the front room now. It seemed too big for the two of them.

'Never having had children,' said Blessings, by way of explanation. 'You must regret that.' Peter was surprised. 'I presume you haven't had children – from your choice of clothes.'

'I haven't, no.'

'So would you like to have had children? Of course you would! Of course you would, Abbot!'

'If you speak on my behalf, Blessings – and inaccurately – I may decide there's no value in me being here.'

The judge smiled. 'Well, would you?' she asked. 'Would you like to have had children?'

'It has crossed my mind on occasion.'

'You see. I was right.'

'Right about the wish but wrong about the decade. I haven't thought it for a while.'

'The world misses a little Peter, I think!'

'Or a little Petra?'

'Quite. Though a boy would be particularly special, don't you think?'

'You clearly think so.'

'Oh yes.'

'Well, as I say, it's all a little late for me, so it's not something I

150

dwell on. Seasons change – and things once carried by the thrusting tide of desire sink down into the silt of the past; forgotten things.'

Though, in truth, he had dwelt on it recently, with things from the past so stirred. Could he and Rosemary have had children?

'Well, perhaps it isn't too late, Abbot. Have you ever considered that?'

Peter laughed. 'You have a time machine in the garage?'

'No, I have something better – a younger body in the house, of child-bearing age.' Peter froze. 'You are still fertile and able, I presume?'

Peter was struck by how normal this all felt, sitting with a judge in Stormhaven discussing his fertility . . . when it wasn't normal. And what was Blessings suggesting?

'I'm sorry, I don't quite . . .'

'I only want a donor, Abbot! Your *face!*'

'A donor?'

'It would be nothing more than that. A sperm donor. The world is crying out for them.'

'I hadn't heard.'

'There's been a shortage of them since the anonymity laws were changed. The offspring can now come and find you, by law, which has made men think twice about a brief spillage at the clinic. The donors have dried up, so to speak. But I'm a little choosy anyway.'

Peter relaxed into his chair and pondered the unfolding scene.

'I'm not sure what to do with this conversation, Blessings.' She smiled mischievously. 'I mean, we seem to have moved at a deceptively fast pace and – well, as I said, I don't know what to do with it all.'

And he didn't.

'That doesn't sound like a no, Abbot. And really, you don't need to do anything – well, only a little. I mean, I'm not looking for a husband. I'm not even looking for a father for the child; that would be quite up to you. I'm just looking for a boy who will grow to be a man . . . a proper man.'

Peter remembered the story of her father's unfortunate demise, as told by Martin. Death in the toilet. But he held back from comment. The longing for a child – a male child – was clearly some search for redemption. He wanted to help; but not in that way.

'I'm sure you'll find someone.'

Other men's names came to mind, possible volunteers, suitable sperm donors ready and waiting in Stormhaven, and he nearly offered some names. ('Have you ever thought of Martin Channing? An intelligent man, no question of that.' He'd leave out his morality. 'Or Terence, even? Such a brave soldier, and a much loved leader of men.') But he didn't. It wasn't as if Blessings was an impetuous soul. She'd have thought through these matters carefully, sifted Martin and Terence like a medieval flour merchant. Blessings did not suggest things casually. And, more importantly, he was not responsible for her solution. A son was her issue, not his . . . he needed to leave.

'This conversation will remain confidential, I trust,' she said.

'As confidential as it can be, given that no promises were made.'

'She never would have been good enough for you, you know.'

'Who?'

'Rosemary.'

'Rosemary?'

'I saw you having lunch in the deli. All very cosy.' They'd been seen. 'Should you really be on the case – given such intimate connection?'

Blessings was not making a casual enquiry.

'Everything has been cleared,' he said, and it was almost true. 'I am neither a suspect nor a beneficiary.'

'But close to the deceased.'

'I have spoken more words with you in a few days than I have with Rosemary in the last forty years. I'm not sure how close that is.'

Was she going to be difficult?

'We must not speak ill of the dead, Abbot,' she said, preparing to speak ill of the dead. 'And her death is a tragedy, of course. But she would not have been a good pond for you to return to. Really she wouldn't, quite unsuitable.'

And that appeared to be that. As Peter walked home, he found some peace in the sea that evening, the waves unusually calm.

Though sometimes a storm followed such water.

'He likes to be whipped,'

said Tamsin.

'Who?'

'Major-General Terence Blain.'

Abbot Peter sighed. They were back in his small front room, catching up. Tamsin had brought her own coffee.

'Try this,' she'd said, 'and you'll never go back to the Lidl brew.'

And while it did taste very good — really very good indeed — the abbot was finding the case less pleasing. The whole thing was beginning to feel like a conspiracy against men: a critique of his own inadequate love life and the inadequate lives of others of his gender, and all the more uncomfortable for being true.

'And we have this on good authority?'

'The best . . . the one who whips him.'

'Cherise?'

'How did you know it was her?' asked Tamsin.

'An educated guess.'

'That's who you'd choose?'

It wasn't who he'd choose.

'We're here to catch a murderer, I believe,' he said.

'And I was thinking of your Venn diagram, Abbot, the shared circles.'

'Oh.'

He was surprised she'd taken to his idea. The ideas of others were not usually acknowledged by Tamsin. She preferred credit focused firmly on herself.

'It wasn't such a ridiculous idea, you know,' she said.

'Remarkable.'

'With a little tweaking by me. I showed Cherise photos of the men in the Etiquette Society, you see. Terence, Martin and Geoff.'

As suggested by Peter. Had she forgotten that? 'OK.'

153

'And what do you know? There's the man she knows as "Curly" but who is in fact Terence Blain. One out of three isn't bad!'

'It isn't a crime, I suppose, being whipped; and the major-general has been through a lot.'

'But it's all so depraved,' she said, shaking her head, as if this was about much more than mere crime. As if a little terror on the battlefield went anywhere near justifying *this*. 'Don't you find men depraved?'

He was an unlikely advocate for the male gender but he couldn't help but attempt some sort of defence. Tamsin brought out such reactions in him.

'Is it really any more depraved than someone who goes shopping to cheer herself up?'

'That's what you tell yourself, is it? Being whipped is the same as retail therapy? I hardly think so!'

'We all live with the unresolved inside, buried in the layers of our ego. We all feel the need for escape, for release.'

'Cherise could fit you in tomorrow afternoon apparently.'

Ignore her. 'He won't find this easy,' said Peter.

'Who won't?'

'Terence. He won't find the spotlight of investigation easy.'

'Men like that are beyond shame, believe me.'

'I don't believe you. Men like that are consumed by it. Enter his mind if you can.'

'I'd prefer not to.'

'There's a theme of self-punishment here, the *need* to be punished. Here's someone who can't forgive himself for being deficient. There's a deep sense of deficiency there, from a long time ago.'

'We used to call them perverts.'

'And he wants it covered up, of course. It's a difficult feeling to look at. Yet now his worst nightmare beckons: he's facing the prospect of his deficiency being exposed.'

'I think he's the one who's been doing the exposing.'

'He's a proud man, Terence, a very proud man. Don't let the relentless self-deprecation fool you. He would not want this intrusion.'

154

'Then he should have killed Cherise, not Rosemary. Well, shouldn't he? It's Cherise who holds his guilty secret.'

The abbot didn't respond so they sat in silence. Why would Terence kill Rosemary? There was no apparent reason. But he'd certainly be uncomfortable right now.

'So how did you know he chose Cherise?' asked Tamsin. It had been niggling at her.

'Oh, just something she said. It wasn't rocket science. She told me of a man who was keen not to meet Rosemary, and who sent her out on a "recce" to make sure she wasn't around. That was the word she used and it struck me as odd; it wasn't her vocabulary. Who in Romford takes a recce? It's too military.' He took a sip of Tamsin's coffee. 'It's very good.'

'Your schoolboy detective work?'

'No, the coffee; it's very good.'

And Peter found himself wondering if coffee was, after all, something you shouldn't cut corners on. The Christian tradition had struggled with coffee ever since the advisers of Pope Clement VIII had pressed him to denounce the drink. They believed that coffee was the 'bitter invention of Satan' because of its popularity among Muslims. But experience trumped prejudice, when on tasting the brew the pope had declared that 'this Satan's drink is so delicious it would be a pity to let the infidels have exclusive use of it'. And now Peter, in a hot beverage epiphany, could see what Pope Clement had meant.

'And what did Blessings want with you last night?' asked Tamsin, glad that she'd led her uncle into a higher truth.

'Blessings? Well, an unexpected conversation,' said Peter. 'Unexpected, yes.' He relayed its content, about Blessings' wish for a child . . . though without mention of the role she wished him to play. He didn't wish for more sideways glances from Tamsin.

'So Blessings opened her heart to you?'

'In a manner.'

'And told you how desperate she is for a child?'

'A boy child.'

'She doesn't want a girl?'

'This is about bringing a decent man into the world.'

155

'Oh, and there goes a flying pig!'

'There's something here about her father, though I don't know what. Martin alluded to it . . . some shame.'

'But father-shame does not a murderer make. I'm not so impressed by mine, but I'd need a better reason for murder than that. Whereas a former arsonist who likes eavesdropping on private meetings sounds a great deal more suspicious. What's young Francisco really doing in Stormhaven?'

'Perhaps he's short of alternatives. Offenders usually are.'

'My heart bleeds . . . almost. Though I hope it's Geoff.'

'You what?'

'I hope it's Geoff. I hope Geoff is our murderer.'

Peter sat with the comment for a moment. 'Is that allowed?'

'Police do it all the time.'

'Why do you imagine that commends it to me?'

'I'm just saying. It's not a moral crusade or anything! You have a suspect you don't like, and simply hope it's them. It's quite natural. I'm sure you do it.'

'I don't do it.'

'It's just a game, in its own little way, and it doesn't mean it *is* them, obviously. Tara's the much likelier candidate and I wouldn't mind if it was her. She has murder in her, that woman, in a way that Geoff doesn't, and she's the main beneficiary. Who knows what went on between her and Rosemary? We have no one's word but Tara's. I mean, I don't wish to be mean about your present love interest . . .'

'And Martin?' said the abbot, quickly. 'His fingerprints are all over this case.'

'Except where they matter.'

'But could anyone but Martin have gathered that group of people together? And if so, why?'

'He's not a murderer, though, Peter. Do you think he's a murderer?'

The abbot submitted. 'No, I don't think he is, really.'

'No, I don't think so either. So we're back with Tara.'

'And with Terence, with whom we started. He's a very good murderer, qualified at least.'

'But does he care enough about anything? I'm not sure he cares enough to kill. So who would you like it to be?'

'I can't play that game, Tamsin.'

'You can.'

'No, really, it's not in my nature.'

'I'm waiting.'

'Well, Geoff, probably – if I did have to play the game.'

Tamsin laughed. 'I knew you would.'

'I mean, I'm not going to play it, but if I did . . . yes, definitely Geoff. He poses the greatest test for my compassion muscles.'

'It's hurting,'

said the abbot. He was wearing only his underpants.

'Just strip down to your undies,' she'd said calmly when he walked in, and Peter had obliged, as if this was entirely normal in his life; something he'd been doing for years with women he hardly knew. And now he was lying on his front with Tara's finger pressed firmly into his left buttock . . . and it was hurting terribly.

'It's meant to hurt, you baby. Not that hurt is the purpose, of course. Healing is the purpose – but sometimes there's only healing in hurt.'

'How very profound, you should be a vicar – aargh!'

'As long as you're within your pain threshold, that's the main thing. Are you within your pain threshold?'

'How would I know?'

'You'll know.'

'Is there a red button I can press?'

'It's the rotation muscles around your hips,' she explained. 'They're a little tight.'

'They were fine when I came in.' Tara laughed, ignoring him.

'You may need to put a little ice on them when you get home. You probably know that already – or peas.'

'Peas? What, fresh peas?'

'Frozen peas.' This man had been too long in the desert. 'But not on the bare skin.'

'Not on the bare skin – oooh!' More pain.

'And only for ten minutes, otherwise the muscles will react and start warming themselves again and we don't want that.'

But Peter's muscles were reacting now and so he tried to think beyond it, mind over matter, to reach a place beyond the pain.

'So you'd never been to Bybuckle Asylum before yesterday?' he asked.

'Why do you ask?'

'Aargh!' Her fingers were again tormenting his buttock, harassing the secret, hidden-away muscles. 'I'm interested in the place,' he said, recovering.

'Well, you and Rosemary alike, then.'

'How do you mean?'

'It's why she wanted the sheltered housing built there. Do you want me to stop?'

'No,' he said, truthfully. 'As you say, sometimes the truth must disturb before it heals. But what was that about sheltered housing?'

'Obviously Rosemary felt a duty to the space,' she said, now working the base of his spine.

'Obviously?'

'But then that estate agent – the gross one – pulled the rug from beneath her plan and changed the proposal.'

'What proposal?'

'All very last minute, Rosemary said – and she was angry about that. I knew when Rosemary was angry.' Peter had now forgotten the pain.

'What proposal?'

'She felt they'd used her to get planning permission, that's what she said, and then suddenly the plans changed, and her ideas were jettisoned from a great height.'

'I see.'

He didn't see . . . but he wanted to.

'All right, let's have you on your back now, so I can do the front of your legs.'

Peter sat up and turned himself over. Tara covered his upper body and right leg with towelling and then started to work on his left. 'Can't have enough towels,' as she'd said to him yesterday. She put a little more oil on her hands.

'So who's the "they" in all this?' he asked, trying to sound conversational.

'The estate agent fellow.'

'The gross one.'

'The gross one, yes. I don't know the others in the syndicate. There was someone else.'

'Oh?'

'Rosemary was particularly angry with him.'

'It was a "him" then?'

'I think so, I'm not sure. Is that hurting?'

'Not really, no. A little perhaps . . . actually, it's hurting a great deal.'

'She used to call him "the snake", so I'd imagine it was a man.'

'Can't a woman be a snake?'

'Possibly.'

She now covered his left leg with the towel, and started work on his right, but whether it was painful, the abbot wasn't sure now. His mind was too busy with connections – and questions.

'So the estate agent wasn't the snake?'

'No, the estate agent was Geoff Berry, the one who likes dressing up – well, you know, acting. No different from us, really. Most people like us to dress up.'

'Yes.'

'And some like dressing up themselves.'

'Model Service is the local theatre, really,' he said.

But with that revelation – the link between Berry and the asylum – the abbot lost track of his prior question, still hanging in the air. He lay still for a moment and felt the pressuring hands on his flesh, so intimate, so satisfying . . . and he was suddenly back at the monastery.

The nearest he'd got to such intimacy in the desert was when the barber Moussa came from Cairo once every two months to cut the monastery hair. He was not a gentle barber; no one would call Moussa gentle. He would grip the head in his strong hands and drive the razor over the skull with the roughness of a man who had many heads to shave before he could go home. Yet the abbot had enjoyed the pain, the fierce touch. It was the only touch to be had in the big sand; the only connection.

And then he remembered his question. 'Why did Rosemary feel a duty of care to the site of the Bybuckle Asylum?'

'How do you mean?'

'You said she felt some duty towards it. "Obviously", you said. I was just wondering what you meant and why it was obvious?'

'Well, of course, she felt a duty towards it! I mean, don't you know?'

'Know what?'

'She felt guilty in a way, given some of the consequences.' Peter lay still, alert. 'Very guilty ... there was a lot of distress, you see, and some people never forgave her.'

'Never forgave her for what?'

'Your muscles are tensing. You'll have to relax.'

It was like an anxiety dream. 'Just tell me what she did, Tara.'

'I can't believe you don't know. I just assumed you knew. Do you really not know?'

'Tell me,' he said quietly.

'It was Rosemary's report that closed down Bybuckle Asylum.'

Silence.

'Rosemary's report closed the place?'

'She was commissioned to write a report on the asylum, which she did, quite objectively according to ... well, people I've spoken to. I mean, she blamed herself on some level, but it was never her fault.'

'You mean the closure?'

'The place was dead in the water, everyone knew that. There used to be terrible stories about it. There was a room called "The End Room".'

'Yes, I know about "The End Room".'

'And she tried to brush it all aside, all the vindictiveness that came her way, and believe me, there was a lot of that. But I could tell, when I got to know her.'

'What could you tell?'

'I mean, years had passed, but she always felt responsible for closing it down and what happened next. I always said to her, "You've never really escaped from the Bybuckle Asylum, have you, Rosemary?" And let's be honest, she didn't, did she?'

161

'Do you remember

the report you wrote?' asked her interrogator, who sadly had returned.

'What report?' said Rosemary.

What was this? And what were they doing?

'Your current predicament might give a clue,' they said, indicating their lonely setting.

'My report on the Bybuckle Asylum?'

'Very good. You were quite feted after that, I believe.'

'It was not a job I asked for; but one I did to the best of my abilities . . . and one with a correct outcome.'

'Would have been better if you'd turned it down, Rosemary; a great deal better. Better for everyone . . . better for you.'

She'd interviewed many people here in Gladstone Ward, staff and patients. And those in Victoria Ward – or 'The End Room' as they all seemed to call it. It was probably a better name. It was assuredly the end if you got dumped there. And the staff had been surprisingly open about that; there comes a time when speaking the truth is a relief, however much it condemns you. They'd spoken very freely, most of them.

And now here she was again, back in Gladstone Ward. Only this time she was the one tied to the place, strapped to one of the few remaining beds.

'You closed it down,' said her interrogator.

'The health authority closed it down.'

'No, your report closed it down; everyone knows that.'

'And why does this matter?' asked Rosemary. 'It was a blessing, believe me.'

'A blessing? A blessing for who exactly?' This line was almost snarled.

'Bybuckle wasn't fit for purpose. It was run by the staff for the staff. Not for the patients. No one should have to live like that. And some didn't. There were at least four deaths in the bath over the last three years before it was closed. People shouldn't die in the bath. Did you know about "The End Room"?'

No response.

'It was where the elderly were put, those with dementia and others reckoned beyond help.' She could still smell the place after all these years. 'It was where people were left to rot. Some hadn't had a conversation in twenty years . . . or a smile. No one mourned the death of Bybuckle — apart from the small group of sadists, inadequates and time-servers who ran the place.'

'And the residents, of course.'

'They were all found alternative—'

'Do you remember the day the cameras came in, Rosemary? Do you remember that day?'

It was like a cross-examination, leading her blind through the evidence, when she didn't know the charge. Though Rosemary did remember the cameras, and she now believed it had been a mistake, allowing them to film her conversations with the patients.

'Yes,' she said wearily. The ties around her wrists were hurting.

'Remember the one who spat in your face?'

'Yes.' She remembered very well.

'What did you reckon about her?'

'What did I reckon? I remember that even the staff were cowed by her. She was a bitter, spiteful woman — and I don't think she was mad at all. Malice and madness are not the same. One of the therapists said that her only pleasure in life was tormenting the other residents. She'd found a new form of power in her old age and didn't want to let it go. Her name was Myra — Myra someone.'

'Myra someone, yes. That sums up your attitude rather well. Myra someone. Also known as my mother.'

'Your *mother*?'

'We need to talk,'

had been the gist of Peter's phone call to Tamsin. And now they sat together in the interview room at Stormhaven's quiet police station (and Tourist Centre). When open, it mainly handled missing dogs, aggressive dogs, lost property, found dogs, anti-social behaviour in Vale Road and incidents outside the school, where sharp-elbowed parents in large cars were becoming ever more dangerous at drop-off time. The police said the parents were the school's responsibility while the school said it was down to the police. A community police officer from Newhaven had been told to 'keep an eye'.

So the recent murder of Rosemary Weller was a change of gear for the Stormhaven constabulary, and while the Lewes mob were handling the case, the Stormhaven nick enjoyed the reflected glory . . . and from time to time, some scraps of excitement. Like DI Shah's occasional use of their interview room.

'Geoff Berry is part of a syndicate trying to buy the land,' said Peter, who always felt trapped behind a table.

'How do you know?'

'Tara told me.'

'And she wouldn't lie, of course.'

'I don't think she's lying. Why would she lie?'

'And remember this?' Tamsin put a clear bag on the table. It contained the sticker left in Model Service.

'Yes, Tara gave it to me.'

'She did, yes. But now we know who put it there. Fingerprints all over the place. Like to take a guess whose wonderful fingers they belong to?'

'Francisco?'

Tamsin tried to hide her irritation. 'Well, it was fairly obvious, I suppose.'

It hadn't been obvious, so how had the abbot known? A lucky guess, probably . . . just a lucky guess.

'He wanted Cherise to stop working there,' said Peter by way of explanation. 'He told me in the kitchen at Black Cap.'

'Right,' said Tamsin.

'He was obviously trying everything to make things difficult for the business.'

'Obviously.'

'I mean, I presume he has his own key to Model Service, which made things easier, and Blessings' supply of stickers to hand. Katrina assumed it was her client, but it didn't have to be and always seemed unlikely to me. Why would a client do that? It just needed someone with a motive, a key and access to the stickers. Francisco.'

'So perhaps he went a little further to stop the business?' ventured Tamsin.

'How do you mean?'

'Well, like murdering the owner, for instance. He wouldn't have known that everything was left to Tara. And he's an ex-con, remember.'

'He is. But there's a more pressing matter,' said the abbot firmly.

'Allow me to be the judge of that.'

'I won't allow you to be a bad judge, Tamsin. There *is* a more pressing matter.'

'What?'

'Are you ready?'

'Oh, for goodness sake.'

'Rosemary wrote the report that closed down the Bybuckle Asylum.'

Peter sat back and Tamsin took this in as best she could, though frustration made a blur of it. This was huge. Why hadn't she known?

'*Rosemary* wrote it? How do you know?'

'Tara told me.'

'Oh, it's Tara again, is it? She's feeding you a lot of information all of a sudden. Was she drunk or something?' He wouldn't tell her the nature of their meeting. It would become something it wasn't. 'What, she *was* drunk?'

'No.'

'Then where were you?' Tamsin could sense some hesitation, some weakness in her uncle.

165

'She was giving me a massage.'

'She was *what*?'

'It was just that.'

'A massage? She was giving you a massage?'

His fears proved prophetic. He'd have to see out the storm. 'She gave me a massage. She's a qualified masseuse.'

'I'm sure she is.'

'And we talked. It helps a case to talk with people where they're in charge; helps them to relax.'

Tamsin shook her head in disbelief. 'And yourself?'

'Believe me, I wasn't at all relaxed.'

'So this massage with an attractive forty-something – it was all for the good of the cause, was it?'

'It was, yes. And means we now know Rosemary wrote—'

'Some big sacrifice?' Her tone was layered with the thick slush of sarcasm. 'And was it a massage with happy endings?'

Peter got up from the table; he couldn't stay seated. There was a window out on to a car park. He could take in the view, though there was no view to take in beyond Tamsin's insecure reactions.

'Tamsin, you're making an idiot of yourself.'

'Oh, *I'm* making an idiot of myself?' She could hardly believe she was hearing this. 'I thought you were taking the lead in that.'

Peter looked at her and felt a moment of compassion. 'I'm going to pause, Tamsin, count to ten, sit down and then attempt an adult conversation with you . . . rather than try to talk to an insecure five-year-old.'

'You've got a nerve!'

'I have great sympathy for the five-year-old, believe me, but right now, I need someone displaying less baggage in this investigation . . . as you might say.'

They lived the silence in the room.

'That's so pathetic!' interrupted Tamsin.

Peter stayed silent, starting the quiet count again. Tamsin felt rage at the final accusation, rage with it all; though she needed the abbot, foolish as he was. She needed him, and that was worst of all.

'Just who is the professional here? Answer me that.'

Again Peter stayed silent, starting the quiet count again.

'She thought we knew,' he said quietly.

'About what?'

'About Rosemary writing the report that closed the place; and perhaps we should have.'

'Speak for yourself.'

'But it doesn't matter. We do now and nothing is lost. The report that brought down Bybuckle was written by Rosemary.'

'I don't see this is really so pressing.'

'You don't?'

'This information may be of no consequence at all, Abbot.'

'That's possible. But it was your question when we were at the asylum yesterday: why there?'

'And you think you've answered it by having a massage with Tara?'

'Maybe. I have an idea, certainly. We're checking some records; someone was very angry about that closure, I think.'

But Tamsin wasn't interested in the records. In fact, she wasn't listening. Hearing but not listening. It was time she took charge and had the information to do that.

'We heard from the Health Authority this afternoon.'

'And?'

'They are going to sell to the syndicate you mentioned. I knew all that.'

'Of course.'

'And yes, Geoff Berry is involved. But here's the thing: he's not fronting the consortium.'

'Rosemary spoke of "a snake".'

'And I know who the 'snake is, Abbot. And *that's* what I call a pressing matter.'

'I want you to leave,'

said Blessings firmly. 'You'll be gone by six. That gives you an hour to pack.'

Francisco was quite thrown. He hadn't expected this. He'd sensed a cooling of the atmosphere, but the judge had always been cool. A few degrees lower was neither here nor there.

'But Blessings – Judge!' He'd never known what to call her and he didn't now. When you live alone with someone, you don't have to call them anything, which had been a relief.

'You'll find two hundred pounds in an envelope in the hall. Don't take anything else.'

The bitch, thought Fran. 'I burned down a church hall. I'm not a thief!'

The two were not the same and it was so unfair to link them. But that was what prison did, tarred you with a very large and indiscriminate brush. Not that Blessings cared, not when she felt so betrayed. Fran was a disgrace, an embarrassment, that's all she knew.

'It's to help you with lodgings until you get sorted.' And then she sniffed a little. 'But perhaps that won't be a problem with your new-found friend.'

'I don't have anywhere to go, your honour.'

'Then learn to tell the truth.' She wouldn't look at him, making herself busy with kitchen tasks, cleaning up and putting away. 'Learn to tell the truth. And then you might find a bed easier to come by.'

'I do tell the truth,' said the plaintiff.

'Well, you behave in an odd manner for a gay man, Francisco, that's all I can say; a very odd manner.' So that was her issue. 'You did tell me you were gay, do you remember?'

'I mentioned it.'

'You made quite a thing of it.'

'I'm attracted to men *and* women.'

168

'Oh, please!' Blessings found this very distasteful. 'You say whatever you need to say to get whatever you want. I found you in prison, remember.'

'After putting me there.'

'No, you put yourself there, Francisco. I didn't burn down the church hall.'

'I burned down a memory and I've said sorry. I just want a normal life now. I want to take back control.'

'Odd way of showing it.'

So much was welling up inside Francisco . . . this was a mystifying life, which always caught him out, left him in the wrong. He was always left in the wrong. He wanted to hurt the judge.

'A prison record – it's like walking round with a corpse tied to your leg. Do you understand that when you send people down? And when they finally let you out, you're free from your cell, but never free from the prison of people's assumptions. I'm learning that.'

Now Blessings swung round and faced him. 'Try being a black woman in the legal profession.' She had no interest in the boy's self-pitying drivel.

'Then you understand,' said Fran, chastened by her fury. 'Understand how I feel.' There was a moment of connection between the two, but it didn't last.

'No, I don't understand, Fran, because I can't change what I am. I'm black and I'm a woman. Neither of these states will disappear with soap. But you can change what you do, that's the difference. You want my advice? Don't burn down a church hall and don't hang around brothels. Is that really going to help how people perceive you?'

'I – met – a – girl.' Each word with the emphasis of the desperate. 'That's all I did.'

'I'm sure you've met plenty of girls there and you may even know the name of one or two.'

'It's not like that. I didn't know she was a prostitute. We didn't meet there.'

'You didn't meet at the whorehouse?'

'No.'

'But you're still seeing her.'

'Yes.'

'Still lapping her up despite what you know?'

Silence. Blessings didn't understand . . . but what was there to say? She'd never hear.

'The police have got you on camera,' she said. 'You're aware of that? They've got you on film entering the premises. And do you really think that someone in my position can have someone like you in my house? Someone dating a slut, a pornographer – whatever!'

Francisco breathed deeply, shamed, confused and now raging himself. 'A pornographer?'

'It's all the same, the consequences are the same – men doing abnormal things, debased activity.'

What was going on here? What the fuck was going on? And then Fran was remembering. Something stirred in him, it was the word that did it, 'pornographer'. The conversation he'd overheard, one night after the meeting of the Etiquette Society. Yes, he remembered now. All the others had gone home – the Three Strange Men, as he called them. Blessings was left talking with Rosemary, the charity woman, in the hallway. She was just taking her coat from the hook, when she turned to Blessings.

'I want you to know that I'm very sorry about your father,' Rosemary said in her matter-of-fact sort of way. The prison psychologist, who'd worked with Francisco, would have called it a door-handle statement. You say the most awkward things, the most difficult things, when you're about to leave and your escape route is clear.

'What about my father?' Blessings had asked. There had been such a hard tone to the judge's voice.

'With the pornography.' That's what Rosemary had said. 'With the pornography.' Francisco had seen nothing, standing there on the stairs, but had felt the shock of his landlady. 'I'm aware of how he died, Blessings.'

'Really?'

'Yes, well aware. But you must never think less of him or of yourself,' continued Rosemary confidently, as if this was a palliative,

170

as if she was somehow leaving things better than she'd found them. 'Many men enjoy pornography, wherever they look at it, and heart attacks in the circumstances are not uncommon. But they don't have to be defined by it when they're gone. You're not to let the death of your father in that toilet destroy his life or his memory. He's worth more than that.'

Francisco remembered the difficult hallway silence. He then heard the front door open and close without a word spoken. Fran had walked into the kitchen attempting nonchalance as if he'd just come down from his room. Blessings came in and went out, saying nothing. She could not believe what she'd just heard and Francisco never mentioned it . . . until now, because he was desperate.

'I heard the conversation, you know.'

'What conversation?'

'The heart to heart with Rosemary . . . in the hallway.' He was nervous as he spoke. How far to go with this?

'I've spoken often with Rosemary in the hallway,' said Blessings, coldly.

'The one about your father, the toilet . . . and the pornography.' He didn't really know what he was saying, but she did and the embarrassment was clear. A shameful family secret.

'Are you blackmailing me?'

'No! I'm just saying.' This wasn't blackmail, he didn't want anything. Well, he did want something – he wanted to stay, but that wasn't going to happen now, was it? And then it just came out, unnoticed in his psyche until now: 'Is that why you killed Rosemary?'

'You'll be gone by five and forget the two hundred pounds,' she said, walking towards the door. 'You're trash, I'm afraid. But they tell me there are still free beds in the Bybuckle Asylum. It's about all you're fit for.'

She'd deal with Francisco.

Tamsin would see him alone.

She didn't have time for the banter between Martin and the abbot. It was not productive and rather exclusive. It didn't include her, and as she didn't feel included it wouldn't be happening. Martin had suggested they meet at Costa Coffee in Lewes, rather than the *Silt*'s riverside office, and this was fine by her. If he wanted the humiliation to be public, then so be it.

'I don't like mixing business with pleasure,' he'd said on the phone, explaining the venue.

'I'll keep the pleasure to an absolute minimum,' replied Tamsin.

Martin ordered a flat white, Tamsin a sparkling citrus drink.

'I trust you're paying,' he said. 'If it isn't a date – and I sense that may be the case – then the one who most needs the meeting should pay. And that would certainly be you in this instance.' He smiled.

'The Bybuckle Asylum,' said Tamsin, waiting to see the fear in his face. But Martin merely took a sip of his coffee.

'What of the dismal place?' he asked.

'A good site, I'd imagine – for someone with vision.'

Martin put down his coffee. 'The selling of the Bybuckle land has been rather on and off down the years. More off than on, obviously, which is why it still sits there in all its bleak and disintegrating glory. I think the sane have all but given up on it.'

'Leaving just you and the ChanBerry consortium. Why didn't you mention that?'

Martin was only momentarily surprised. 'Because it has nothing to do with anything.'

'Nothing to do with the murder there?'

'I see no possible connection.'

'I can imagine some might disagree. I might even include myself among them.'

Martin smiled. 'What possible benefit would there be for me and my backers in a murder on a property we'd like to buy?'

172

'Well, that's the question, isn't it?'

'It is, yes.'

'The obvious reading is that you simply wanted revenge, maybe to get even, after Rosemary pulled out of the consortium. Perhaps she knew things about you all.'

'Revenge does have its delights, I grant you, and I can't say I'm above it, not at all. But there are better ways than physical murder, believe me. A few well-chosen words at a vulnerable moment can cause infinite and perhaps more satisfying hurt to someone. Bring hell to them on earth, I say! And anyway, the situation you describe simply didn't exist. The vision for the place changed, nothing more. And dear Rosemary had to have her say, as she always did. But that's business.'

Tamsin was struggling. Rosemary had likened him to a snake, but an eel would be a smoother fit, slipping through the questions. She'd sat down with a strong hand, or thought she had, with a fine ace to play. But the ace had achieved nothing, had been trumped with ease. She now looked vainly for her next move.

'I suppose a murder lowers the asking price,' she said. 'Who wants a property where there was a killing?' It sounded pathetic.

'Oh dear, Detective Inspector, you really are missing your abbot.'

And the trouble was, he was right. She *was* missing Peter. He gave her space in interviews to think, while he prodded and probed in his own particular way. And now she had no space; she felt as one beneath a stampede, crushed mercilessly.

'Stay with the question,' she said.

'Really?' said Martin, shaking his head. 'Because we're in the Land of the Laughable here. Do you not follow the property market? Mr Berry will tell you. A house in Newhaven was recently sold. Nothing remarkable there, you say. But this particular house, six months previously, had hosted a most grisly killing, involving a coffee grinder, an axe and the loss of three pints of blood over the kitchen floor. Following an open day, they had three offers, all above the asking price, one of which they accepted.'

'Proving what?' She knew exactly what it proved. She just hated his easy confidence.

'Proving that death – apart from the Dallas killing of JFK – is a temporary interest, Detective Inspector, to you and everybody else. A brief headline at best. But if you want some help with this investigation – and you do seem to need it – why not ask Blessings why she so disliked Rosemary?'

'What makes you think she did?'

Martin leant forward and Tamsin pulled back slightly.

'I never told you this, but Blessings was very keen for her to be removed from the Etiquette Society; very keen indeed. Not at first. They seemed quite amicable initially, but, well, who knows what happened? I'm not sure that Rosemary was too keen when the Welsh toy boy arrived on the scene, skulking around in the kitchen or on the stairs, always slightly out of view. Perhaps she didn't trust what was going on. It was none of her business, of course, but she may have said something, I don't know. Rosemary did tend to say something.'

Tamsin hadn't yet touched her drink. 'On the subject of Rosemary,' she countered, 'I'm told Geoff made a pass at her at one of the Etiquette Society meetings. Is that true?'

'Who told you that?'

'A good source.'

'Geoff makes passes at everyone, Detective Inspector. He makes more passes than Lionel Messi.'

He was the one footballer Channing had heard of, but clearly Tamsin hadn't, so he continued.

'The fact is, Geoff can't help himself. He's always trying his luck. Well, he hasn't tried it with me yet, but it wouldn't surprise me.'

'That's all sounding pretty seedy.'

'When is a pass not a pass? When it's a confusion, Detective Inspector, which is Geoff through and through, bless him. He has no boundaries at all, so it's all a bit of a blur.' Tamsin's disdain was evident. 'He could be married to three different people at the same time and not notice the problem. It's why he likes acting. At least he knows who he is for a moment – a cliché but true.' Martin paused and sipped at his coffee. 'Now, I really feel like I'm doing your job, and I'm acutely aware I'm not being paid for it – so did you have anything else to discuss? My print deadline is quite merciless in its demands!'

174

'You're not off the hook, Martin.'

'Or do you just like my company more than you care to admit, Detective Inspector?'

And then came the phone call, which Tamsin took – and was soon wishing she hadn't. As far as she could tell, amid the hubbub of Costa, it was an accusation of sexual harassment against Peter.

'Sexual harassment? The abbot?' There was some explanation down the line. 'I'll be with you shortly,' she said, still wondering what exactly they'd been saying.

'An accusation of sexual harassment against the abbot?' said Martin, rising from the table. 'Not a good day for you, Tamsin – not a good day at all.'

And a bad night in Stormhaven was to follow.

'Unforgivably late, Geoff,'

said the voice on the phone, full of apology. 'Really I am!'

'A little warning might have been helpful,' said the estate agent. I mean, it was quite a request! And rather out of the blue, even for a seasoned performer such as himself.

'Yes, I know, I know, Geoff. But sometimes the best ideas come late in the day and you know, something inside me just said we have to have you with us. We really have to have you, you lovely man!'

'Well, I'm glad you thought of me, of course I am,' said Geoff, at ease behind his desk and warming to the call. 'And you know I'll do anything for the kids.'

He said it so often he was beginning to believe it; though he hadn't done much for his own.

'I know you will, Geoff, it's in your bloody DNA! And it's a council thing really, with the mayor and all that, but I just had to mention you, I hope you'll forgive me. Of course, everyone thought it was a smashing idea – if we could somehow get the great showman to agree.'

'Well . . .'

'We did consider violence, obviously!'

Geoff laughed heartily. 'I just think it's great the place is being used in this way,' said the now glowing estate agent, 'and I'd be delighted to be a small part of the evening – as long as it's not *too* small! And I mean, if it's for charity . . .'

'Every penny.'

Geoff paused for a moment, surveying his office, from which he ran the business – his own business. But he wasn't thinking about property as he spoke on the phone. He was thinking of tonight and waking up the showman within.

'I haven't done my clown turn for a while,' he said. 'So I may be a little rusty . . . though people do say it's one of my best.'

'That I can confirm.'

'It's amazing what a little greasepaint can do,' he remarked, feeling the excitement in his veins. His evening was looking up, particularly with the mayor involved. It was always good if the mayor was there – more coverage in the press, better class of audience. And he had the time, plenty of time ... evenings were not completely satisfactory at present. He'd been on the computer more since Mandy had gone, on websites where he shouldn't be, because you had to fill the time and he liked his time well filled ... and then filled again. And he was thinking of his clown act, and wondering if he might extend the performance in some way. 'I could bring along my unicycle and the plate-spinning gear if you wanted.'

'That sounds very good. It's going to be a memorable evening, Geoff. But remember to keep it secret.'

'Oh, yes!'

'No telling anyone. I want the surprise to be magnificent!'

'Message understood.'

And with the details sorted, Geoff put down the phone with a large smile. Millie, his bouncy receptionist – this is how he referred to her – pushed open his door and asked him if he wanted a cup of tea.

'I'd like a glass of champagne, Millie!'

'I'm not sure we've got any bubbly!' she replied, nervous and excited. Was he serious about the champagne? 'Have you had some good news, Mr Berry?'

'You could say that.'

She had heard his wife had walked out on him. Perhaps she was coming back?

'Would you like me to buy some? It's quite cheap in Morrisons. You know, the Cava stuff.' She'd like a little wander round the shops.

'No, Millie – I jest, me thinks. Tea must suffice!'

'Sorry?' What was he saying? You didn't always know what Mr Berry wanted. He could become someone different every day, as if he wasn't too sure who he was himself. He did a lot of acting, so perhaps that's how it was with them lot. She thought Geoff was a bit of a joke, to be honest.

'Just a cup of tea, Millie ... and some chocolate biscuits, perhaps.'

'Yes, Mr Berry.'

Millie withdrew smirking, made a discreet 'nutter!' face to one of her colleagues, who laughed, and went to the small office kitchen where the kettle was housed.

While alone in his office, Geoff enjoyed a moment of well-being, a singular sense of rightness about the world . . . well, his world, at least, because things were pretty good right now. He surveyed his kingdom with some pride. He had an office, a company with four staff and a very decent property. And he had photos – of his kids, of happier days, of his performances down the years, including his famous Fagin turn in a 2004 production of *Oliver!*, which the local press had been somewhat ecstatic about. And on top of all that, he had pretty young Millie asking him if he wanted tea every day. He'd keep her . . . he liked the way she looked at him.

So yes, young Geoffrey had come a long way since his early days as a property hustler . . . rather more reputable now. *Definitely* more reputable! But everyone has to start somewhere. Everyone has some shade in their past, Geoff always said. You have to start somewhere, and it's not always pretty. You can't make an omelette without breaking eggs.

And let's be honest, they'd mainly been loonies, who wouldn't know a palace from a hen-coop, so no harm done . . . and much money made. *Kerching!* They'd been rehoused from the asylum, that was the main thing; that was the bottom line. And who did the quality of accommodation really hurt, apart from the fine consciences of the bleeding hearts brigade? And Martin was absolutely right: Geoff *was* something of a local celebrity. People approached him in the street, and sometimes he performed in front of the mayor – and this was why he was smiling today, why he spoke of champagne. A great sense of well-being was running through his estate agent's veins . . .

'Sexual harassment,'

said Tamsin. 'You mentioned sexual harassment.'

'I did.'

'So what exactly do you mean?'

She sat in Blessings' front room, having again declined the offer of tea.

'I'm not claiming sexual harassment, Detective Inspector. You mustn't put words in my mouth.' She'd made herself tea, and sat with it now, facing Tamsin across the room. It felt like a courtroom, with a touch of Ghana. 'I'm just noting how quickly the scent of scandal got you round here.'

It was dark outside and things were not much clearer inside. What *was* she saying?

'So you're withdrawing the claim?' asked Tamsin.

'I never made the claim.' Tamsin stared at her. How could she say that? She'd as good as made the claim, over the phone. Or was it different for lawyers? 'I merely ran the claim by you, so to speak, the idea of a claim . . . which is not the same as making it. And you're here because you were worried, because such a claim – were it made – could be a very damaging allegation, particularly for this murder enquiry. Who wouldn't be worried by an allegation made by a senior figure in the legal world? Especially when the object of that allegation, someone on the investigation team, had links to the deceased? What a mess that would be!'

Tamsin didn't like the power play at work and neither did she know what the judge was talking about. It left her defensive when she preferred attack.

'And the point of all this?' she asked.

'I don't know if the abbot has spoken with you.'

'About what?'

'All I'm saying is that I expect my conversation with him to remain private as it has no bearing on this case.'

179

What conversation? wondered Tamsin. Was this the conversation about Blessings wanting a child?

'The abbot is a very private person, Mrs N'Dayo.'

'Then that makes two of us.'

'He's not a gossip.'

'Then the matter is closed.'

'But there was no "matter". At least, not from where I'm sitting.'

'And we'll talk no more of counter-allegation.' The words lingered in the air.

'If I thought that was a threat . . .'

'It is no threat! Please, Detective Inspector!' She attempted a laugh. 'That would be a quite ill-founded assumption from the presented facts.' She calmed herself, regathered, took a sip of her tea. She then smiled. 'Rather, consider it a celebration of peace, an affirmation of the good character of the abbot.'

But Tamsin was not celebrating. She was angry. She was being used by this woman as some lackey go-between to keep the abbot's mouth shut about, well, whatever it was that had passed between them. She needed to find out what that was. Had he held something back? And if he had, why? Too busy with his massages . . .

'But perhaps there is something I *could* usefully share with you, Detective Inspector, to make your visit worthwhile. Off the record, of course.'

'Yes?'

'My lodger – now former lodger – Francisco Cornwell. Catholic family.'

'It's no longer illegal, I believe.'

'You may want to watch him.'

'Why?'

'He's a troubled boy, who's done time. I myself put him behind bars, as you know, so I'm quite aware of his rather sordid story. But I hope I've done my best for him since then, giving him a home.'

'I'm sure you had your reasons.'

Tamsin did not wish to encourage her righteousness. Charity was never free, not in her experience.

'Well, I asked him to leave after he made threats against me.'

'What sort of threats?'

'It doesn't matter, this is not a formal complaint.' Here she goes again, thought Tamsin, everything as rumour . . . and unattributable. 'But he's now homeless, I suppose, and hanging around with prostitutes, from what I can gather.'

'Do you know which prostitutes?'

'They're all alike to me, Detective Inspector, all of the sluts. And he'll need money, of course, but I'm not sure where he'll be getting it. You can see the dangers, I'm sure.'

'I can see the dangers in many situations, Mrs N'Dayo, but until a crime is committed—'

'Stormhaven may not be a good place for Francisco at present. That's all I'm saying. He's an unreliable presence in the community, to put it mildly; so maybe a police word in his ear? You'll know this better than me, Detective Inspector, but prevention is better than cure, surely? I'm just passing this on . . . informally, of course.'

'The matron's outfit,'

said Cherise.

'What of it?'

'Can I borrow it? He's asked for the matron's outfit later.'

Katrina nodded absentmindedly. She felt like the girl's mother sometimes, really she did, providing clothes for the latest fancy dress. Cherise could have the matron's outfit, it was washed and ready. It helped that they were the same size and could share these things. Costumes were requested more by middle-aged clients, and there were plenty of those in Stormhaven. But there was something about Cherise that rang alarm bells for Katrina.

'You don't look yourself, Cherise, you look – are you all right? I mean, you do know him?

Katrina didn't want a row. She just wanted the girl to be sensible and Cherise was not always as sensible as she could be.

'Of course I know 'im! He's a nice man, bit of a sweetie really. Very polite. Likes a good whippin'.'

'So he must be a judge.'

'I think I'm like his social worker in a way.'

Katrina laughed in derision. 'You – his social worker? That is what you think?'

'Only bein' funny.'

Why did Kat have to take everything so seriously?

'So what's his name?'

'How would I know his name? He's secret squirrel, he is! He's a soldier man, I know that.'

A soldier man? And now Katrina's stomach was churning.

'His social worker, if he had one, they would know his name, I think, Cherise.' She spoke reprovingly. 'You are nothing to him, if you do not know his name.'

'What's got into you all of a sudden?'

'We do not know their names, we never do, so we are something

182

different. Not their social workers, I think – something hidden away and shameful. Not precious.'

Katrina was never far from shame; it was always a short journey for her. Cherise had learnt this, so she was hardly surprised now. Katrina bloody hated herself and moved quickly into self-flagellation, always had, ever since she'd known her. She beat herself more than the clients! But what was the point of it? For Cherise, there was no point. Why punish yourself? It was probably the Catholic thing – but really, what was the point?

'We know how they treat us, Kat,' she said kindly. 'We don't need to know any more than that . . . and maybe it's better we don't, eh?'

'Better for who?' said Katrina, and it was probably at that moment that she decided she wanted out – to be out of this trade. She'd look around, consider other things. Yes, it was time for change, a fresh start. She'd found a man, a man who liked her. She was sure of that, and he could change his ways; he could change. She would help him to change.

'And I mean, "Cherise" is hardly *my* real name, is it!? It's not like any of us are telling the truth. I don't know his name, he don't know mine. So we're quits.'

'Katrina is my name.'

'Is it? I never knew.'

'So what is your real name?'

'Mine?'

There was hesitation.

'Is it so hard to tell me?'

They'd never had this conversation and Cherise was struggling. She felt safer with 'Cherise'. It was a protection, like a coat in the cold wind. It meant that in a way she wasn't here. To expose the soft flesh beneath it, to reveal her childhood name, the name she grew up with . . .

The doorbell rang.

'Saved by the bell,' Katrina said drily as she got up to welcome her next client. He was new, had sounded young on the phone. She didn't know what he wanted, he hadn't specified. Sometimes they didn't know themselves and had to be guided, like your first day at school.

She opened the door. He was mid-twenties and nervous. Definitely a first-timer.

'I have an appointment,' he said.

'First time?'

'Maybe,' he said, blushing.

'It won't kill you,' said Katrina with a smile. 'Follow me.' And then turned and led him upstairs, having looked him briefly in the eye. She'd start with a bath, with 'hunt the soap'.

But there was more on her mind than bath games tonight . . . a great deal more.

The abbot felt awe and fear

as he gazed on the photocopied list of names. One name in particular stood out . . .

The document lay on the fold-up table in the Stormhaven nick, placed there by PC Chris Richards, fresh back from the East Sussex Records Office.

'An easy find?' asked Peter, settling down on the uncomfortable chair.

'Easy? You must be joking.'

'I'm sorry.'

'The Bybuckle Asylum records – should anyone ever need to know – are twenty-five feet in width, file after dusty file. Thick, clinging dust, the sort that's hard to get off the hands. Oh, and hidden away in the farthest corner, away from the light.'

'In death, as in life.'

'I think they were about to be thrown out, a little past their sell-by date.'

'I've never believed in those, Chris, neither for coleslaw nor asylum files.'

'So what are you looking for?'

There before them lay the final roll-call of residents in the Bybuckle Asylum, ten days before its closure. The remarkable thing was how many were still there at this late stage. He'd read of some panic in finding them accommodation before the deadline for eviction, which was what it had been. Peter's eyes moved slowly down the list, resting on each name in turn, trying in some way to honour them. One hundred and thirty-seven patients: Maisie Patricia Eleanor Donaldson, Frank Edward Styles, George Herbert Stanforth, Maud Ann Sprackley . . .

'Must have been a Dunkirk-like evacuation in the final days,' said Richards, who had a degree in history.

'Though less glorious, perhaps, much less glorious. It was a fairly brutal clear-out.'

'I suppose care in the community had to be better, though.' PC Richards liked to look on the bright side of life, otherwise things could get a bit dark. Life was better sunny side up; he had to believe that.

'If it had existed, yes,' said the abbot.

'How do you mean?'

'Care in the community didn't exist, Chris. It was a sound bite, a mere phrase, an ideal – it didn't exist as anything other than a slogan. So most of these ones,' he said, pointing at the list, 'the last to go – the incurables – well, they'd have drifted into homelessness. Not easy for their loved ones to behold . . . ah, here we are, here we are. Oh my goodness!'

He ran a highlighter pen through one of the names. His hand shook slightly at the discovery.

'Is that them?' asked Richards.

'I think so,' he said as one reaching out for the Holy Grail. And Peter felt both awe and fear.

Awe at the discovery; fear for who might be next.

'Who the hell's this?'

yelled the young man beneath Katrina. It was his first time at Model Service and while hadn't known what to expect, he certainly hadn't expected this – a bloody monk in the doorway!

'I'm sorry,' said Peter.

Katrina, interrupted at work, turned her naked upper body round to the open door where he stood. She was wearing skin-tight leather boots and – apart from the cross round her neck – nothing else.

'What are you doing here?' she asked, with confused aggression.

'I need to know where Cherise is,' said Peter, trying to deal with Katrina rather than the scene before him. 'I'm sorry to interrupt, obviously, but it's important.'

Katrina covered herself with a towel, while staying astride the client.

'I'm sorry,' she said, looking down at the IT man beneath her. (This was all he'd said about himself – that he worked in IT.) 'He will go away.' And then turning to Peter: 'You go away!' This wasn't good for business.

'Cherise?' asked Peter stubbornly.

'She's downstairs.'

'She's not downstairs; and she's not at home.'

Katrina thought for a moment, caught between two worlds, two bodies.

'Then she's still at the asylum.'

'The asylum? What's she doing there?'

'I can't talk right now.'

With her head, she indicated the IT man, who now lay still and silent, like a trapped bird. Could the abbot not see this was bad timing?

'What's she doing at the asylum?' he asked.

Katrina gave up. 'Meeting a man.'

187

'Who?'

'I am not her keeper!'

'Who's the man?

'I don't care.'

'But you do know.' Her voice was troubled, angry. She clearly knew.

'Excuse me,' she said to her client as she dismounted. And to Peter: 'We talk outside.'

Throwing a bathrobe over herself, she pushed the abbot through the doorway and out on to the landing.

'Terence, all right?' said Katrina.

'Terence Blain? Cherise is with Terence Blain?'

'I think so.'

'Why do you think so?'

And so Katrina recounted her conversation with Cherise earlier that evening. She'd wanted to find out more, so she'd run the bath and asked the client to undress and settle in, while she returned downstairs.

'I'll see you later,' Cherise had said.

'Where are you going?'

'He wants to meet outside the asylum, bless 'im.'

'Who?'

'Secret!'

'Bybuckle Asylum – the one where Mrs Weller was killed?'

'It's all right, the police have all gone home!'

'And that's why I worry.'

There was discomfort in Cherise's voice, Katrina could hear it, despite the overlay of confidence.

'Why go there, Cherise? Why go to the asylum?'

'We're not going inside or anythin'. He just wants to show me the gaff.'

'And why would he want to do that? It is not like a tourist attraction or anything. It's a ruin.'

'Most tourist attractions are ruins, Kat, that's the point, isn't it?! Lighten up!'

'I'm just asking: why?'

'The place means a lot to 'im, all right? I don't know why and I don't much care! I don't mind being paid for a walk down memory lane.'

'It depends on the memories and whose they are. Not all memories are good.'

There had been silence between them, Cherise feeling angry because it wasn't like Katrina was her mother or anything. Not that she listened to her mother; they hadn't spoken in years. And she wouldn't be listening to Katrina either.

'And then we'll come back 'ere. That's the plan, all right?'

'You're coming back here afterwards?'

'That's why I need the matron's outfit!'

Katrina paused now, standing on the landing in the bathrobe. The story was told.

The abbot nodded. 'And that's the last time you saw her?'

'Yes, it is. You happy now?'

'Happier than Cherise, I suspect.'

'He doesn't like her anyway, I know that.'

'Why do you say that?'

'I just say it because it is true.'

'You know the man? You know the man she's meeting?'

'You go now!' She opened the door, revealing her client getting dressed. 'I cannot believe you inconveniencing me – really! How did you even get in?'

'Pervert!' grunted the young man.

Peter decided to leave. 'I'm sorry to interrupt.' He turned and started down the narrow stairs.

'Is she all right?' called out Katrina. But Peter was gone, moving fast.

'Cherise is in trouble,' he said on arriving in reception where Fran loitered. He'd let the abbot in.

'How do you mean?'

'In the asylum, that's where she is. Scenes I never thought I'd see.'

'Sorry?'

'It doesn't matter, I'm talking to myself.'

And he *was* talking to himself, because the danger was acute and he needed to focus, to calm the world around him, and calm the world within, to make good decisions . . . to think '360 degrees', as a therapist once told him. Peter remembered him now. He'd spent six months in the monastery, burned out with the care of others and needing a break – a bit of desert respite, the healing of rock and sand.

'We generally think about forty degrees, Peter,' he'd once said over supper in the refectory. 'We're aware of about forty per cent of what is happening, within us, around us. Forty per cent, max . . . some a lot less. To think three-sixty degrees is pure mindfulness.'

And that's what Peter wished for now . . . 360 degrees.

'You say she's at the asylum?' said Francisco.

'What are you doing here, Fran?' asked Peter, suddenly pausing. Why was he here?

'Me? Well, Blessings has thrown me out, hasn't she?'

'The judge has thrown you out? What have you done?'

'I haven't done anything,' he pleaded in his Welsh lilt. 'Absolutely nothing.'

'She wouldn't throw you out for nothing.'

There was a brutal fairness about Blessings; some sort of moral logic.

'I've been thrown out for *not being gay*, I suppose. Usually the other way round in seaside towns, isn't it?'

Peter took this in. 'Explain – quickly.'

'I told her I was gay when she visited me in prison – and it wasn't absolutely true.'

'So she's angry because you lied to her about being gay.'

'It's not a complete lie.'

'Lies rarely are.'

'But I'm with Cherise now.'

'Really?'

'I'm with her, all right? And that's why she's thrown me out. The judge doesn't like what Cherise does, calls her slutty. And I don't like what she does, mind. I don't like it at all. It *is* slutty . . . right slutty, in my view. But that's all going to change, I know it. She just needs to learn.'

'So you're trying to fix Cherise.'

'I will fix her. It's not right what she does.' The abbot's eyebrows rose. 'Makes a fool of me.'

'It's her life.'

'Not any more it isn't. It's *our* life now. She needs to learn that.'

He'd met the man

beneath the street light by the Bybuckle Asylum. James was making his way along the empty seafront towards the shelter of the beach huts when he saw the figure at the foot of the steps, looking around as if wondering what to do. With a shaved head and military bearing he assumed the man was homeless; he'd hardly be the first old soldier out on the drift. Why else would he be standing here on a night like this, with a cold moon above? There was nothing here but the wind and the sea.

'I'd warn you against that place,' said James, eyeing the gloomy silhouette of the asylum.

The man looked surprised to be spoken to. 'Why would you do that?' he asked, pulling his coat tighter around him.

'If you're thinking of kipping there, I mean.'

'Kipping there?'

'Do you know what it was – what it once was?' said James, who could still feel the damp of the walls and didn't mind a little company now.

'I know enough,' came the reply.

'It was a nuthouse,' said James.

'Is that what they call it?'

'It's probably not what the mayor called it, or not in public at least!'

'More of a crime scene,' said the old soldier, looking up at the building. 'From what I hear, it's more of a crime scene.'

'No, I mean *before* the murder.' James had read all about the killing of the charity woman. The homeless do see newspapers; they just tend to be second-hand, extracted from bins or picked up at stations. 'It was a mental asylum before that, the Bybuckle Asylum. And I reckon you can still hear the cries.'

'You think so?'

'The place spooked me, and damp as hell. I was in there a few weeks ago, but couldn't stay.'

James liked this man. He was drawn by his stillness.

'As you say, you can still hear the cries,' said the stranger. 'They don't give up, do they?' He spoke quietly.

'You heard them?'

'But I don't want to keep you.'

'I don't mind a chat. What's life, if you can't—'

'No – I don't want to keep you.'

'No,' said James, understanding. It was a dismissal. This was not a man who encouraged small talk, he could see that now. 'I'll be on my way.'

'It's good to get home . . . or so I'm told.'

'Yes,' said James. 'Well, I'm aiming for the beach huts, a kinder holding than this place.'

Had he really said that? There was something about the man, as if he too had spent his life walking into the wind; as if he too had missed kindness along the way. Yet here they both were, passing ships in the night, and a space between them that could never be crossed.

'Good night to you,' said the man.

'And to you,' said James. 'I didn't catch your name.'

'I don't think you need to.'

'No, well, see you around, no doubt.'

Terence smiled and James disappeared slowly down the road, in and out of the street light. He thought of looking round, looking back – he wanted to know what the man was doing by the asylum. Something had seemed strange. But he decided against it; it was best that he didn't, that he simply kept on walking, looking ahead.

And then he was thinking about the stove in the beach hut. He could make something hot. Soup – he had two sachets in his pocket, mushroom and minestrone. Though he'd prefer to be going home. He knew that now as he walked along the seafront. He wanted to go home. For years he'd known he couldn't go home, that he'd only disappoint his wife and children again, and he couldn't do that. But now he wanted to try . . . to try again. As the man said, it's good to get home.

He passed a girl walking the other way – well, a young woman, walking quickly and quite dressed up. He said, 'Good evening,' because he couldn't ignore her, he had to say something, and she looked at him as though he was a perv.

He wasn't surprised; he knew how he appeared. The woman might have looked at a solicitor – his old self – but she wouldn't look at a tramp, who must be rejected and determinedly not seen, as one too frightening to contemplate.

James wanted to make for home; but instead, he kept walking towards the beach huts and the stove.

Who knows what that bloke was up to at the asylum?

'So why is she angry with you, Francisco?'

'I don't know,' he said. 'I really don't—'

'Please don't waste my time.' It wasn't a request from Tamsin. 'She gave you a home. You must have done something to make her angry.'

'Why have I been arrested?' he asked calmly. He wouldn't be kicked around any more. He had plans for this evening and this interview wasn't part of them. 'I don't understand why I'm here.'

'You haven't been arrested, Francisco. You've been detained . . . for questioning.'

'I'm not black, am I? I mean, if I was black I'd expect to be stopped and searched without cause.'

'Don't try and be clever.'

'She organized this, didn't she?'

'No.'

'It's the sort of thing she'd do to get her own back. Get her friends in the police to give me some grief. Bloody typical!' Fran felt angry now.

'We are not her friends.'

'She barked and you jumped, eh?' That irritated Tamsin because it was true.

'No one's jumping, Francisco.'

'Then what are we doing here when I've done nothing wrong? Or is Welsh the new black in Stormhaven?'

'These are just routine enquiries.'

'*Routine enquiries?* She's frightened of what I know and that's a fact.'

'What do you know?' Tamsin was suddenly interested – but Fran laughed. He actually felt quite powerful. He wasn't going to be pushed around by *her*. Nor by any woman . . . no more being pushed around by women.

'She doesn't like me being with Cherise, all right?'

'And why doesn't she like Cherise?'

'She's a prostitute. Well, a sex worker. She prefers to be called a sex worker. But that's a prosy in my book, a slut. Blessings calls her a slut.'

'So?'

Fran paused. 'And I told her I was gay.'

'Told who you were gay?'

'The judge.'

'Really? That's an odd thing to do.'

'I'm not gay.'

'If you say so.'

'It was when she visited me in prison. I played up to it a bit, you know, for the sympathy, I suppose.'

'And then she discovers you, on video, visiting a brothel?' Fran made a face. 'It's not playing out well, I can see that.'

'It wasn't like that anyway – between me and Cherise, I mean.'

'How was it?'

'I didn't know Cherise's job when we met. I was doing her garden. I'm "Gardener Man".'

'I'll bear it in mind.'

'I only discovered later – you know, what she did.' Should Tamsin mention the sticker yet? 'Then I mentioned something, and she got really angry,' he added.

'Who, Cherise?'

'No, Blessings.'

Hold back on the sticker for a moment. 'And what made Blessings angry?' asked Tamsin.

'Ask her about Rosemary and her father!'

'Why would I do that, Fran?'

Fran was beginning to twitch, his legs unable to keep still.

'Pay her a visit and ask her about her father – ask about Rosemary and her father!' Somehow he knew this was important, that it might get him out of here. 'She just froze when Rosemary spoke of him . . . totally froze.'

'What did Rosemary say?'

'And I didn't mean to blackmail her or anything – it just came out. About the pornography.'

'What pornography?'

'It just came out. I just wanted to stay, wanted a home – or to get my own back. I don't know.'

Tamsin raised her hand to quieten him. She wanted to mention the sticker, but she also wanted clarity; this was important, possibly urgent. She glanced down at her phone. A new text message had appeared, from Peter, or ABBOT as her phone put it:

It's about the sexual shame. Bad tonight. Going there now. Ring.

What was Peter talking about? He shouldn't be let loose on texting. She'd finish with Francisco and then ring.

'So what did you mention, Francisco, that made her so very angry?'

'Like I said, I heard a conversation between her and Rosemary. It was after one of their meetings.'

'What sort of conversation?'

And so he told Tamsin what he'd heard. Rosemary talking about Blessings' father with the pornography. And the heart attack . . . how he'd died in the toilet surrounded by dirty magazines.

'Rosemary was trying to be kind, I think. She was quite forthright, that lady, and trying to be kind. But it didn't sound kind to Blessings, that was very clear. She went quite ape when she'd left. And the milk turned after that.'

'The milk turned?'

'She didn't have a kind word for Rosemary, ever. "I find it quite repulsive the way she chases after Terence," I remember her saying. But then, of course, Terence fancied Rosemary; you could see that, even from the kitchen.'

'You saw a lot from the kitchen.'

'And Blessings fancied him as well, so that wasn't going to work, was it?'

Tamsin's mind had just gone up a gear: a shameful end, an unlikely love triangle . . . and a sense of acceleration in the investigation. Things were becoming very clear.

'I want you to go downstairs and make a statement, Francisco.

And then you're free to go. You've been very helpful.' They could forget the sticker for now.

'No apology, then?'

Tamsin looked at him with disdain. 'PC Wells will go with you.'

And with the two of them gone, Tamsin glanced again at Peter's message. 'Ring' he said, but she didn't need to ring. Different paths through the wood, perhaps – but they'd come to the same clearing. The Welsh Wonder Francisco had made everything very clear and she needed to act, to make an arrest in Firle Road. She texted a reply:

Understand. See you at the front door.

This was going to feel very good indeed . . .

He'd worn a hat and beard

on arrival and departure at Model Service, aware of the corridor cameras. It had made Cherise laugh at the time.

'It's not so bad!' she'd say. 'It's not like it's illegal!'

Terence would smile. She didn't understand how bad it could be . . . and how 'bad' was a great deal worse than 'illegal'.

'I mean, who cares what anyone else thinks?' she asked. 'It's not like my mum and dad are exactly thrilled at what I do.'

He hadn't thought of her parents. 'Do they judge you?' he asked.

'I suppose. I mean, they still love me; they still really love me. But, you know—'

'You do not think judgement poisons love, leaving it cold and dead?'

A crucifying pain in his gut, like sharp nails pressing. He did not like talk of love.

'I don't know what you mean!' said Cherise. Was he off his bloody rocker?

He was aware that something had grown between them over the months . . . like a flower in a dry land. Trust grows discreetly between vendor and buyer. No commercial relationship is ever just that; it is either less or more, and his time with Cherise had been more. She was paid to act, of course she was, but you can only act so much. She was a sweet girl and he wanted to protect her, though nothing mattered, not really . . . nothing had mattered for a long time.

*

'Hello, Curly!' she said now, looking up from the foot of the asylum steps.

Cherise looked lovely in the lamplight.

'Hello,' he said.

When she'd asked what to call him, he'd said 'Curly'. He had a shaved head now but it had not always been so. He'd had curly hair when younger, 'when I still had hopes and dreams!' as he put it. 'And hair.'

'You're still Curly inside, that's the main thing,' she said cheerily. She liked to cheer people up, liked the last words to be hopeful words; life was better that way, better when it was hopeful.

But Terence wasn't still Curly inside. Hope had left the house some time ago. Young Curly, who'd dreamt of being good, dreamt of arms to hold him, warm against cold, had left quietly by the back door, his departure unnoticed.

'You must come up here for a moment,' he said, through the chill night wind.

Cherise was hesitating, her hair blowing wild. 'Can't we go back to Church Street? It's bloody freezin' out 'ere.'

'I want to show you something. And then we'll go back. I've ordered a taxi.'

Cherise liked the idea of a taxi. 'I've got the matron's outfit,' she said and Terence nodded.

'Good.'

'So what is it I must see?' she asked, climbing the ten steps to the asylum front door with difficulty. The Bybuckle steps were not made for high heels.

'Give us a turn, Mr Clown!'

one of the children shouted. They were bored after school, standing outside Morrisons. And Tara watched the clown respond, clearly delighted to be asked.

He was riding the unicycle he'd been carrying, up and down, round and about, while attempting to juggle two oranges. Everyone was happy, cheering away, and he stayed on his bike, even though he dropped the oranges. And this was the good thing about clowning: things could go wrong, and people still liked you. They were liking him outside Morrisons, Tara could see that, and she was almost enjoying it herself – until she recognized him as the estate agent fellow. And that changed everything.

She'd found him creepy when buying a property through his agency. After the first viewing, she'd made sure she was never in a house alone with him again; his lack of boundaries was uncomfortable. And seeing him in full make-up now made her feel ill.

'You're a rubbish juggler!' shouted one of the children.

And instead of hitting him – his initial desire – Geoff made a 'What *do* you mean?' gesture and picked up the oranges again. He looked at them for a while, polished them with his sleeve and then attempted to juggle again. He gave himself a few successes, drew some applause, threw them higher and higher, looked pleased with himself – and then deliberately messed it up, to everyone's amusement . . . and his own deep chagrin.

With big gestures, he indicated he would try again, and with his fingers held high, got them counting down from ten, building the tension.

'Ten! – Nine! – Eight! – Seven! . . .'

On reaching *One!*, he started juggling again, getting ever more excited at his success – he was a pretty good juggler – until he rather deliberately dropped them again. He hit himself in theatrical fashion on the forehead and fell over to more laughter.

He got up, bowed, took the evening shoppers' applause, picked up his unicycle and continued happily on his way, still angry at that rude little sod of a child, but somehow enlarged by the performance – more content in himself, a bigger and better person and made so by the applause.

Tara watched him disappear into the darkness, going God knows where, but thought only of Katrina.

She hadn't been herself recently, Tara was well aware of that. And now a client had turned up, a booking made – and no sign of her! Just a ridiculous note on her desk saying, 'I have to go out. Sorry. But I have to.' Tara had had to explain that Katrina was 'unavoidably detained' and send the poor man away.

And this wasn't good, not good at all. She had never had to do that before. Katrina had always been so reliable and she didn't want to lose her. But what was the girl thinking?

She followed the clown down the street towards the sea.

The torchlight wobbled

in the asylum dark. Held by an uncertain hand, it moved slowly and silently towards him.

'Hello,' said Peter to the shadow behind the light. 'Is that you, Cherise?'

He'd entered the asylum by the front door; he needed to find the girl. She hadn't been at Church Street, so she must still be here. There'd been no sign of Tamsin on his arrival. Perhaps she was held up, but he couldn't wait. He texted again but got no reply. The time for waiting was over, so he went inside and stood in the hallway for a while, listening. There was nothing to be heard but the damp drip of a leaking roof, well soaked in recent days; the smell of a rotting mat was strong tonight.

He moved quietly through the hallway and then down the dark corridor, feeling his way along the cold walls before stepping through the rusted swing doors into the cavernous Gladstone Ward. Here was the largest single repository of madness in Stormhaven, through which generation after generation of the struggling and insane had stumbled. The abbot feared further insanity tonight.

The faint light at the windows – diluted orange from the street lamps – left the space strangely obscured, blinding the night eye for the middle darkness. He was immediately aware of Rosemary. She felt present.

'Are you here?' he asked quietly. 'Can you see me now? Rosemary?' Her final moments had been lived in this desolate ruin of a room. Did she loiter, perhaps, a ghost – or angel – tied to the place of the unresolved? 'Can you help me?'

It was then that he saw the torchlight moving towards him, and at first it seemed kind, almost an answer to prayer. Here was a light in the dark – the lady of the lamp, walking the ward, calming troubled souls, until all were at rest. But the torch jerked a little and stayed silent. The light moved towards him, but not in hope. This was no kindly light . . .

'Is that you, Cherise?'

Silence. The abbot stood still but the torch continued its approach.

'He loves me,' whispered the voice behind it.

'Who loves you?'

'And you won't spoil this. You have spoiled enough this evening.'

The torchlight had come to a halt, a few yards away. It now shone steadily in his face. Only slowly did he see the gun, held in the unsteady hand like an open-mouthed goldfish.

Peter sensed that this was the whisper and the body of a woman.

'What are you doing here?'

asked Blessings, who'd noticed two police cars outside her house. They were hard to miss.

The homes that surrounded the south side of the golf course, where the clubhouse sat proud, were not much bothered by traffic at night. Estate agents called it 'a haven of idyllic calm'. So when two cop cars arrived at speed, with full bells and whistles, they received attention from the householder.

'You weren't going anywhere, were you?' asked Tamsin, walking towards the judge, a silhouette in her front entrance.

'Only to bed,' she replied, pulling a shawl around herself in the cold. Tamsin wasn't noticing the cold.

'Because we just wanted a little chat about Rosemary.'

'Really?'

'Can we go inside?'

Tamsin almost felt sorry for this lone figure in her elegant doorway. She did seem very alone.

'No,' came the reply. 'Not unless you have a warrant. Do you have a warrant?'

'I just thought it would be warmer for you.'

'Such concern, Detective Inspector. But why would you – and half the Sussex constabulary, it seems – want a conversation about Rosemary at this time of night?'

Tamsin had arrived with four other police officers in case of trouble. They lurked at a discreet distance, though obvious enough in the shadow of the gates.

'New information has come to light, Mrs N'Dayo.'

'I hope it's good.'

'You didn't like Rosemary, did you?'

The judge paused. 'I'd be very careful, Detective Inspector.'

But Tamsin was bored with the judge pulling rank. 'I'm not sure we need to be too careful, Mrs N'Dayo. Indeed, maybe the time for being careful is quite over. Is the abbot inside?'

'Inside where?'

For the first time Tamsin faltered a little. He must be here. How could he not be here by now? And then a voice called out in the darkness.

'Ma'am,' said one of the police team. She turned round. 'A message.'

She'd given him her phone, to keep an eye. 'Give it to me.'

He stepped forward, exposed now in the security light that splashed across the gravel driveway.

'It's from the abbot.'

'Give it to me.'

'What's going on, Detective Inspector?' asked the judge.

'Excuse me a moment.' Though something inside her already knew. She gazed down on the message.

I'm at the asylum. Where are you? Get here now.

Tamsin drew breath and saw only an abyss before her eyes . . . an abyss into which she was falling.

'There's been a mistake,' she said. Her mouth could hardly speak.

'A mistake?' said the judge, smiling horribly.

And of all the people to witness this cock-up, to be the victim of this cock-up . . . Blessings N'Dayo, the high court judge! Did it get any worse? She could kill Francisco with his damn stupid story.

'We were merely patrolling in the area.'

'Patrolling for what?' asked the judge. 'Lost golf balls?'

With amused disdain, Blessings was quickly in charge.

'A false lead,' said Tamsin.

'And there was I thinking you were accusing me of murder.'

'No, nothing like that . . . a misunderstanding.'

She heard herself sounding ridiculous. The cars were parked square across the driveway to foil any getaway, and lit up like a funfair. Blessings' smile was one of contempt . . . and then pity.

'We're leaving,' said Tamsin.

'I'd invite you in for a drink, Detective Inspector; but incompetence so exhausts me, I simply don't have the energy. But I'll manage a phone call to your superiors in the morning.'

206

Tamsin nodded. There were no words available in her head, no polite words, no usable words to a judge familiar with her rights ... to a judge so misused.

'I'll bid you goodnight, Mrs N'Dayo.'

And with that, Tamsin turned, cheeks burning, and walked towards the car. She bent down and climbed into the back seat. She hadn't been able to speak an apology. She'd tried but it hadn't happened.

'We need to get to the asylum,' she said.

'Bybuckle Asylum?'

'Just drive, for God's sake.'

'You let me handle this,'

said the voice behind the torchlight. The abbot sat in a corner, the gun still pointing towards him. It was a voice he recognized but also one that confused him.

'How did you get here?' he asked.

'I ran.'

She must have run quickly. The abbot had hardly dawdled.

'And why the gun, Katrina? There's really no need for a gun.'

'Because maybe you are not so helpful here and need persuading a little.'

'And you are helpful here?'

The figure in the dark stiffened. 'Yes, I am helpful. I believe I am. I can reason, he listen to me; and you will just be a big noise, trust me.'

'I don't trust you, Katrina, not in this affair. And sadly, neither does he.'

'He trust me!'

'He doesn't trust you. You're going to be in his way tonight.'

'I called out to him, he knows I am here, that I love him. So Cherise will be all right now.'

The abbot paused . . . listened to his breathing. Sometimes it was all there was to do.

'He trusts no one, Katrina. That's why he's alive today.' Silence. It was the second encounter of the evening that they shouldn't have been having. 'Does he know you have a gun? Is it his gun?'

'You won't spoil this, Abbot. Like I say, you have spoiled enough this evening.'

Katrina was determined to stay in control. She just had to be here, to make sure nothing went bad. Terence was a good man. She wanted to live with him, she knew that, but he needed to stop seeing Cherise, to stop talking with her . . . because he was a good man. And he was her man, Katrina's man. But then the abbot was rising to his feet.

'So let's go together,' he said. 'Where are they hiding?'

'Sit down!'

But the abbot did not sit down.

'You're badly mistaken, Katrina.'

And then out of the darkness, Fran appeared.

The stone steps were steep,

slippery and narrow, leading down from the street, a half-hidden access. The two police officers moved cautiously in the dark, closed in by creviced walls either side, the paint eaten by salt.

'We used to come down here when we were kids,' said PC Goss. 'The place still had nutters in then and we just wanted a laugh.'

Tamsin nodded. She could see why he'd never made sergeant. Enlightenment was yet to bother his consciousness.

'And did you get in?' she asked.

'Sometimes, if they left the door open.'

'There *is* a door down here?'

'Well, there used to be, ma'am. I mean, if they haven't blocked it up. It's basement access, so it was, well, pretty spooky. Dark. I remember it as pitch black. It's like a secret floor, really.'

'Beneath the wards?'

'Yes, I think maybe the Grade A crazies were kept down there, as a punishment. That's what someone said. Who knows? I mean, what can you do with a nutter? I think they put 'em down in some countries and you can see why.'

Tamsin neither wanted nor needed his company any more.

'I'll take it from here, Constable. You know what you have to do.'

'Yes, ma'am.'

'Don't let me down.'

'No, ma'am.'

'And three bags full, ma'am,' he felt like saying as he turned to go back up the stairs. He didn't say it, he wouldn't dare. A bit stuck-up, that DI. A looker, obviously, everyone knew that, but an ice maiden, never let you near, always keeping you away.

As for Tamsin, this was her best chance of redemption. She'd reckoned on being too late to enter the asylum by the front door; it would surely be locked, or watched, events having moved on? A more private entrance seemed wise. And then the revolting Goss had revealed a back way in; not a well-known path, so perhaps, Tamsin thought, she could be clever. And she needed to be clever after the night she'd had.

Goss disappeared back up the steps. He could help the armed response unit, local knowledge and all that, or he could crawl back under the stone he came from, Tamsin wasn't bothered. She continued down, step by hidden step, a cold handrail for help, the smell of urine, arriving finally at a pile of sodden rubbish, cans and the like, thrown down the steps.

And before her now, an old metal-framed door. Would it open? And what lay behind it?

*

'What's going on?' asked Fran, standing in the damp gloom of Gladstone Ward.

'Stay away,' said Katrina, still waving her gun. 'Leave now. You should both leave now.' She pointed the weapon towards Fran. 'Leave now!' she shrieked.

And something inside the young man turned. He was sick of women telling him what to do: the judge, that detective, now this woman. Like his old Sunday school teacher, the witch. He moved towards Katrina.

The abbot watched.

'Give me the gun,' said Fran, holding out his hand . . . but she stood her ground. 'Give me the gun, you stupid woman.'

Katrina was shaking.

'Give him the gun, Katrina,' said the abbot, gently. 'It will be all right. He doesn't want to harm anyone. You don't want to harm anyone do you, Fran?'

'*Give me the gun,*' he said.

'Do as he says,' said the abbot, rising slowly from his crouched position. Had he misread the situation? He was beginning to wonder, but Katrina did as she was told. A desperate figure, she shouldn't be here, why had she come? Slowly, she handed the gun to Fran, relieved to be rid of it and scared.

'I don't want anyone hurt,' she said. 'You mustn't hurt anyone.'

211

'Now where's Cherise?' asked Fran, pumped up. There was no answer. 'Where's Cherise?!'

'We don't know,' said Peter.

'Of course you know.' He was becoming familiar with the gun in his hand, the power it gave.

'And how can you help Cherise?'

'I think I can teach her a lesson, Abbot.'

'I'm not sure she needs a lesson. Not from you.'

'Oh, she needs a lesson. You don't make a fool of Fran.'

Tamsin stared at the door.

Beyond this place, this entrance, there was no going back. Open the door and, like the gladiator, you leave the tunnel and enter the arena.

The arena would be a risk. But she had to be there. It wasn't a choice, tonight of all nights, because she'd be crucified in the morning. The judge would see to that. Death here might be preferable . . . and with the decision made, she reached forward, took hold of the handle and turned it gently. Something gave, the mechanism clicked and slowly she pulled open the rusted door, felt the cellar chill and stepped inside.

It was dark, so dark . . . Goss hadn't been wrong. No light: sheer black as she pulled the door shut behind her and inched her way forward. And silence . . . the silence of a tomb, below ground and away from sound, apart from the drip-drip-drip of water.

There was a click behind her. Was that simply the door closing? She'd pulled it shut; it could simply be the mechanism settling. It was possible. Or was it the door being locked behind her? It sounded like a locking, a dead lock. Tamsin stood terrified. Was there someone with her in the basement silence, another presence in this tomb?

And then a hand on her wrist.

'You should be dead,' said the voice.

'You should get out of here,'

said Katrina. 'Get out of here while you can, Abbot, before you cause trouble.'

'Come over here,' said Peter.

'And you, Fran,' said Katrina. 'People with guns cause trouble, they do bad things. You should get out of here.'

'Don't tell me what to do.'

'Come over here,' said Peter again. 'Katrina – please.'

She began to move towards him, leaving Fran alone in the large space, a restless silhouette by an old metal bed.

'So where's Cherise?' he asked again. 'She's here, isn't she? You told me she was here, Abbot.' Something Peter now regretted. 'And if she's with that man . . .'

And then Fran dropped to the floor, like a puppet with its strings cut, the gun removed from his hand in one swift movement. And out from behind one of the old cubicle curtains appeared another figure.

'It's not good to play with guns,' said the voice.

'Then you shouldn't provide them,' said Peter. 'I always blame the suppliers. Is Fran OK?'

Fran was moaning in pain. It had been so quick.

'It's only a broken wrist. You're lucky – bones heal.'

'Is that you, Terence?'

'Don't follow me.'

'Where's Cherise?' asked Peter.

'The detention of civilians is authorized for security reasons or in self-defence,' said Terence. 'So please leave now, Abbot . . . and you, Katrina. And take your friend. His pain will ease.'

'Can we talk, Terence?' asked Peter.

'There's nothing you can do. I want both of you to leave, and I ask this politely.'

'Or what?'

214

'Or it will not end well.'

'So you're a soldier again, Terence?'

'It's good to have rules of engagement. It simplifies war.'

'War? I didn't realize this was war.'

'What you realize is not my concern, Abbot.'

'And deadly force?' asked Peter. 'Is that permitted here?'

'Deadly force is permitted in certain combat situations.'

'Only self-defence legitimizes deadly force, Terence.'

'You know your rule book, well done.'

'And no one here's trying to shoot you. Is anyone trying to shoot you, Terence?' Again, no response. 'And my guess is, Rosemary wasn't either. I don't think Rosemary was trying to shoot you, tied to the bed frame. So the war is a little one-sided. There's a battle-field – but only one army.'

'Don't follow,' he said, withdrawing. 'Neither of you follow. Do you hear me?'

'Why can't we follow, Terence?' Peter watched the image fade into the big dark.

'Tactical withdrawal . . . but don't follow . . . for your own safety.' He was just a voice now, calling across the night ward. 'Do you understand? Don't follow.'

'But I love you, Terence!' shouted Katrina.

'You don't love me. You need me. They are not the same, not the same at all. Grow up.'

The major-general was rigid with concentration. He was having to adjust, playing the game in front of him. Katrina's arrival at the front door had not been part of the plan, neither had her discovery of his gun on the table. He should be gone by now; but he was still here. This was complex now, a different game to play.

But it was good to have rules again, rules of engagement. He'd missed them. In hostage-taking, always ensure the captives understand the nature of their confinement – and the penalties for disobedience. Establish boundaries. It's kinder . . . harsh at first but kinder in the end. People know where they stand.

'Don't follow!' he shouted one more time.

This is the difference between the soldier and the terrorist. The soldier has boundaries; though every combat soldier will become a terrorist on occasion . . .

'I understand,' said Peter. 'We won't follow. If you free Cherise.'

And then silence in the ward – the groans of the mad, their midnight screams, long gone from this strange outpost by the sea. Only the jerky sobs of Katrina could now be heard. Terence had dissolved in the darkness, made his own way out. He'd returned to wherever he came from . . . returned to Cherise. They must be in the End Room, and now Peter wondered about Tamsin. Where was she? Had she got his message? What was happening out there? Was the place surrounded yet?

'Terence!' shouted Katrina. She got up and moved towards the darkness. 'I want to help you!'

'Katrina!' shouted the abbot. 'Come back!'

'I want to help you, dearest.'

She was running past the body of Fran, following the shadow.

'Come back, Katrina!'

'I love you, Terence!'

'*Come back, Katrina!*'

But it was too late. The trip-wire explosion smashed the asylum sky, a terrible flash ripping at the roof, a flying silhouette, the deafening wall-shuddering roar, the falling masonry, the settling dust . . . and the silence.

'Oh my Gawd!'

said Cherise, in terror.

'Just stay calm,' said Tamsin, handling her shock – because whatever was happening in there, they needed to stay calm.

'But what the 'ell was that? What the—'

'Stay calm.'

Tamsin didn't know what it was, and her handcuffed hand was sore from the jolt. Terence had said he was being kind. The basement door had been booby-trapped, and he'd made it safe when he saw her coming – but what could she believe?

She'd found herself marched up some stairs and into the space where she now sat. Though God knows what was happening around them.

'I heard Katrina,' said Cherise. 'She was shouting. I know it was her. Katrina's here.'

'We're getting you out, all right?'

Cherise was showing signs of panic. She needed calming.

'Like that's going to 'appen.'

'We will, there's a way.'

'You think so?'

'I think so.'

But she didn't think so. This was not a situation they had any control over. And where was the abbot? Dead? She didn't want him to die; she couldn't cope with that.

'And we can't leave without Katrina,' said Cherise.

'There's nothing we can do for her,' said Tamsin firmly.

'But what's she doing 'ere?'

'I don't know what she's doing here. I don't know what you're doing here, either.'

'He invited me.'

'And a night out in this god-forsaken asylum seemed a good idea, did it?'

'It wasn't like that.'

'And how did she even know you were here?'

Cherise paused for a moment. 'Well, I told 'er. I mean, she was askin' – she was like that. So I told 'er. I just said we was meetin' 'ere. That ain't my fault.'

But why had Katrina followed her? Cherise didn't get that. Apart from anything else, she had a client, and Katrina never missed a client. Unless – oh, *of course*!

'We're getting you out of here,' said Tamsin. 'Help is coming, you can be sure of that. The place is probably surrounded now.'

She looked up to see Terence standing in the doorway and aiming the gun straight at Cherise.

'The armed response unit takes a while, doesn't it?' he said. 'I trained them, you know.'

'Where's Katrina, Curly?' asked Cherise. 'And why the bloody handcuffs?'

'Katrina had no business being here.'

*

Terence and Katrina had met outside Model Service last month. She'd been enjoying a fag break in the wintry morning sun of Church Street. Terence dropped his beard when trying to remove it, she picked it up, and a moment that could have been awkward became one of comedy. She laughed . . . and he laughed, and Katrina had loved his eyes. And she'd known instantly that he was military; everything about him said soldier.

'My father was a soldier,' she said.

'I'm extremely sorry to hear it,' he replied and was about to move on when he realized she was an attractive young woman who liked him. 'You work round here?'

He didn't mind a short conversation. She was easy on the eye and he was not in a hurry.

'Up the road, yes. I'm in hospitality.'

'I have no idea what that means,' he said. 'But I'm sure you're quite brilliant at it. I've always wanted to be good at something.'

She knew he was single; he had to be.

'Perhaps we could meet for a drink, and you could tell me what you are good at? And why you wear a false beard!'

'If I told you that, I'd have to kill you,' he joked, and she liked this funny man. Older, but that was OK.

And they had met for a drink, and then another – and on one occasion he even came back to her flat for supper, with her son, who liked him very much. They talked about guns, after Terence had told him that you never hear the bullet that kills you – 'because the bullet travels faster than the speed of sound'.

'It's reassuring, really,' he added. 'Best you don't hear it, eh? That's a bullet you don't want to hear.'

She liked him more and more. He was civil, polite, darkly humorous; a better man than her father. He didn't need to know where she worked. Who'd be helped in the telling of that story? And neither did she know of his own interest in Model Service. Until the shocking day when, from behind the screen in reception, she saw Cherise answer the door, welcome Terence inside and then watched the two disappear together upstairs. The sense of betrayal was immense, which became anger towards Cherise, the little slut. That relationship would have to stop, there was no question about that.

But first, *she'd* have to stop, get out of the business. And then he could come home to her.

*

'She loves you,' said Cherise in the cold darkness of the asylum. 'I know she does, I can tell.'

'I'm afraid there's no love on the battlefield,' said Terence quietly. 'Just operational imperatives.'

'*Operational imperatives?* What the fuck's that supposed to mean, Curly?' She was wondering where he'd gone, the man she knew. But the man she knew was struggling. Terence knew it too; different worlds invading the operational mind. You couldn't allow that.

'What happened in there, Terence?' asked Tamsin, picking up on his hesitation.

He remained straight-armed, gun-pointing . . . but strained. Tamsin knew the look – a dangerous look, an uncertain state. She didn't want him making decisions from a state of distress; she'd engage him.

'The consequences of war,' he said.

'And in English?'

'You want a lecture?'

'I've always enjoyed a good lecture,' she lied. 'It's never too late to learn.'

Terence smiled. 'Is this called "playing for time"?'

'Call it what you like.'

'You can feign a retreat, Detective Inspector, to lure the enemy from a well-defended position. William the Conqueror at the Battle of Hastings, for instance. He did just that and the prize was England.'

'Do you have anything more contemporary to draw on?'

'Harold's infantry followed the retreat like fools and were annihilated by the Norman cavalry.' He'd lectured at Sandhurst – easiest job in the world. An expert in hindsight, like all the rest. 'But tonight was different.'

'Tonight?'

'Is that more contemporary?'

'How do you mean, different?'

'This was not a feigned retreat. This was a mined retreat, a protective move.'

Cherise felt sick.

'A protective move?' said Tamsin. 'But what are you protecting?'

'The prisoner will be quiet now.'

But Cherise took no notice, because she didn't want to be quiet and this was Curly and he was acting like a bloody lunatic. She needed to find out.

'So where's Katrina, Curly?'

Peter moved slowly

across the disintegrating terrain, formerly Gladstone Ward, passing two bodies on the way.

He could hear muffled voices in the End Room. Voices were good. Cherise must be alive, there was still time . . . though time for what, he didn't know. Terence, it seemed, had left Civvy Street and was a soldier again with a different set of values from those of the Stormhaven Etiquette Society. But what was his plan? He must have a plan. Soldiers always had a plan. Peter thought that plans were overrated. He'd never had a plan that hadn't fallen through, like the bomb-shattered roof now crumbling above his head.

His feet kicked some masonry on the ground, debris from on high. It made a scraping noise; cursing himself, he stood still. The asylum air was a dusty damp in the lungs, plaster still falling and bent metal creaking above. Was the roof safe? He moved on, a little quicker – and then cursed. Sharp pain. He'd walked into the mangled remains of an iron bed, his shin screaming. But his shin must wait. Breathe into the pain. He stood still surveying the traumatized landscape. There was a six-foot crater in the floor to his right, the eye of the blast, a black and open wound in the concrete offering a quick drop down into the asylum's underground corridors.

Ahead of him, appearing slowly in the asylum gloom, was the silhouette of a figure in the doorway . . . Terence. But who was with him? There were two other voices. Peter moved step by cautious step, breath by unarmed breath, towards the soldier . . . towards Goliath. Yes, the story of David and Goliath came to mind; a contest that was no contest, a boy who rejected the king's wise armour for absurd weaponry of his own choice.

Terence had a gun. What did Peter have? Where was his catapult and pebble?

The end game had begun

and he knew the end game well. Terence expected the armed response unit along shortly, dragged from their pre-cooked meals round the telly, out into the cold night. Most would be glad to be leaving their families for a gun spree with the boys. And he knew what was coming; he hadn't lied when he said he trained them. They'd used the SAS facilities in Hereford. They'd always laughed at the Plods – little wannabe soldiers the lot of them. But it was the Plods who'd be laughing tonight. 'We only took out that instructor fellow – you know, the one with all the medals!'

It would start with the megaphone, reminding them they were surrounded. Snipers in place, the inevitable Home Office-approved psychologist feeding lines to the Operational Commander, the food sent in. 'Is there anything else you want?' Slowly, slowly, relationship established, the softening process, nice, nasty, nice, the guard lowered, then – he'd taught them well, but he wouldn't be following the script. There'd be no polite way out of this. And surprises awaited them on their arrival.

'So where's Katrina, Curly? You got to tell me.'

Cherise was getting on his nerves, like a mouthy corporal the night before a strike. She was invading his thinking time.

'Against my orders, she followed me,' he said quietly. 'Against my orders.'

'Don't I have a name any more?' He wasn't using her name and she didn't like that. 'She loved you, she did. Katrina loved you. Was that against your orders too? I tell you, no one loved you like Katrina did.'

Terence felt the discomfort again. She shouldn't speak of love, the stupid girl. She didn't know anything about love. It wasn't good talk. The rage in his blood and guts. 'No one loves you like I do, Terence,' that had been his mother's line: 'No one loves you like I do.' If that was love . . .

And then disturbance behind him. The human body is never silent, there's always noise in the air, it just can't help itself . . . someone was approaching from the main ward.

'I know you're there, Abbot,' he said, adjusting the angle of the gun in his hand. He needed to cover two lines of attack.

Peter pulled back, like one caught out on the lake, surprised by thin ice – but with nowhere to step but forward.

Gun still pointing

at Tamsin and Cherise, Major-General Terence Blain turned round towards the emerging form of the abbot.

'I hoped you'd leave.'

'I could hardly do that,' said the abbot, rather primly,

'Foolishness and courage can look alike,' said Terence. 'The difference is in the outcome. You're a fool if you fail, courageous if you win. Death or glory? Welcome to the lottery.'

'Thank you.'

'You can join the other hostages. We won't be long.'

He stood back from the doorway to allow the abbot inside – inside the End Room.

'Hostages, Curly?' said Cherise. 'Is that what we are?'

'Sit down,' barked Terence and Peter moved to obey before looking down and seeing . . . *Tamsin*? Impossible – but there she was in the half-light and Peter, amazed, suddenly felt better. They exchanged a look of solidarity. He sat close to her, on the other side from Cherise, backs to the wall, Terence still standing in the doorway.

'Just give up,' said Tamsin, as if faced with a tiresome teenager. 'This is a crime scene, we need to clear up.'

'It was a crime scene long before you and I turned up,' said Terence.

'You mean someone stole some lead from the roof?'

She was mocking him.

'Bybuckle Asylum became a crime scene the day they decided to close it down and threw the patients to the wolves.'

'They were rehoused, Terence, it's a well-known story. No wolves involved.'

'Thrown to the wolves.'

'Did your mother speak of wolves?' asked Peter.

'We're going downstairs,' said the soldier.

'Why are we going downstairs?' He didn't like the idea. 'Is that where you shoot us, Terence, like those cowards in the revolutionary army killing Tsar Nicholas and his innocent family? There's only innocence here, Terence. And you're no coward.'

If Katrina hadn't arrived on the scene, the job would have been done. Cherise would be dealt with and he'd be well away. But he wasn't well away and he needed them downstairs. He needed time . . . play the situation in front of you, soldier.

'Take your shoes off,' he said. 'All of you. Abbot – here's the key. Unlock the handcuffs.'

'Our shoes?' Cherise didn't get this at all.

'Take your shoes off.' The simple command, still quiet, expecting to be obeyed.

'Curly!'

'Take them off!' His shout was as shocking as the blast. With their hands now free, they removed their shoes. 'Now – single file, hands on your heads, no sudden movements – let's walk.'

They rose slowly and obeyed, moving towards the basement stairs. The wet tiled floor was cold on their feet, and jagged. They moved forward carefully, like swimmers on the shingle without beach shoes.

'Left down the stairs,' said Terence firmly. Cherise wasn't happy.

'It stinks down there,' she said.

'Do it.'

'It's gross.'

'Do it.'

And so they did, Cherise leading the way, down disintegrating stone steps that led to the asylum basement.

'This is where the most troublesome residents were taken,' said Terence.

'Is that true?' asked Tamsin.

'Those ripe for more singular treatment . . . and where they kept the records.'

'I've seen the records,' said Peter.

'And do avoid the back entrance, Detective Inspector. It's wired again.'

'We'll get a moment,' said Peter to Tamsin but he wasn't sure if she heard.

'I don't know why you're doin' this, Curly.'

'Well, we're about to meet an expert in all that.'

'What?'

'An expert in the "why" of it all. I've flown him in especially – tremendously knowledgeable about rehousing schemes. So who'd like to meet an expert in inhuman housing?'

'What are you talkin' about?'

Cherise began to get scared again. This wasn't Curly any more, or not the Curly she knew. She'd lost him and they were now standing in the asylum basement.

'Sit on the bench,' said the soldier. Like the star over the stable, his torchlight rested above a rotting wooden bench that ran along the underground corridor. Already sitting there was the resident expert, who could explain everything: Geoff Berry, local estate agent, though dressed tonight as a clown.

'I'm sorry if it's a little damp,'

said Terence. 'Perhaps you could move along a little, Geoff, as much as you're able.'

His right wrist was cuffed to the underside of the bench.

'Who's Geoff?' asked Cherise, sitting down next to the stranger. The darkness was musty, damp and thick, untouched by warmth or the seeping neon of the street.

'Geoff's in property,' said Terence.

'Are we here because of your mother?' asked the abbot. There was no reply.

'I can't see a fing!' said Cherise.

'I feel your mother, Terence,' persisted Peter. 'Is she the meaning of all this?'

'There is no meaning,' said the soldier.

'So what's the story, Terence?'

'That's probably a question for Geoff to answer,' he replied. 'Wouldn't you say so, Geoff? Would you like to fill them in on the housing story? Not your finest hour – in a life of un-fine hours.'

Geoff coughed.

'Well?' said Terence.

'Your mother didn't like her new accommodation.' He spoke it in a monotone, as a line given to him and told to repeat a hundred times.

'That's why you're here, Geoff . . . because some easy money knocked on your door and you thought, "Why not?"'

'It wasn't my idea . . .'

'So we can't even credit you with originality.'

'It was just something I was told to do. I was young, I didn't really understand—'

'And didn't really care, either. Well, the misery of others is always a leg-up for someone, is it not? There wasn't any care in the community on offer. Just cold-hearted fraudsters like you.'

'Asylums were far from perfect, Terence,' said Peter. 'Before we get too nostalgic.'

'Baroness Elaine Murphy is an expert witness for the prosecution,' said Terence.

'Is this a court?'

It was a court, apparently.

'She wrote about care in the community between 1960 and 1990 . . . and do you know what she called her book?'

'I'm sure you're goin' to tell us,' said Cherise, fear now turning to anger. 'Not that we bloody care.'

'*The Disaster Years.* That's what she called her book. The disaster years. They didn't "bloody care" either.'

'We need to be leaving, Terence,' said Tamsin firmly. 'We do need to be leaving. People will be worried about us.'

'Some benefited, of course.' Terence paused. 'Not the patients, obviously; nothing is ever done on their behalf. They were offered low-grade and isolating accommodation for high prices – but then, the local authorities couldn't be choosy, with all those bodies to house. And they *were* bodies rather than people . . . to the developers.'

'We did our best,' muttered Geoff.

'They were called "group homes", which sounded rather nice. But they were dustbins for the difficult; halfway houses for those on the path to homelessness.'

'Can we go now?' asked Cherise, who felt cold.

'I just want to apologize, if, in any way, I—'

'I think we're in a land beyond apology, Geoff. Even if I believed it. Like every criminal, you're sorry you've been caught, not for anything else. You're a worm.'

Geoff sank back. They could feel his spirits deflate; a sad clown in handcuffs.

'Of course, Geoff was expecting the mayor to be here and an adoring audience. Weren't you, Geoff? It didn't take much to get you out. So you're bound to be a little down.'

And then Peter spoke: 'You do know your mother hated you, Terence.'

Tamsin looked shocked. What was the abbot doing?

'Be quiet, Abbot,' said Terence.

'She didn't love you. She hated you. It's important to know the difference. She couldn't love; quite incapable of it.'

'Be quiet, Abbot, before I blow you apart and make you truly holy.' He'd impose operational silence from here on. The pain was starting again.

'So we must stay truthful and not call it love. It was something very different. It was only she who believed that you had a heart of shit. No one else thought that.'

A heart of shit? Tamsin was now alarmed. Terence, a clear figure in the dark, now tensing up, finger on the trigger. Peter wondered how many more words he'd be allowed. But only words could help them now, down in the chill belly of the asylum.

'Not kind words, Terence – but do you know what I think?' Silence. 'I think she was speaking of herself, not you. She hated you because she hated herself. That's what I think. *She* had a heart of shit, or that's what she felt – while you had a heart of gold. It's called projection. People put on others what they can't face in themselves.'

The major-general kept the torchlight on them, hiding in the shadows behind.

'One more word and you're dead.'

Clear enough, thought Terence, and he wouldn't say it again. He needed to think about the end game, the exit strategy. He'd shoot the abbot if he spoke again. He wouldn't mind shooting the abbot. Operational requirement.

'"No one loves you like I do, Terence,"' said Peter – and now Terence staggered slightly. 'Isn't that what she said? "No one loves you like I do." Well, that was a lie, of course. Possession isn't love – and that's all she wanted: to possess you, to have you as her lackey, her whipping boy, endlessly at her command. So why are you still listening to her?'

Tamsin was furious with Peter. Why goad a man with a gun in the basement of a madhouse? Insanity was in the air, in the cold cellar walls, in the chill tile floor beneath their shoeless feet.

'One more word, Abbot—'

'Have you forgotten how to kill?'

'I haven't forgotten how to kill. I killed Rosemary, Abbot.'

'You did, yes.' Tamsin felt the shift in Peter's breathing, as one punched.

'And I can picture their faces, some of those I've killed. Killing happens . . . there's no plan to all this.'

'There is a plan, Terence, and it's yours. Your plan. Take responsibility. Who else's plan is it?'

'It's not my plan.'

'So it's God's plan, is it?'

'The army chaplain used to speak of God's plan.' His tone was dismissive. 'But that was tosh. There never was a plan, was there?'

'There's still a way back.'

'A way back to where?'

'To life, to kindness.'

'You ought to get out more, Abbot.'

'It hasn't helped you much.'

'And what if I don't want to go back?'

'But you do.'

'And where the hell would I want to go back to? What if I'm happy if this is the end – the end for all of us?'

And then Cherise threw up. She couldn't help herself, it was all too much, the anxiety, the terror. She was throwing up, jerking, heaving . . . and the torch slipped from the soldier's grip. He liked Cherise.

'Run!' shouted the abbot, as the arm straightened for firing, the abbot moving forward, Tamsin reaching across, a shot in the dark, blood on the walls – a shriek.

And then silence in the cellar, broken by a muffled, pitiful sobbing.

*

'The building is now surrounded,' came the voice over the tannoy, though no one much cared down below. 'But we're concerned for the safety of those you have with you, Terence. Could you confirm that everyone with you is well? And if they aren't, is there any help we can offer . . .'

It's a terrible sound, a soldier crying – and then the eye-watering smoke.

Smoke everywhere . . .

230

There were holes in the roof

of the Bybuckle Asylum, due to recent explosions. This caused contractors in hard hats to be brought in to plan its demolition. No one wanted the place left standing now; and to that extent the explosives had been kind, if violence can be kind, forcing an issue avoided for years by red tape, committee work and legal objections.

Like an alcoholic at the end of the road, the Bybuckle Asylum had finally touched the bottom; it could fall no further, there was no more abyss to explore. After madness, murder and bomb blast, the only way was up. The wrecking ball swung into action soon after.

Rosemary Weller was remembered well, as a stalwart of the charity scene – respected, perhaps, more than loved. The death of Katrina Pulskaya, a Polish hospitality worker, was also lamented briefly. It wasn't yet clear why she was at the scene of the crime; she left a son who was currently 'staying with friends'. The *Sussex Silt* was restrained concerning these tragic events. They ran a stirring piece on Rosemary, with the headline 'Stormhaven's very own Mother Teresa', focusing on her charity work and early days in the field of mental health, starting as a nurse in the Highgate Asylum.

'Major-general turns mass-killer' was another headline, detailing Terence's remarkable war record before his fall from grace 'in the dark caverns of Stormhaven's shameful madhouse'. 'War was easier than peace for this latter-day Lawrence of Arabia, whose twisted mind turned to murder and abduction in Stormhaven.'

'"Katrina was both a friend and colleague," said Daisy Watts, fellow hospitality worker and terrified hostage in the asylum on that tragic night.' She'd wanted to do the interview under her real name. It seemed right after their recent conversation. And there was nothing wrong with the name Daisy. She hadn't liked it as a child, but maybe it was time to return. Maybe Cherise had travelled as far as she could go.

The paper also reported a police raid on a brothel in the town with a Mrs Hopesmith taken in for questioning, though later released without charge.

'We acted as soon as we heard of it,' said Inspector Wonder in a press conference. 'There's no place for this sort of establishment in Stormhaven – or anywhere, for that matter. We want to keep this town a decent town. Model Service has been closed down.'

Nowhere in the reporting of these incidents was mention made of the Stormhaven Etiquette Society. Most of the column inches were given over to the county-wide manhunt for the murderer, Terence Blain, who'd escaped from the crime scene that was supposed to have been surrounded. The *Sussex Silt* wasn't impressed: 'Major look stupid!' was the headline above a piece that chronicled how 'the murdering major-general' escaped through the drains to walk free. 'His whereabouts are now unknown but police say that he is dangerous and should not be approached by the public.'

'So did you know?'

asked the abbot.

'You're sounding pompous, Peter.'

'You mean the question sounds pompous?'

'No, you and the question sound pompous. It's the tone of the question, which is a combination of you both.'

'I must work on my tone.'

They sat in Channing's large open-plan office in Lewes, overlooking the River Ouse. He'd seriously wondered about relocating to cheaper premises in Stormhaven – namely the Bybuckle Asylum – but he'd now decided against it. A ghostly lunatic army seemed to pervade the place and he really couldn't be doing with them. There were no lunatics in Lewes; they wouldn't be able to afford it.

'I'm simply asking if you knew of their connections with one another – Terence, Geoff and Rosemary?'

'You're not simply asking, Abbot. No one simply asks anything. You're a prosecuting counsel. You're accusing.'

'That may be how you hear it but it's not my intention.'

Channing got up from his editorial chair and gazed out through the large windows. The tidal river was full-bodied today, and on the opposite bank the large Tesco was busy with trade. He was not unattached to the scene – another reason to stay away from Stormhaven. There really were so many.

'Do you know your problem, Abbot?'

'I know of several.'

'You seem to imagine that there's some set and reasonable reality out there – some reality to which we're all accountable in some manner.'

'You pile your assumptions high.'

'But there's no such thing, believe me.'

'I'm not with you.'

'Everyone has their own reality. That's what I'm saying, Abbot.'

'OK.'

'And I've met some pretty strange ones in my time. I know people who believe they travel to Saturn every day – twins who live in Peacehaven, God help them. Absolutely convinced they travel through space to Saturn each morning and return in the evening. And I know others who believe they simply commute to London and back. But who's right?'

'Is that rhetorical?'

'And then some people know there is a God while others know there isn't one. And again, which of them is right?' Peter remained in silence. 'We must allow everyone their own realities, Abbot, without pressuring them into ours.'

'I see.'

'Which rather removes the "one-reality" preacher from the scene, don't you think? I think so ... *and* pompous questions like the one you posed.'

'Well, the ghost of Hitler will be most comforted,' said the abbot with a smile. Channing looked quizzical. 'I mean, he might have been worried that you'd object to his outlook on life; that you might pressure him into some other reality. But your cleverness gives him generous permission to proceed. The new morality: "Our reality is right if we believe it so, if our alternative facts suit us."'

Martin regretted his attempts at philosophy. He didn't usually do this sort of thing, and he wouldn't again. It had sounded good in his head but stupid as soon as it was spoken. So he'd move on.

'Just forget Bybuckle, Abbot. I recommend forgetfulness on your part.'

'That won't happen quickly.'

He still had the place in his clothes and his dreams.

'I mean, obviously it's the story on top at the moment, but believe me, the *world* is a lunatic asylum ... one big nuthouse. We have the notionally sane and the officially mad, but let me tell you, between the two there is no between. Which makes marvellous copy, of course. But it's now all about what it's always all about: the next story. We've gorged enough on the Bybuckle carcass and it's time for something new. Was there anything else?'

'So you did know of their connections?'

'I do applaud your investigative persistence, Peter.' He said this with a smile and clapped his hands loudly. 'And, of course, I remember now why I once offered you a job.'

'That wouldn't have worked,' said the abbot. 'We would have fallen out.'

Martin winced. 'A terrible thought.'

'But you still haven't answered the question.'

Channing paused by the window, a newspaper man in silhouette, black against the bright winter sun. He returned to his desk.

'I was like a hound with a distant scent in my nostrils.' He had to tell. 'One of my interns, clever fellow, dug up the link between Rosemary and Geoff with regard to the closure. I sensed an untold story there and intended to tell it. And then while trying to persuade Terence that he needed me as his book agent, he let slip his own connection to the place, which I thought rather interesting . . . well, more than rather. I'll deny it all, of course, and we won't pretend you've recorded this, because you wouldn't know how.'

Which was true. 'So you gathered them together in the Etiquette Society and played with their souls.'

Channing laughed. 'You make me sound like some *deus ex machina*, but it wasn't like that at all. The scientist can assemble the chemicals, but how they react is quite out of his hands. The death of dear Rosemary had nothing to do with me. Remember, the world is a madhouse without any help from my good self.'

What did the abbot think of Martin Channing? He was erudite, funny, a charmer; and determinedly playful in his insistence on taking nothing seriously. But was he also a monster? Perhaps he simply inhabited the fields of audacious assault, of untethered scheming, of cynical risk and dare, that lay in the mist beyond right and wrong. This is what the abbot was thinking on the bus back from Lewes to Stormhaven.

He would see Tamsin that evening. He'd bought tickets for an Elton John tribute act in the Barn Theatre. He'd seen him in the desert, twenty years ago now . . . though not in person. There hadn't been an 'Elton John Monastery Tour'. But a screen and video machine had been hired by the monastery so they could watch the funeral of Princess Diana, and he'd sung rather well, rather winningly about a candle . . . and a rose.

Though now, as the bus passed Tide Mills, the soldier was on his mind, the missing major-general.

'You don't know where Terence is?' had been Channing's closing question. 'Not hiding him, are you?'

'Hello, Blessings,'

said the visitor, cold on the doorstep.

'Well, well, well.' She stayed in the doorway. 'You shouldn't be here, of course.'

'I'll be gone shortly. And I expect nothing.'

'You expect me to let you in.'

'Maybe.'

'I can't help you, you do know that?'

'I don't want help,' said the soldier.

'No, you never did, Terence. Not the helpable sort.'

He shrugged. 'Though maybe I can help you,' he said.

'I doubt that.'

Blessings was looking around. Had anyone seen him arrive? She doubted it. She trusted his discretion and her own high walls.

'Before I leave, I mean. I could help you before I leave.'

It was the look in his eyes. They both knew.

'You mean?'

'You know what I mean, Blessings . . . what you asked for.'

'And what you turned down.'

'Not now.'

'What could possibly have changed?' said Blessings with a smile. 'You'd better come inside.'

And the front door of Black Cap closed behind Terence – a fox free from the pack . . . for a while.

'What will you do?'

asked Peter.

'Sell up and move on,' said Tara, sipping a glass of red wine.

They sat in the reception area of No. 9, Church Street, the business formerly known as Model Service, a joint venture between Rosemary Weller and Tara Hopesmith, though now closed down by the police amid a public outcry led by the *Silt*.

'It's that easy?'

'No, it's a nightmare. I have to ask what I want to do with my life and I'm not sure I know. Should you know what you want to do with your life?'

'The zero hour breeds new algebras,' said Peter.

'I have no idea what that means.'

'Well, not one for the scrapbook then.'

He'd chosen a whisky from the well-provisioned drinks cabinet – whisky and ginger ale.

'You don't want to marry me, do you?' said Tara, looking him in the eye.

'Marry you?'

'I could do worse.' She smiled.

'I'm not sure you could.'

They sat in silence, slightly shocked at where they'd reached.

'Rosemary loved you; I mean, as far as she knew how to love. She did things for people rather than love them.'

'She did do things for people. She saved me, in a way.'

'It's a sort of love, a practical love . . . but not a romantic love.'

Peter drank again from his whisky. He was enjoying this moment, there was something about it. Alcohol softened him.

'There was a desert between us,' he said, confessionally. 'Between Rosemary and me . . . a desert, both real and metaphorical. We couldn't quite cross over into each other's territory.'

'Whereas I'm a complete romantic, of course.'

'That sounds threatening, like a prelude to invasion.'

'Not all invasions are bad.'

'Now there's a thought for the day.' More silence. 'You'll note that I don't actually know what to say at the moment. I don't even know what I'm feeling.'

Tara simply sat, which drew Peter out once again: 'They say separate houses are the best form of cohabitation.'

'Cohabitation in separate houses. How does that work?'

'I have no idea. I know only my cell . . . and my lust.' Had he said that? 'So what I could give you, I have no idea.'

His phone rang. 'I'm sorry, that's my niece.'

'The detective?'

'Yes. We're seeing an Elton John tribute act this evening at the Barn Theatre. My treat.'

'Hah! Well, good luck with that!'

'You've seen him?' said Peter as he picked up the phone. Tara nodded and then mimed the cutting of her throat. 'Oh. So not good then?'

God knows,

it was never meant to be like this.

War was a good deal simpler and happier – this was Terence's sense as he lay on the bed. You left right and wrong at home, where they should be, with no voice in the field of conflict. You simply did the job that was asked of you, with no other considerations. It wasn't your job, it was their job. Others could take the blame – the politicians, whoever.

But the events at the asylum had been his job with the rights and wrongs close at hand. And his head ached, because his mother hadn't shut up all day, the evil old witch. You give her what she wants, but there's no sense of thanks or applause, and when had that ever been different? There was only failure with her. And it makes no difference when they're dead – this is the thing, they carry on talking, carry on gnawing at your existence, voice lingering like the plague in the pathways of the brain. Did he have more blame in his body than blood?

And perhaps that's hell. The eternal judgement of another, though he knew she was gone, snuffed out; he knew there was nothing left of the dead. He hoped there was nothing of his mother right now, nothing left of the harridan, no flesh left on the bones in the cemetery off Vale Road.

But for Blessings, he wished for birth, for new life. He had done what he could.

It was their final meeting.

'And then there were three,' said Blessings, devoid of emotion.

Empires come and go, rise up and fall away . . . and the Stormhaven Etiquette Society was no different. It was not advertised as the final meeting – no speeches were prepared or bottles of fizz made ready – but that's what it became for this awkward trinity in the judge's large front room: Geoff, Martin and their host.

'No Terence?' said Martin with mock surprise. 'And he's always been so regular.'

'I can't abide the man,' said Geoff, who was frightened and wouldn't relax until he was found. Handcuffed to the bench in that god-forsaken cellar – that wasn't funny. And who knows what would have happened if – well, it didn't bear thinking about. The man was insane, evil. And to think they'd sat here with him, as if he was normal.

'And I like to think we've done our bit for the area,' said Martin, breaking the silence. Conversation had not arisen easily on arrival, when polite banter must flourish or all feel awkward. But the empty chairs – once occupied by Rosemary and Terence – could not be ignored and an unsettled tone prevailed. Nor had any tea been offered to the guests.

'I'm sure we have,' said Geoff, aware of nothing achieved at all. What had the Etiquette Society ever achieved apart from notoriety and bad feeling? Perhaps that was enough for Martin, but it wasn't enough for Geoff, who preferred applause, otherwise what was the point of anything? 'And I'm also sure we've enjoyed every second in Blessings' lovely home. Quite a property – and I've seen a few!'

Always worth reminding people that he knew about property.

'We have perhaps kept people on their toes,' said Blessings, and the other two smiled. No one had liked getting their stickers; there was little doubt about that. They were the secret society from whom no one liked a visit. 'Though not Rosemary,' added Blessings and the smiles faded. 'Not Rosemary. She won't be needing her toes six feet under. No dancing there.'

'I'm not sure she was a keen dancer,' said Martin, by way of reassurance.

'So did we kill her?' asked Blessings, to the surprise of her guests. 'I do wonder that. I do wonder whether *we* killed her?'

Her words hung in the air for a moment.

'A rather odd question, Blessings,' said Martin.

'Well, it seems that at least three of our number had a history, Martin – a shared history. And two of them are now dead, just leaving . . .'

Geoff felt the sweat pricking at his neck.

'Well, so it transpired,' said Martin casually. 'So it transpired.'

'Coincidence?' asked Blessings.

Martin managed some mock laughter. 'We'll ignore that!'

'Well, was it? Was it all just one very big and unfortunate coincidence?'

'These things happen, Blessings.'

'But why did these things happen?'

'I've never believed in conspiracy theories myself. I mean, good copy obviously – but normally quite unbelievable . . . rumour and intrigue invented by the sad and lonely.' And then, as an afterthought: 'You're not sad and lonely, are you, Blessings? I'd hate to think of you as sad and lonely.'

Blessings looked at him, without movement of head or face.

'What are you actually suggesting, Blessings?' asked Geoff, leaning forward and disturbed. He'd already decided he wanted out of the society; he'd come here tonight to hand in his resignation. Martin had been rather mocking of his experiences in the asylum that night – but Martin hadn't been there, so how could he possibly know what it was like?

'"A clown in the asylum" – not a good epitaph, Geoff!' Those had been his words.

But ever since then, Geoff had woken each night in that awful cellar, tied to the bench in the silence of dripping water and fear. He could swear he'd seen figures down there, the cracked and the crazed, moving in the shadows.

'It's PTCS, Geoff – post-traumatic clown syndrome!' joked Martin.

Geoff hated Channing, he realized that now. But what was Blessings suggesting? That Martin had known of the connection? That he'd . . .

'Coincidence doesn't play well as a defence in court,' said Blessings.

'Though probably not enough in itself to convict,' said Martin with a smile. 'And of course, this isn't a court. It's a meeting of the Stormhaven Etiquette Society, which is why I sit in a comfortable chair, why there is no court recorder present and why I, as its creator, now declare the society to be defunct, finished – deceased.' He said it with a bit of a flourish, like a showman. 'So, if there's no other business—'

'Just a game was it?' said the judge, with the levity of a head teacher on the prowl.

'You did once tell me you were bored in Stormhaven, Blessings. Don't tell me you didn't. And I'm an incorrigible people-pleaser, after all. It hasn't been dull, has it?'

He had been powerfully attracted to Blessings at the outset. He'd wanted her as much as he wanted anyone and the chance to sit in her front room once in a while . . . well, who knows what might have become of that?

'You bastard,' said Geoff.

'I'll give you that one for free,' said Martin. 'Gratis. But I wouldn't repeat it.'

'Oh yes?'

Geoff was feeling feisty. He didn't add 'You and whose army?' but that's what he was feeling. You could only push Geoff so far and Channing had better believe it, however many readers the *Sussex Silt* might have. Geoff had his pride.

'Yes,' said Channing coldly. 'Or you might find all sorts of unfortunate stories creeping into the Stormhaven consciousness. Local celebrities can quickly look rather jaundiced . . . the gutter press and all that. I'll show myself out.'

'I'd convict you,' said Blessings as he walked towards the hallway. 'I'd send you down.'

243

He turned – and for a moment a haunted gaze passed across Channing's face, like a boy caught out, like a child told to sit on the stairs. He recovered himself to act out mock-fear and then the familiar smile. But his smile did not reach his eyes and Geoff realized for the first time that Channing's smile never had.

The front door closed quietly behind him and he was gone into the night.

'So!' said Geoff, relieved at Martin's departure. He was glad he'd made a stand; he didn't regret it. Channing had that coming to him. Had Geoff gone too far, though? You wouldn't want Martin as an enemy. But, well, here he was anyway and looking to the positives, glad to be alone with Blessings, even if he wouldn't mind a nightcap in his hand, something to calm him a little. She was a very attractive woman, no question of that, and an evening here was not the worst option available, far from it.

'Wonderful property, Blessings,' he said warmly. People loved talking about their houses, especially with an expert like himself. 'How much did you pay for it, out of interest? Because whatever it was, it would be a great deal more valuable now.' He loved his own expertise sometimes. 'Property prices in Firle Road have risen between twelve and fifteen per cent per annum over the last five years. Brighton overspill . . . very telling.'

'I'd convict you as well,' she replied. 'Now let's find your coat.'

'Of course,' said Geoff, hastily rising. He hadn't expected this. 'But I mean, Blessings, if you ever—'

'I won't be selling through you, Mr Berry, not if you were the last estate agent on earth. And from here on, it's Judge N'Dayo as far as you're concerned.'

'Quite. Well . . .'

'Good night, Mr Berry. And if you've avoided a prison sentence, it's only because injustice reigns.'

She opened the door and closed it behind him. With Geoff gone, expelled, Blessings returned to her chair and sat down.

'They've gone,' she said, voice raised slightly.

'I know,' said Terence, who was standing on the stairs. 'Sorry to have missed the final meeting; as harmonious as ever.'

'And you must be gone as well,' she said.

'I will be.' Blessings had allowed him to stay for three nights while the police hung around known haunts, watched harbours and airports and offered his picture to the press. She'd said yes because he was a proper man, strong, and decent. But now their contract was fulfilled and the welcome over.

'Goodbye, Blessings.' They were together in the hallway. 'You have my will. I can't think of a better witness than you. Make sure they give everything away.'

'I will.'

'And I trust you'll be able to look after my child . . . should my child appear.'

His hand reached towards the door.

'Don't you need anything?' she asked.

'I've taken one or two small tools.'

'What for?'

'It doesn't matter.'

'No food?'

'No food. As Socrates said, "There's so much I have no need of."'

They looked at each other, there in the hallway of Black Cap. He leant towards her and kissed her briefly on the lips. It was a sweet taste, one he'd like again.

'Goodbye, Terence.'

And after he disappeared into the night, Blessings cried.

'I'm still in shock,'

said the abbot, though the Barn Theatre was now half a mile behind them, allowing some recovery time.

'You're not still moaning about the show?' Tamsin was thinking ahead, to a glass of wine.

'I *am* still moaning about the show.'

'Well, stop moaning. Enjoy the view.'

The night sea was magnificent, a calm majesty.

'I still need to moan.'

'Well, what did you expect?'

'That wasn't a tribute act – it was an insult.'

Tara's mimed throat-slitting made deep sense now, and while they had left at half-time it still rankled.

'You do have a harsh tongue, Abbot.' Tamsin enjoyed saying that. 'Though I agree, Joey Long was appalling and there's no defence for that . . . there's no defence for appalling at all.'

'I mean, I suppose he was young . . .'

No, excuses weren't helping.

'Were the tickets expensive?' asked Tamsin. 'Is it the money that's getting to you?'

The abbot's wallet was neither deep nor much opened.

'Well, they didn't seem so when I bought them. They appeared quite reasonable. But ten minutes into the show . . . I mean, was Joey actually playing the piano?'

'I think it was mostly backing track.'

'You mean it was mostly Elton John.'

'Yes, the original artist was playing most of the tribute as well. I could see the boy's problem.'

'Only one?'

A seagull swooped towards them, then climbed again.

'The karaoke screen that he'd fixed to the keyboard – it kept stopping, which threw him, as he didn't know the songs particularly well.'

246

'Which is a shame.'

'It is a shame.'

'For a tribute act.'

'Yes.'

'Not to know the songs.'

'Now can we talk about something else?'

Peter contemplated the night sky, aware that there were bigger problems in the world, more punishing conundrums.

'But it was sold out!' he cried to the heavens, as one utterly bemused. 'How could that – well, how could that sell out anywhere but in his own front room?'

'Stormhaven is not the West End, Peter. It's the Worst End, I keep telling you. People take what they can get here . . . like the seagulls.'

After a chill night walk along the seafront, with a westerly wind in their faces, they were approaching his front door. The light was still there in the upper window, where a candle burned at the top of the stairs.

'I've always meant to ask you about that.'

'About what?'

'The candle.' She pointed upwards. 'And the last time I tried, you didn't answer.'

'We were just off to the asylum, as far as I remember. It wasn't the best of times.'

'It's never the best of times to get an answer out of you.'

The abbot turned the key and they stepped inside. It wasn't the best of times now either.

'And you meant to ask what, exactly? How much it cost? Where I bought it?'

'Don't be dull, Abbot.'

They were hanging up their coats, Tamsin taking longer than usual, learning new ways with her plastered arm. They'd done a good job at A & E, she had no complaints about the care; but the fact was, a plastered arm changed everything.

'I'd just like to understand the question,' said Peter.

'Well, not everyone has a candle burning on the stairs, night after night. That's not normal.'

'It's normal here. Do have a seat.'

He'd give Tamsin the comfortable one, in consideration of her condition.

'But not in the real world, Abbot. So what's it about?'

'What's any candle about?'

He looked up the stairs at the light in the landing dark. He thought back for a moment to the light in the asylum, approaching him in flickering silence, refusing to declare its intentions. It had been a disturbed and unsettling light. But this light was something else.

'I don't know,' said Tamsin. 'I'm not a fan of candles. Everyone imagines they're great, but I don't see it. Wax is messy . . . occasionally for a dinner party, perhaps.'

'Well, I look forward to my invitation. The previous ones have clearly been lost in the post.'

'You hate dinner parties.'

'Which is just as well.'

'So what is it about?' She wouldn't give up.

'I'm not sure you'd understand, or perhaps I don't. But it's always burned for . . .' And then he stopped. 'If you don't mind, Tamsin, I think I may leave it for the moment.'

'Leave it?'

'Yes, I'd best keep the oven door closed for now.'

'Your oven door is always closed.'

'Then let me open it with some gratitude.' From his position on the herring box, he looked at her with a smile. 'You took my bullet, Tamsin. Down there in the asylum cellar, you took my bullet.'

'I did, didn't I? God knows why.' She looked down at the plaster cast on her right arm, the one that had moved to shield him, though her shoulder had taken much of the force. 'You were being an idiot, goading him. In hostage situations, you're meant to talk people down, not talk people up. The idea is to calm them.'

'It was better he touched his rage.'

'You didn't get shot.'

'I was thinking more of Cherise. He never wanted to kill her. He couldn't really go back to being a soldier. He thought he could, but he couldn't.'

'Well, I'm glad *Cherise* is OK.' Tamsin waved her plastered arm in the air.

Peter smiled. 'You took the hit, but we all walked free.'

'Including Terence. So where's the old soldier now, Abbot?"

'I don't know.'

'He's not here, is he?'

'He'll be holed up somewhere, like he has been all his life. But he's not free, poor man. Wherever he is, he's not free.'

Tamsin looked at him with strange intent, almost wonderment, as if she couldn't quite believe what she saw.

'You like him, don't you?'

'Of course I like him.'

'What do you mean, *of course*? He killed Rosemary.'

'Formative attachment patterns are not easily disposed of in later life.'

Tamsin snorted her derision. 'You mean his mother was a cow, so that's all right?'

'I mean, our emotional identity is modelled and cultivated by family, whether for wounding or harmonizing. And it's a long goodbye from such modelling. I'm still saying goodbye to mine.'

'Too long a goodbye for Rosemary, killed in cold blood,' said Tamsin. 'Yet you like him?' Her words dripped with disbelief. 'Those two facts don't seem to you a little, well, contrary?'

'I host them both, that's all I'm saying. I think Rosemary liked him as well.'

'Until he tied her to a bed and . . .'

'I know,' said the abbot.

'You'll be a better copper when the romantic in you dies.'

'I don't want to be a copper.'

'He could have killed us all.'

'Fortunately, I had a saviour.'

'That's not a name I want on my tombstone.'

Peter got up. He'd been sitting for too long that evening.

'You'll be disappointed to hear this, I know. And you'll disagree, Tamsin – but I fear there's strong evidence for the existence of kindness in you.'

'It was nothing of the sort. I just . . .'

'You just what?'

Tamsin glanced down at the plaster cast and waved it a little, like one might a medal.

249

'The doctor said I'll be able to remove it in six weeks. Injury in the line of duty . . . could get me promotion.'

The abbot chuckled. 'So this sacrificial act was ambition rather than kindness?'

'And only a flesh wound.' Outside, a car sounded its horn. 'My taxi's here.' She got up. 'Good teamwork, though.'

'I'm sorry?'

'Good teamwork.'

Good teamwork? When did Tamsin ever work as a team? And when did he?

'Is that the post-case debriefing?'

'Do we need more?'

The abbot indicated that her summary would probably cover it. 'Want help with your coat?' he asked.

'I'm not disabled, Peter.'

'No – but you have a disability. Your right arm is broken and your shoulder recently dislocated.'

'I'm fine. It's only change.' She hung her coat over her shoulders.

'You need one of those capes,' said Peter, 'like the nurses used to wear.'

'This isn't the brothel, Abbot.'

He opened the door and she stepped out into the still night, a January moon over the rippling water, gentle waves breaking contentedly on the Stormhaven shingle. He couldn't remember the last time he'd seen them so content . . . or felt so himself. The lights of the Newhaven ferry glowed in the distance, like a birthday cake on water.

'Thank you, Tamsin,' he said.

'Cold, isn't it?' she said, pulling her coat round her.

'Terence was aiming at me.'

'You were saved by the dark.'

'And by my colleague. Teamwork, as you say.'

'So let that be the end of it. And I won't hug you. It'd be too painful.'

She never hugged him; it wasn't her way, but tonight she had a reason she could name. She walked to the road and eased herself

250

into the taxi. The engine was running and the taxi pulled quickly away along the seafront towards Newhaven, but wouldn't stop until it reached Hove, another land completely.

*

High in the dark sky above, out over the sea, Terence put the plane on autopilot. He wanted to look around, un-busy himself. This was something like freedom, clear of the world below.

He'd left Blessings' house and walked two miles through the night to the village of Ripe. He'd then gained access to the little Deanland aerodrome, and the aircraft of a friend, a Cessna 120. He'd have liked one last flight in his Sierra, but knew the police would have Shoreham airport covered. So he exchanged a tarmac runway for grass, and a speed of fifty knots with twenty degrees of flat had taken him up into the night over Sussex.

He headed for the coast, found a good horizon and took the plane high, 5,000 feet over the sea. No police dogs here. And perhaps he'd have a child, a child through Blessings, something of him continuing – or was that just sentimental rubbish? Still, it made him feel glad – perhaps as glad as he'd ever felt. He reached for the Cessna's limit, one last stretch of the legs, before turning back towards Stormhaven and lowering altitude. He wouldn't be going to prison; it would remind him too much of home.

Down below, a homeless man called James, with whom he'd recently exchanged a few brief words, saw it all unfold. He'd remained in the beach hut with the stove, found respite there, and had just come out to Splash Point for a pee, when he saw the plane's downward approach.

Fascinated by flight, and sensing danger, his hand went to his mobile phone, which his wife still paid for every month. He looked to the sky, as Terence looked down . . . there, a distant figure on the shore, a figure at Splash Point looking up.

Terence had company – a man had come to watch him fly. A brief moment of connection between them as Terence felt the rush of the steep decline, down towards the water, feeling alive, this was life . . . and then levelling out, altitude of 150 feet. So close to the sea and on to autopilot, the plane could do the work now. He'd

251

worked enough in his life, and in some dusty and dangerous places. He wished to rest.

The craft flew level with the skyline, the ball of the Slip Indicator safe between the hairlines, the plane balanced and happy, moving towards the white cliffs. They say that death is white – a white arrival, a clean slate; that would be good.

And James filmed it all on his phone. He could just see the pilot, who seemed at rest, flying towards rock, the terrible smash of plane and chalk, the flash of fire in the night sky, the fractured aircraft falling on to the shingle, into the waves, the debris of death.

James had never had that courage . . .

*

'Homeless hero films murderer's sick suicide.'

That would be the *Silt*'s headline, along with the story of renewed contact between James and his family after the publicity surrounding the incident. He found himself suddenly feted – the homeless hero, valued now by people who'd been passing him by for years. There weren't many who didn't want to interview him, get a slice of his story, including an abbot, would you believe – an abbot, in Stormhaven! And accompanying him, her arm in plaster, a rather glam detective.

'Life's tide, eh?' he remembered saying to the monk, who seemed a perfectly reasonable fellow.

'Life's tide indeed,' he'd replied, as if he'd seen some ebb and flow himself. 'Who knows what the morrow will bring?'

James was meeting his family later. They'd wanted to come to Stormhaven and a local paper was paying.

'Not me,' he'd replied. 'And I've given up trying.' He didn't want to get his hopes up . . . but couldn't help himself.

'Well, whatever it brings, I wish you a *good* morrow, James.'

Even the detective managed a smile.

'It must be strange,'

said Terence.

'What must be strange?' Rosemary was cold.

'Returning to the place of your fame.' He'd found a chair and sat by the bed where Rosemary lay tied. 'The TV documentary you invited in, your moment of power and glory.'

'It wasn't like that, not at all.'

She'd just been doing her job. It had felt neither powerful nor glorious. The care in Bybuckle Asylum was abominable; she'd merely highlighted the fact and grasped a nettle everyone else had avoided.

'And here we are again in this ruin of a place; once a home but now a shell.' He sat slightly hunched in his large overcoat with its deep pockets. 'I once went back to a place of fame.'

'Where was that?'

'A battlefield – well, it was a small village at the time of my first visit.'

'This was with the Special Forces?'

'Some hostages were being held and it was our job to get them out. And I made a bit of a name for myself there, I suppose.'

'You deserve a name.'

'A rather violent face-off, nothing pretty. Thirty-seven dead by the end – mostly theirs, but some of ours. We laid the bodies out in the high street, like in a spaghetti western, the silence . . . I remember the silence.' He paused. 'But we were heroes, we knew we were heroes.'

'You're clearly a very brave man.'

'And then I go back there again ten years later.'

'Why?'

'There's something in me that wants to go back to my scene of triumph. And what do I find?' Rosemary didn't know. 'I find children playing where the bodies lay. No bloodstains, no bullet-ripped walls. And the terrorist hide-out, the focus of most of the savagery – that was now a bakery . . . a bloody bakery.'

'Your work was done.'

'My work was done, yes. I should have been happy. Do you think I should have been happy?'

'I think you should have been proud of your work . . . and bought a nice loaf for your troubles!'

'But I wasn't, you see. I wasn't proud – or pleased. Naughty boy, eh? Rather a shock, that, I don't mind admitting. I think I still needed it to be a battlefield where I was the hero . . . but it wasn't a battlefield, not any more. All of that was forgotten; I was forgotten. They had new memories, new hopes – they didn't want some bloody soldier disturbing their charming life. They'd had enough of all that; they didn't even remember the soldier. I was just another tourist.'

Rosemary lay on the metal frame, listening. He had returned . . . though what his intentions were she had no idea.

'My mother kept the video, by the way – the bit of the programme when she spat at you.' Rosemary began to feel ill. 'She could never forget, my mother. Determined old hag – could hold a grudge for ever.'

'And you?'

'It can't have happened far away from where you are now . . . could be the same bed, even. Was this her bed, perhaps? That would be a bloody thing, wouldn't it? If it was the same bed – she'd like that. She wasn't always kind.' Terence paused. 'She was never kind.'

'No.'

'Though she didn't last long after the place closed down. Got dementia.'

'It happens, sadly.'

'Lack of company, I think.'

'They didn't encourage friendships in the asylum. You do know that, Terence?' Silence. She couldn't even hear his breathing. 'Friendships among patients were broken up; the staff found them too threatening. Friendships made patients seem more normal, more human, more like the staff . . . and the staff didn't like that. It's all in the report. They broke up friendships.'

254

'Don't interrupt.'

'It's called the truth.'

'She ended up like a battery chicken in substandard accommodation, courtesy of Geoff Berry – that's all that need concern us.'

'Is that what she said?'

'"Care in the community is the new name for hell," that's what she said. "The new name for hell."'

'She made plenty of hell for others, as you well know.'

'She walked out in the end and never came back. I don't know where she died.'

'Your mother was held together by spite, Terence, not community.' She might as well say it. 'It was her victims that kept her alive. When this place closed down, she had no one to crucify any more. Except you. She could always get to you, even when she wasn't there: "No one loves you like I do, Terence."'

He didn't move.

'Isn't that what she said?'

'Doesn't matter what she said. She's dead now.'

'I wish she was, Terence.'

Rosemary remembered their conversations in the car. He'd never answered her question – always avoided it. He simply got out of the car and started walking, as if that was an answer. So she asked again.

'Does nothing matter to you, Terence?'

'She always joked that I should shoot you. "Get her address from the TV company!" she'd say. She'd never written me letters before, but she started writing then. Lots of them – you were on her mind. I didn't pay undue attention because I never thought we'd meet. But we did, you and your accomplice.'

'My accomplice?'

'At the Etiquette Society, the property louse Geoff. So it proved to be good for something at least.'

'How is he my accomplice?'

'And then you told me what brought you to Stormhaven – the report on the Bybuckle Asylum. So let's do it, shall we? Get the bitch off my back.'

'Do what?'

But the gun was already out of his pocket. Two shots into the head, one through the eye, the other in the forehead. He paused to confirm the killing, unscrewed the silencer, returned the gun to his coat pocket and turned to leave. There was no happiness.

'Now we're evens, Mother,' he said, wrenching the door of Gladstone Ward shut behind him. He walked down the dark corridor, through the hallway and out on to the empty seafront. 'I never want to hear from you again. *Ever.*'

Epilogue

Peter stood in his kitchen, aware of a quiet certainty. He'd have to do it; it was a force inside. And it was the conversation with Sarah that had done it.

Something had seemed to shift as they spoke, for she was so like Rosemary yet quite unlike her as well. Were all sisters like this? They'd talked after the funeral, over tea in the church hall. They'd found a small table in the corner and their own supply of flapjack.

'So how did you know her?' she asked, glad to be out of the crowd. Sarah found crowds difficult, especially when they contained family . . . and friends of the family, with whom things had not been easy. Strangers would have been easier today. She'd almost not come.

'Well, a long time ago I was a patient of hers.'

'Where?'

'Highgate Asylum.' He hadn't wanted to mention that.

'So you were a nutter?' She said it with charm; you could not take offence.

'We all have our moments, Sarah,' he said defensively.

'You'll be pleased to know I've had my own.'

'Your own moments?'

'Well, one moment really – it just went on for a while. I'm not sure how long a moment is permitted to last. But it wasn't good.'

Peter did not push the matter. He'd only just met her, and this was her sister's funeral.

'But you must have kept in touch?' she said. 'With Rosemary, I mean.'

'We did on and off. More off than on. I was away in the desert for a while.'

'Another asylum?' Her questions were childlike in their simplicity, and quite disarming.

'Some would say so, though it was called a monastery.'

257

'Oh, yes!' she said, looking at his clothes. She was mid-fifties but seemed so much younger.

'And you were Rosemary's younger sister.'

'I still am.'

'Of course.'

'We didn't always get on. But we got on better when she stopped trying to save me or tell me what to do.'

'And you reached that happy place?'

'I should probably tell you something.' She leant forward. 'I mean, everyone else in this room knows, which is why they aren't so keen to talk with me.'

'And what do they all know?'

'I was a prostitute for a while.'

'OK.' It came as a surprise.

'Or as good as . . . no, I was, I was. Why disguise it? Not that I knew what I was doing at the time. I mean, you can look back on your life, on moments, on times, and wonder what on earth you were doing.'

'I do it frequently – not the prostitution, the other bit.'

'But that's what I did. That's where I found myself, in that sort of life, and it was hard to leave, very hard. There were others involved, forceful people; and I wasn't very forceful.'

'No.'

'And then Rosemary saved me – well, organized the inter-vention – and she thought I should be grateful to her.'

'That's what she said?'

'I don't know if she actually said it, but you don't have to say it, the demand is still there – or that's what I felt. And I mean, I should have been grateful, in a way – but it was my life, and I wanted to make my own choices. And we got on better later when, as I say, she stopped trying to save me; or stopped as much as she could ever stop. She was always my big sister and very free with advice.'

Peter smiled. 'Perhaps she turned to saving others instead.'

'I imagine so. She did a lot for people, or so I hear.'

'You are aware she ran a brothel?' said Peter after a pause.

'She *what*?' Both tea and table almost went flying.

'She ran a brothel.'

258

'Rosemary!'

'Yes.'

'You're joking.'

'I'm not joking.'

'Really, you are.'

'I'm really not.'

Sarah was in a state of shock, smiling and shaking her head. 'I can't believe that.'

'Well, in your own time.'

Sarah breathed deeply. 'It's true?'

'It's true.'

'Then no, I was not aware. Can I tell everyone else here?'

'Well, some of her employees are present.'

Sarah looked incredulous. 'Oh, this is too good. Just too good! I somehow love her more now.'

'She was very eager to look after her girls. Their well-being was really at the heart of the business.'

Her mood suddenly darkened. 'Not for the clients – it's never their first concern.'

'Well, no.'

'Unbelievable. The things we don't know.' She held her tea tightly, sipping occasionally. Peter allowed her time. 'Still in shock, I'm afraid.'

'Well, it's a bit of a boulder to throw in the pond.'

'And I'm sorry, I've forgotten your name.'

'Peter. Abbot Peter.'

'Very grand.'

'Not from the inside.' And then as casually as he could: 'I don't suppose she mentioned me.'

'Rosemary?'

'Yes.' He felt a fool.

'Not that I can remember, no.'

'Well, I wouldn't have expected it.'

'She was pretty secretive, though. There was much she didn't speak of. She had an outer shell like a crab, and nothing behind the shell or beneath it ever got out. But I mean, you should ask the rest of the family. They saw more of her.'

259

'It doesn't matter . . . it really doesn't matter. And it's probably time I was off anyway.' He'd seen Tamsin signalling and he began to get up.

'We must meet again,' she said. 'I hope so.'

'Yes, we must, Sarah, we must – it's been very good talking.' And that felt strange, because she looked so similar to Rosemary. Perhaps a little prettier . . .

He had known then that it was time. He'd been awaiting his moment . . . and this was it.

And so now he left the kitchen and slowly climbed the stairs, looking up at the simple flame burning, climbing towards the light. It had danced delicately in the window for so long – and often forgotten. A light of longing, even in the dark, a calling out, the whisper of a homecoming. But there'd be no homecoming now, for Rosemary was dead. Or perhaps the dream was dead, for Rosemary had merely given this longing a name.

'Goodbye, Rosemary,' he said. 'Rest in joy.'

He bent down and blew out the flame, staying still until the last ember had died on the wick and the winding column of smoke had dissolved into the dark space at the top of the stairs.

'Rest in joy.'

Acknowledgements

A book is always the work of a community and I am indebted to mine. So my thanks to Shellie Wright, Elizabeth Spradbery, Alison Barr and Rebecca Parke for kindly reading early versions of the manuscript and sharing their delights, quibbles and bugbears; to my keen-eyed and trusted editor, Karl French, whose questions opened new asylum doors; to my neighbour Dave Burton for telling me all about planes and taking me up in his; to Marylebone House, whose fine craft is to make good books happen; and to all those kind readers whose encouragement along this fictional way (you won't have known) would sometimes save my fragile day.

A story is just an introvert's way of starting a conversation . . .